AT THE
GEORGE

AT THE GEORGE
And other essays on Rugby League

GEOFFREY MOORHOUSE

Hodder & Stoughton
LONDON SYDNEY AUCKLAND TORONTO

The author would like to thank Peters Fraser & Dunlop for permission to reproduce the extract from Tony Harrison's poem '*v*' on page 50.

British Library Cataloguing in Publication Data
Moorhouse, Geoffrey, *1931–*
  At the George: and other essays on Rugby league.
  1. Rugby league football
  I. Title
  796.33'3

ISBN 0-340-43040-0

First published in Great Britain 1989

Published by Hodder and Stoughton,
a division of Hodder and Stoughton Ltd,
Mill Road, Dunton Green, Sevenoaks, Kent TN13 2YA.
Editorial Office: 47 Bedford Square, London WC1B 3DP.

Typeset by Hewer Text Composition Services, Edinburgh.
Printed in Great Britain by St Edmundsbury Press, Bury St Edmunds, Suffolk.

CONTENTS

AT THE
GEORGE

One

At the George

If you are in Huddersfield on Sunday, you go to the George. For all that times have changed enormously since its textile heyday, Huddersfield retains many of the airs it began to wear halfway through the nineteenth century, when it prospered on the manufacture, design and colouring of woollen shawls and mantel cloths. Nothing is much more memorable of that period now than the buildings round St George's Square in the centre of the town, which still speak of Victorian confidence and growth. One side of the square is occupied by the colonnaded length of the railway station, which J. P. Pritchett designed on ambitiously Corinthian lines in 1847–8; and at right angles to it is another of his compositions, the George Hotel. Four storeys high, Late Classical from quoin to pediment, this might easily be mistaken, were it not for its name in huge gilded letters across the front, for some quite important hôtel de ville in Burgundy or the Dordogne. Its greatest significance is that a very English revolution was once proclaimed within its walls.

It is to the George that people go on Sunday if they feel like celebrating, or merely expanding, in the middle of the day. They can eat a three-course lunch, at a fixed price, in the pastel-shaded dining-room, where long mirrors are ranged along the walls and the deep windows are curtained heavily in chintz. The Trust House food seems often to be washed down not by traditional Yorkshire beers, but by beverages from Huddersfield's later experience: flasks of Mateus rosé, half bottles of sparkling French white, or even more trendy mineral water with, in this case, a patriotic emphasis on Ashbourne rather than Perrier. Middle-aged couples treat great-grandparents to this fare; youngish couples treat themselves and their children; still

1

childless pairs make the most of each other while the opportunity remains. Occasionally, at a long table in the middle of the floor, a function is simultaneously held, a twenty-first birthday party or maybe an octogenarian event, and everybody in the room looks genuinely pleased while the flash-bulbs pop; including the young people who are waiting on and who are clad, both male and female, in a uniform black and white with a bow tie at the throat. The George at lunch-time on Sunday is as homely as one of Mr Forte's establishments can possibly be.

But the revolution, I ask one of the waitresses, after she has sweetly enquired if everything is to my satisfaction, sir; whereabouts did the revolution take place? She hasn't a clue, which is sad. But (and this is much more important) without being prompted, she goes to find out and comes back five minutes later with a delicious grin. 'It was in the Tudor Bar, sir,' she says.

Ah, the Tudor Bar, which Mr Forte's architects have done their best to render in a Home Counties stockbroker mode, full of dark beams and white plasterwork and spurious wooden dowels, and the sort of wrought-iron chandeliers that Errol Flynn used to swing from when he was Robin Hood. And in a not very conspicuous corner, where you would probably miss it unless you knew what you were looking for, a little monument to the revolutionary act. Three small bronze figures are mounted on a stainless-steel plate affixed to the wall. One figure, carrying an oval football, is about to pass it to another, but is already tackled by someone else. Below is the relevant inscription, engraved on the steel: 'In this Hotel, at an historic meeting on August 29th 1895, was founded the Northern Rugby Football Union, known since 1922 as the Rugby Football League.'

It may be thought exaggerated, quite out of proportion, to speak of a game and revolution in the same breath. This will almost certainly be the response of anyone who has never felt the powerful affiliation of a whole community with the group of players representing it in a team sport: for among the many divisions of humankind is that which separates those who enjoy various forms of athletic or other sporting activity, and those to whom these things are an unmitigated bore, even anathema. Yet it is at least a matter for argument that man at play down the ages has been as significant as man at war and man at work. The American historian Barbara Tuchman is one who has argued this, and gone so far as to suggest that, 'In human activity, the invention of the ball may be said to rank with the invention of the wheel.' But we do not need to invoke this judgment in order to see revolution in the meeting at the George in 1895. What happened that day in Huddersfield was, with smaller repercussions, as much of a social, economic and political insurrection as the resistance of half a dozen farmworkers at Tolpuddle, sixty-one years earlier, to a reduction in their wages. It, too, was fundamentally about artisans and labourers making ends meet.

The game which gave rise to the dispute, although the result of a popular evolution across centuries, had been systematically organised in the nineteenth century by the upper and middle classes, who played a similar role at approximately the same time in the development of golf, soccer, athletics and cricket. William Webb Ellis's famous handling of the football at Rugby School is supposed to have occurred in 1823, but it was not until 1871 that the Rugby Football Union was founded, to be followed within a few years by the formation of similar bodies in Scotland, Ireland and Wales. By then, rugby was no longer the sole preserve of the well-to-do, as it had originally been. It had become the people's game as well, most notably in South Wales and in the North of England, for reasons connected with the great industrialisation of these areas in the nineteenth century. 'Sport provided pleasure where work did not, and the more strenuous the physical labour the more strenuous the physical release it demanded.'

In time, the majority of rugby clubs in the North drew their playing strength from the mills, the foundries and the coal-mines of the region, and these footballers were not often from the salaried management: they were wage-earners of the rank and file. Such were the men who started to play rugby in Huddersfield in 1878, when the local team was formed.*

Though managers and people in trade from the outset appeared on its committee, folk from that class and age group generally enjoyed themselves in less robust ways than on a football field. Some of those belonging to the textile communities strung out along the Colne Valley of the West Riding gravitated with their wives and daughters to the Huddersfield Choral Society, which had been launched in 1836 and was by mid-century widely celebrated for its performances of oratorio. One step ahead of the artisans and labourers in organising their lives,

---

* The rugby team was a development of the Huddersfield Football, Cricket and Athletic Club, which had been founded in 1864.

these middling citizens who had an ear for music and a voice to match, found their own release from work by opening their lungs in harmony.

The five-day week was still two or three generations away and Saturday was no different from Monday, whether you were labouring on piece-work or on shifts. If you wanted to play football or otherwise pleasure yourself on the seventh day, you forfeited that part of your wage. There was the rub. Many of the finest rugby footballers in the land simply couldn't afford to. These were rules codified by men who could take time off from their properties, their businesses and professions whenever they had a mind to play games, to go fishing, to hunt fox, to shoot birds. But gradually a number of northern clubs sought to revise them, and it is likely that they were impelled by a desire to maintain their success on the field as much as by any considerations of equity off it. For the North had become the English stronghold of rugby.

The very first fixture between county sides was Lancashire versus Yorkshire, arranged up there the year before the RFU was formed. After only 4,000 people turned up at The Oval to watch England play Scotland in 1878, home internationals were removed to Manchester, where 'an unprecedented crowd' was overflowing the ground within a few years. When the ardent Welsh sought opponents who could match their own mettle in club matches, it was to the crack sides in the North that they looked most of all. The dominance of Northcountrymen, not only in English but in British rugby at this time, may be seen in the team selected to tour Australia and New Zealand in 1888, which was as follows:

BACKS, J. T. Haslam (*Batley*, Yorkshire and North), A. Paul (*Swinton*); THREE-QUARTERS, H. C. Speakman (*Runcorn*, Cheshire), H. Brooks (Edinburgh University, Durham), J. Anderton (*Salford*, North), A. E. Stoddart (Blackheath, Middlesex, England); HALF-BACKS, W. Bumby (*Swinton*, Lancashire), J. Nolan (*Rochdale Hornets*, Lancashire), W. Burnett (Hawick); FORWARDS, C. Mathers (*Bramley*, Yorkshire, North), S. Williams (*Salford*, Lancashire, North), T. Banks (*Swinton*, Lancashire), R. L. Seddon (*Swinton*, Lancashire, England), H. Eagles (*Swinton*, Lancashire, England), A. J. Stuart (*Dewsbury*, Yorkshire), W. H. Thomas (Cambridge University, Wales), J. P. Clowes (*Halifax*, Yorkshire), T. Kent (*Salford*, Lancashire, England), A. J. Penketh (Douglas, Isle of Man), R. Burnett (Hawick), A. J. Laing (Hawick).

Precisely two-thirds of that touring party belonged to clubs (italicised) that would, within a few years, have turned to playing the Northern Union game.

The issue of paying players to compensate for the loss of their Saturday wages, for their 'broken time', was debated openly in English rugby's governing body in 1893 when, at an RFU general meeting, a motion was proposed and seconded by two Yorkshiremen, 'that players be allowed compensation for bona fide loss of time'. It was defeated by 282 votes to 136. The northerners went home, reluctant to sever their connection with the parent body, certainly not wishing to introduce anything as dire as professionalism into the game, but none the less resolved that things could not go on as they were. Meanwhile, the authorities hardened their own position the moment the forces of York and Lancaster had returned north. The RFU hastily reconvened and passed a new by-law which emphasised the inflexibly amateur nature of their game and, just as significantly, stipulated that the Union's headquarters should be in London, where all future meetings must be held. At a stroke they underlined the fact that an economic and social dispute was a geographical one as well.

For many months afterwards an uneasy truce was maintained between the two factions, while the northern rebels held one meeting after another on both sides of the Pennines. The Yorkshire venue was usually the George, while in Lancashire the insurgent committee deliberated in one of Manchester's innumerable Spread Eagle hotels (the one in Corporation Street). The committee-men, it should be said, were not much different in substance from the men who led the conformist rugby clubs farther south. Tony Fattorini, who represented Manningham, was a manufacturer of trophies and medals; Joe Platt of Oldham, who became the breakaway union's first secretary, was partner in a firm of accountants and surveyors; and their colleagues were likewise in a different income group from the footballers whose livelihoods they sought to protect.

Though they had hoped to organise their own competition, with payment for broken time, they wished to enjoy their rugby still under the auspices of the RFU: they had no wish to topple its authority. But by the start of 1895 they had come to accept that this would never be tolerated by the metropolitan overlords. And so, in the last week of August, they met in Huddersfield yet again; conclusively this time. A dozen Yorkshire clubs and nine from Lancashire resolved 'to form a Northern Rugby Football Union, and pledge themselves to push forward, without delay, the establishment of the principle of payment for broken time only'. They followed this pronouncement with their official resignations from membership of the Rugby Football Union in London – all except Dewsbury, whose nerve suddenly went, not to be recovered until the new competition was three years old. But before that September was out, the Northern Union's first season was under way, each player receiving six shillings per match, provided he could demonstrate that he was in employment and had lost a day's pay. It was at this point, as if to claim the legitimate succession, announce the one true blood, that the southern authorities at last got round to putting a plaque on a wall at Rugby School, commemorating William Webb Ellis's own historic disobedience seventy-odd years before.

The RFU, for reasons which are understandable enough, has always chosen to represent 1895 as no more than a hiccup in an otherwise stately advance along the years: 'its progress was impeded for a while', according to one chronicler of the Union code. The reality was more uncomfortable than that. The England XV, weakened by the withdrawals from the North, began to lose international matches at an unheard-of rate, and when Wales crushed them 26–3 at Swansea four years after the great schism, the defeat was specifically attributed by many observers to the loss of Yorkshire and Lancashire forwards who had traditionally provided the backbone of the pack. A correspondent of the *Morning Leader*, a London newspaper, smarting in the aftermath of the Welsh victory, saw a more fundamental reason for England's humiliation that day.

> For many years the Rugby Union has been a closed corporation, composed of men with the mistaken idea that only public schoolboys and University men could play the game. The middle-class and working-man footballer was barely tolerated. And yet it is the latter class rather than the University player that furnishes the majority of the best footballers today . . .

The point about the closed corporation was to remain valid for many a year, with lasting effect. One consequence of 1895 was that the Rugby Union's version of football ceased to be a working-class game in England except in a few margins of the realm: the Celtic fringe of Cornwall, the secluded Forest of Dean, the fastnesses of Cumbria; scarcely anywhere else. The lost ground has never been recovered. Another consequence was a sourness in the air between the old guard and the renegades which has not yet disappeared, so that we are still from time to time obliged to behold the patronising figure of Homo Twickiens, as well as his natural adversary, the aggrieved belt-and-braces character from the North.

Some of the old guard wishfully predicted that the renegade competition would come to an early end, but, although it had its ups and downs, it persisted, sometimes with a flourish, and in time acquired a sort of national identity. Within a few years of its origins, moreover, the Northern Union approach had been taken up on the other side of the world as well, and this led to the code changing its name in Britain. From the moment they adopted this form of rugby early in the twentieth century, the game's followers in New South Wales, Queensland and New Zealand had arranged themselves into Rugby Leagues, and just after the First World War they asked the Northern Union authorities at home to fall into step with them for the sake of symmetry; which was done. If one had to select a point at which Rugby League in Great Britain achieved its majority, then the moment would be a generation or so later, when the game attracted one of the biggest crowds ever to see any kind of football match, when Warrington and Halifax replayed their 1954 Challenge Cup Final, which had finished as a draw at Wembley a few days earlier. At Odsal Stadium, Bradford, no fewer than 102,569 paid to go through the turnstiles that Wednesday evening, and several thousands more were there who didn't.

It was by then not the same game that had been the subject of a rift half a century before. Within a few months of the 1895 meeting at the George Hotel, the northern legislators had made their first change to the rules of rugby, by decreeing that henceforth a deliberate knock-on would be punished with a penalty; and inside a couple of years the line-out had gone. From the outset some had wanted to reduce the number of players on each side from fifteen to thirteen, but this didn't happen until 1907, just before another alteration allowed a tackled man to get up and play the ball with his foot. Thus it was that in little more than its first decade, the game which was to be known as Rugby League had acquired its own shape and rhythms, distinctively different from Rugby Union. The object of the changes was, of course, to speed things up, to make the game as attractive to spectators as possible, for they were vital to the payment of broken time and the other emoluments that eventually came the players' way.

There have always been much greater limits to the financial transactions than some outsiders have supposed. Though at once tarred with the brush of professionalism, the new breed of rugby players were never to become professionals in the manner of top Association footballers. Even in the past few years, when it has been possible for the best of them to obtain contracts with the wealthy clubs in Sydney during the English offseason, not many have done so. It is doubtful whether twenty Englishmen, in any given period, have been in a position to do nothing but play Rugby League throughout twelve months. The great majority have had to balance their playing careers alongside other, longer-term jobs: as miners, as truck drivers, as factory workers, as bank clerks, as schoolteachers, as publicans and as small businessmen. Just occasionally this mould has been broken by some exceptional individual. In recent years Ellery Hanley, the first black man ever to lead the British national side in a major sport, has been so well rewarded for his talent that he has lived in the style of a soccer star without needing to go Down Under except as Britain's captain on tour.*

Before the First World War, St Helens had a fine wing three-quarter in Christopher Chavasse, curate of the local parish church, formerly an Olympic sprinter, subsequently Anglican Bishop of Rochester, and always a figure who might have served as a model for *Chariots of Fire*. But for the most part, British Rugby League players have not strayed too far from their origins in any sense, their payments now representing not so much broken time, as the difference between living their whole lives in a rented house and finding it possible to handle the mortgage on a home of their own.

These things I pondered the day I took my Sunday lunch at the George in Huddersfield. There was a time, not so very long ago, when that dining-room and that bar might have been filled mostly by people heading for the match in the afternoon; but it's over a dozen years since Huddersfield were in the first division, and much longer since they were a powerful side everybody else had to be wary of. If there were any other football supporters in the George that day, bound like me for the Runcorn match, they made themselves inconspicuous and I spotted no one I recognised on the terraces later on.

Rugby League has been enduring a downer in its birthplace lately, though the old woollen town's other great cultural inspiration has never been in better shape, the Huddersfield Choral Society having

---

* Hanley stayed on in Sydney at the end of the 1988 Lions tour to play eight games for Balmain before returning to start a new season with Wigan.

a long waiting-list of people wanting to join. Some of the members, bearing their thumb-stained Novello scores, drive seventy miles in mid-week to rehearse *Messiah* or *The Dream* or something else from the repertoire. A revival in the local fortunes at Fartown, attended by similar enthusiasm, is long overdue; and the match that day, between one team from the middle of the second division and another from the foot, was no great shakes according to the standards set nowadays by the best sides. Yet I had no doubt, even there, when a dropped ball, a bad pass, or some other elementary mistake happened every few minutes, that I was watching a form of football which transcends any other I have known.

That is a subjective judgment; it is not meant to be definitive. Evaluations distinguishing one sport from another can never be much more than a reflection of temperamental differences between enthusiasts. I myself happen to be most susceptible to team games played with a ball, whereas individual ball games (tennis, golf, squash) mean much less to me, and any form of racing, whether by human beings, animals or machines, moves me not at all. I acknowledge, however, that most sports played by experts at the top of their form are worth watching for at least a little while if you are an instinctive gamesman; likewise, they are incomprehensible and dreary if you are not.

I've watched every variety of football and I've played two different sorts, and rugby (in both kinds) is much more attractive to me than any other version. For its grace and its controlled aggression, for its sweepingly swift movements and its moments of brilliant artifice, for its palpitating climaxes where one side is pounding at the other for the couple of points that will mean victory and the adversary is defending as though the end of the world will come with defeat; for all these things and for many individual shafts of daring and courage in every match, rugby is for me incomparably superior to any other winter game.

I would not go so far as a writer on Australian Rules did when he described soccer as 'that most desiccated of games', but it is perhaps of its nature a little anaemic when set against the full-blooded performances of a rugby match. There is, too, a significant ballistic difference between these forms of football, with certain philosophical implications. It is possible to kick a spherical ball with such precision that its behaviour can be forecast exactly: normally it will roll or bounce forward on landing, though the expert kicker can vary this direction to some extent. Not even the finest kicker of an oval ball can be absolutely certain what will happen the moment it hits the ground, when it will move in any one of five directions – forwards, backwards, to the left or the right, or even straight up into the air. On the individual's temperament depends which of these effects, the premeditated or the unpredictable, has the greater appeal.

Of the two handling codes I am stirred mostly by Rugby League, though I recognise that it has not often produced anything more thrilling than the second half of the match between Australia and France in Rugby Union's World Cup of 1987, or more glorious than the battle between England and Australia at Twickenham in 1988. On the whole, though, I would rather watch it than its sibling because more often than not it is the game with the more fluent and fluid movement, as well as the more determined tackling; where, at the highest levels, real inspiration as well as tremendous athletic skills must be summoned to penetrate a defence. The standard of football played at the two Union internationals I have just mentioned is regularly to be seen between the best club sides in League. Yet my preference does not depend only on Rugby League performances on the field. League has my allegiance, too, because it is an expression of who I am and where I come from, the history of my people and our ancestral lands. It is of the culture from which I spring, to a degree that some may never even recognise. My grandmother knew nothing of the game so far as I'm aware, yet when she wanted to praise some person or thing, she would sometimes say that this was 't' best in t' Northern Union'; unconsciously retrieving the words from our collective folk-memory.

I have watched this game a great deal from boyhood to middle age, though there have been periods of my life when I've had to make do with rumour of its progress because I have lived in places at home and overseas beyond the pale. Across these forty years it has changed, though not out of recognition. I think it is faster now than it once was, though some of the old-timers who were my models when I was a boy certainly don't agree with me. Some of its fashions have obviously altered, with Spearmint out and gumshields in, a sidelight on increased dental awareness in our times. Similarly, the old-fashioned scrum-cap has been abandoned in favour of the headband and, latterly, an Australian import that resembles an old track cyclist's protector (such as Reg Harris wore when sprinting at Fallowfield) or even a boxer's headguard.

Substantially, though, Rugby League has remained unusually true to itself, an expression of values as well as a challenge and an entertainment now embedded deeply in the lives of generations on both sides of the world. Among other things, it is a last refuge of the brass band that marches while it plays. It is as well to remember, as disconsolate Fred Tate was reminded at the end of a cricket match in which he had dropped a vital catch, that this is only a game. It cannot be, it should not be mistaken for, the be-all and end-all of anybody's existence. But a game can be much more complex than patterns of athletic energy on a playing-field. It can reflect and embody various habits and attitudes that amount to nothing less than a way of life: and this game does.

Two

Class of '46

Some games you inherit at birth, but I chose Rugby League. My inheritance was soccer and cricket, yet before I was fifteen I had virtually rejected the first of these for a variety of football that had thus far been no more than a matter of rumour in our family, through the sports pages of the old *Daily Herald*. Although I continued to play centre-forward until I left school, my new devotion meant turning my back on Nat Lofthouse on Saturday afternoons, a treachery I had not thought myself capable of, and I am not at all sure what it was that lured me to rugby unless it was simple curiosity, prompted In this case by the enthusiasm of two form-mates, one of whom supported Broughton (soon to be Belle Vue) Rangers, the other Rochdale Hornets. I imagine that either would have been willing to introduce me to his ruling passion, and I think there must have been an element of testing the water carefully, privately, in my choice of where to see my first match. I had noticed from the paper that there was to be something called a Championship Final between Wigan and Huddersfield on Manchester City's ground. Well, I knew my way to Maine Road all right, for I had watched Nat in a torrid struggle with Leslie MacDowell there. And this Rugby League fixture had an appealing intimation of clash about it, that I could appreciate from family tutelage in the lore of the Roses match. I would go to Maine Road, then, for the last game of 1945–6, slipping this novelty into the small space between my footballing and cricketing seasons. It was a momentous spring. Almost one month after going to Manchester to see my first Rugby League match, I returned to the big city, entered Old Trafford for the first time, and watched Lancashire playing the great summer game.

I was bound to go to the football as a Wigan supporter, of course, because of county loyalty, though there were other reasons for the allegiance by the time I set off. I had estimated from the map that Wigan was the nearest Rugby League town to our Pennine spur, and this regularised my position, the bond being sealed by one other thing. One week before, in the Cup Final at Wembley, Wigan had been beaten by Wakefield Trinity in circumstances of high drama and pathos. They had played that match under the handicap of having four men on the high seas, in Gus Risman's touring party en route for Australia. In the absence of Ted Ward, therefore, they had entrusted their goal-kicking to Brian Nordgren, a winger who had recently arrived from New Zealand to subsidise his law studies at Liverpool University by playing for Wigan. He had been well on target in every match until he reached Wembley, but there he flopped completely. He had six attempts at goal and he missed every one; and Trinity won with the last kick of the match, when Billy Stott landed a famous penalty only a few yards in from the right-hand touch-line. This same depleted Wigan team was now to take on a powerful Huddersfield side which had only one man, Bob Nicholson, on tour. It was to be David and Goliath, backs to the wall, six VCs before breakfast, all over again. What more could be asked by a lad who was being brought up to believe that all sport should be played with, and arouse feelings of, chivalry if it was to achieve its potential excellence? Wigan were mine and I was theirs before I had even clapped eyes on an oval football.

I was desperately disappointed by my first sight of them. Their usual strip, I knew, consisted of cherry and white hoops, and I had been looking forward to this distinctive garb of the rugby game. But that afternoon they turned out in plain blue shirts, such as Manchester City and a score of other soccer teams regularly wore; and I am still irritated whenever a rugby side offends against the game's traditions in this way. (Why on earth Widnes have abandoned their unique black and white hoops in favour of the most boring strip in the championship is something that passes my understanding.) I have heard it suggested that rugby deliberately adopted hoops in the nineteenth century because they emphasised a player's powerful physique (his strength), whereas the vertical stripes worn by many teams playing the Association game made the most of a man's slenderness (his mobility): in short, that both kinds of costume were forms of war paint, carefully applied before the kick-off to gain a psychological advantage the moment two sets of combatants strode into each other's view. Though they were, in my eyes, clear sartorial losers to the Huddersfield claret and gold at Maine Road that May day in 1946, the Wigan players looked a hefty lot even in their plainness. Ernie Ashcroft was all of 13 stone without an ounce of fat, and he was in the three-quarter line. Up front, Frank Barton was built like a tank (at the time he was, in fact, a Lancashire Fusilier), and never in my young life had I seen anyone to compare with the muscle-bound, menacing, plug-ugly George Banks.

And they could all shift; even Banks, whose main function when he wasn't propping seemed to be to detach himself from the scrum and scrag the Huddersfield half-back before he could get rid of the ball, thus enabling the back-row men to fan out wide. The speed with which everything happened in that game was one of the things that most captivated me about this new discovery of mine. Tackling came much more swiftly and surely than the kind practised in soccer, and you never saw anyone standing still and 'holding' the ball while he made up his mind which player to pass it to. Consequently the ball was always in motion, except at the scrum and during the brief interregnum when the player in possession was held down.

The scrums fascinated me because they belonged so utterly to a different mythology from the one into which I'd been born. I was enthralled by the way the forwards bound themselves together, front row glaring at front row before they packed down, and by that sudden snapping of tension when the hookers struck for the ball: also by the way it *always* went into the tunnel, for neither Mr Dobson, who was in charge of that game, nor George Phillips, nor any other top referee would have countenanced for one minute today's incompetent scrummaging, where play is often allowed to proceed when the ball has simply bounced off a prop forward's shin straight back into the scrum-half's hands.

There was a eurhythmic grace about so much of what went on out there. I watched admiringly the simplest of all rugby skills, the act of passing the ball, accomplished by an elegant half-turn and tilt of the body, the arms held amply as the hands flicked the pass, generously giving, not meanly transferring in a miserly way. In some of the tackling was the rippling power of a cat leaping to take a mouse or a bird. If I was spellbound by one thing more than any other, then I think it was the way the two full backs stood waiting for the high ball to descend, in those moments of uncertainty I had known when fielding on a cricket boundary, feet beginning to stutter as the last fine adjustment of position is made, arms shaping up to hug the ball tight, the body recoiling a fraction from the impact, but in this game under the threat of an advancing enemy; and the crowd's small stillness while the ball was in the air, giving way to a gust of noise as the catch was taken – or not. Huddersfield's Leake misjudged the arc of one high kick but, turning swiftly at the last, took the ball as it came over his shoulder, on outstretched fingertips, turned again, and ran to set up an instant counter-attack. I had never seen such a marvellously exciting movement before, such an exquisite co-ordination between a man and a football, something that perfectly exemplified high athletic art.

There was also much more courage than had yet come my way. Soccer players of those days had not yet gone in for the histrionics, on getting bumped, that have diminished their sport since; but quite new to me was the unconcern of these twenty-six footballers at taking continuous hard knocks. I happened to be watching from just inside the fence near the halfway line, only a few feet from where Alec Fiddes mowed down his opposite number with a perfect flying tackle. I watched his face clench in anticipation of the crash as he came pounding across and flung himself at Ratcliffe, the Wigan man scarcely flinching as the shoulder smashed into his thigh, the pair of them hurtling heavily straight into touch. It winded me simply to contemplate the damage they must have sustained, but they picked themselves up and trotted back to their places without so much as a limp between them.

This was commonplace, but there was one episode of bravery outstanding even in that company of stoics and giants. Jack Cunliffe, in the match only because Martin Ryan was on tour, started at full back, but was knocked out by a forward rush just after the second half began. This was donkey's years before substitutes were allowed in Rugby League, and as long as a man could stand on his feet he stayed on the field. So Billy Blan took over at the back, scrum-cap and all, and Cunliffe was waved into a vacant space, where he stood swaying uncertainly for several seconds before tottering elsewhere, quite obviously unaware which day of the week it was. And for nearly half an hour he did no more than occasionally, inadvertently, but usefully get in Huddersfield's way. Meanwhile his team hung on to a 5–4 lead, while playing into a fairly stiff warm breeze.

The odds, actuarially, were still against them when they won a scrum just five yards out from Fartown's line, with Cunliffe standing vaguely somewhere to the left. The ball could only have been sent to him because every other avenue was blocked, and what happened next could have been nothing more than an athlete's reflex still operating through the fuddle of concussion. He took the pass and, unbelievably in the small space, side-stepped his way past three men and flung himself over with two tacklers hanging on. Wigan were to score once more before the end, but that was the try which secured them the championship.

I left that match half-wishing there wasn't a full season of cricket to play and watch before I could see this sort of thing again; and there was never any doubt where I would spend my pocket-money when September came. Henceforth, Burnden Park was abandoned in favour of Central Park, which was two bus-rides from home instead of one. After descending to Bolton from our village it became necessary to transfer from the corporation's double-decker to a strange variant run by Lancashire United, built squatly to get under the low railway bridges that festooned the local coalfield, and with long benches on the upper deck instead of the customary twosomes separated by a middle aisle. Leaving the cotton mills and their lodges of water behind, this was soon lurching its way past slag heaps and their attendant flashes, through one colliery village after another.

We were scarcely across the borough boundary before we passed the site of the old Pretoria pit, where at breakfast time one day in 1910 there occurred an underground explosion so huge that it was heard miles away. It cost the lives of 344 men and boys in one of the worst British mining disasters, and it was weeks before they got some of the bodies out, so that they had to soak the coffins in eucalyptus oil at the funerals, to disguise the smell. This was just outside Westhoughton, where they also remembered, with boisterous celebration, a local farmer's stupidity, in their annual Cow Yed Wakes.

Then came Hindley, where Stanley Houghton had sited a comedy that was in the repertoire of every amateur dramatic society in the North-West. At Ince, down blackened-brick side streets, you could still see young women wearing not only clogs but thick woollen shawls as well, these covering them from head to waist and enveloping their babies in the same swathe, just as George Orwell had described them a decade earlier. Before we reached the terminus near Wigan's market-hall, everybody heading for the match got off that bus, which meant that it was virtually empty over its last half-mile. I remember being surprised, the first time I made the journey, at the number who had been aboard since we set off. I hadn't realised so many Boltonians had a weakness for Rugby League.

There was something attractively home-made about Central Park, compared with Burnden and Maine Road and the other grounds I was familiar with. The wooden fence enclosing the playing area might have been tacked together by the supporters' club on a series of summer weekends, and the crush barriers seemed to have been improvised from redundant railway sleepers. The main stand was low and small enough to breed familiarity among those sitting there, and it had been fettled by carpenters with a taste for thick trusses and beams, as had the wide open Dutch barn that covered spectators on the opposite side. That, I found out later, was where Joe Gormley and his cronies from the local NUM always stood, the future president of the union invariably muffled up with a scarf, appropriately sucking one of the town's famous products, Uncle Joe's Mint Balls.

For a long time I restricted myself to the boys' enclosure, which was cheaper than anywhere else (you were admitted as long as you could bend low enough to get under an impeding bar), but this meant that you were penned at one end of the ground from which, on murky winter days, it was sometimes difficult to see what was going on near the far goalposts. On the other hand, it allowed you to hang over the tunnel from which the players emerged, after the long wait through one broadcast advertisement after another ('Write, phone or call for Unsworth's luxury motor coach services . . .'). You could always tell when their appearance was imminent. The broadcast adverts gave way to the tantivy announcing *Entry of the Gladiators*, which is occasionally still heard at Central Park, but never, under any circumstances, failed to herald the Wigan team running on to the field forty years ago.

Before they even came into sight, a draught of Wintergreen would precede the players down the tunnel and drift up into the enclosure, the cleanest smell in the world, it seemed to me. When they hove into sight it was obvious why the pine whiff of methyl salicylate preceded them so pungently, for globs of the stuff were smeared about their knees and ears as thickly as Vaseline, while Banks appeared also to use it on his wiry hair as a macho substitute for the pomade that Denis Compton extensively advertised in those days. It wasn't till I started playing rugby myself that I realised Vaseline was, in fact, mixed up with the liniment, on the principle that it protected the skin to some extent from cuts.

Thus began my education in the game that soon had me under its spell as much as cricket; and while most of the teaching took place at Central Park, before the season of 1946–7 was over I had travelled farther afield in search of tuition. When I was particularly flush with spending money, I used public transport to reach some distant grounds, travelling to Naughton Park on a steam train that was still run by the LMS, getting to Headingley, Odsal, Thrum Hall and Fartown by complex bus itineraries that included the memorable ride provided by the Hebble company across the Pennines, close by the cobblestoned Roman road over Blackstone Edge. Often enough, I got on my bike and pedalled to wherever Wigan were playing away that week, like scores of other lads following their teams across Lancashire and the West Riding.

Near all the grounds was a facility that seems to have vanished with the years and greater affluence: backyards with little notices on match days, which told you that there, for a few pence, you could safely leave your cycle until the game was over; and by the kick-off these yards were as solid with frames and spokes as the outside of an Oxbridge college in term. Once – and only once – I cycled over the hill into Yorkshire, to watch a fixture at Lawkholme Lane, leaving home not long after breakfast so as to reach Keighley in time for the match, returning so late and so exhausted by the ride that I slept till the following noon. By means I forget, I got as far east as Wakefield on one occasion. But Rugby League on Humberside, as in Furness and Cumberland, had to wait many a year, until I had children of my own – and a motor-car.

When Wigan were playing too far away for me to keep up with them, I would select some other match, preferably on a ground I hadn't visited before (for I soon began collecting these, just as, at about the same period of my life, I would go church-bagging on my bike in summer, drawn by a growing interest in architecture). This was how I came to watch Hull play at Lawkholme Lane; and I expect I went because both teams were infrequent visitors to Central Park in those seasons immediately after the war, when there was but one championship division, and only the top teams in Lancashire or Yorkshire met the upper crust from over the hill.

What I recall of that match, apart from its superb setting on the edge of Rombalds Moor, is a prolonged kicking duel between Jack Mills and Fred Miller, which went on for minutes, with the other players brought to a standstill (but ready to pounce), the ball curving from end to end of the field in varying trajectories as each man tried to outmanoeuvre the other: which Miller finally did, placing his umpteenth kick so meticulously close to touch that Keighley's captain was caught in two minds – would it be ball-back or not? – and, fumbling it over the line, gave away thirty hard-fought yards. Full backs do not attempt such passages today, changes in strategy having seen them off to the extent that, when Hampson of Wigan and Auckland's Crequer swapped a trifling couple of salvoes in 1987, you could hear old chaps in the Douglas Stand chortling in a mixture of surprise and recollection of how things used to be.

Some of the Wigan games have likewise fixed themselves in memory because of a single incident, still vivid after all this time. Matches with Leeds supplied a high yield of these, including the unforgettable goal kicked by Bert Cook on an atrocious afternoon in March 1947. It had been raining heavily for days and the pitch was a quagmire of mud and puddles which had both teams slutched up almost beyond recognition before the game was ten minutes old; and still it was tippling down. At every scrum, a cloud of steam drifted off those bent backs, while loose play saw men slithering all over the place and sliding yards whenever they hit the ground. From the kick-off it had been obvious that artful rugby was out of the question, and not long afterwards it seemed likely that whoever chanced to skid across the line first might well win the match. When, just before the interval, Wigan were penalised inside their own half, no one thought much about it, even when Cook was seen to be preparing a shot at goal. You could hear the derisive laughter of the locals all round Central Park – don't be so bloody daft, man! – as he cleaned the ball on his shirt, placed it in the middle of an especially muddy patch and adjusted it as carefully as if it were a watch, stepped back some distance before wiping his kicking boot on his other calf, and stood poised amid those sounds of mirth. Then that rotund figure tiptoed back again, and gave the ball such a thump that goal was written all over it from the moment it rose out of the mire fifty-odd yards from the posts. And though Gareth Price did skid over for an unconverted try later on, that goal alone was enough to put Leeds into the semifinal of the Cup.

I remember the gloom aboard the bus that evening as we splashed across South Lancashire through the still seething rain, the upper deck as steamy as any scrum. The season by then was three-quarters over and Wigan had just suffered only their fifth defeat. They had already acquired the Lancashire Cup, which they would keep for six straight years, and were to win the Lancashire League as well as the Rugby League Championship itself, taking a sweet revenge upon the Loiners at the semifinal of the play-offs. Although the championship was by no means certain to end up at Central Park yet, Wigan had been full of confidence until the Cup-tie that this could just be their year to take every trophy available to them, a feat performed by only three teams in the history of the game, and by no one for a couple of decades. That 5–0 defeat at home in the Challenge Cup was a severe blow to ambition and to self-esteem, and Wigan were still numbed by it when St Helens came to Central Park for the Good Friday match six days later and beat them 12–7. Just over a week after that they went down again, 7–8 to Willie Horne's Barrow at Craven Park. Then they pulled themselves together and won every remaining fixture, nine matches on the trot, to take the Championship. Character had reasserted itself.

And they were a side of great character, approaching their prime. A second New Zealander had joined them at the beginning of that season, gravitating to Wigan like the Aucklander Nordgren, in the course of furthering his wider career. Ces Mountford came from the West Coast, a wild old gold and coal-mining area in the South Island bush, and he was studying at Wigan's celebrated Mining and Technical College for his manager's qualification. At home he had sometimes figured at centre three-quarter, but at Wigan he played stand-off, forming one of the great half-back partnerships of all time with Tommy Bradshaw. A chunky little man (5 ft 4 in, 11½ stone or thereabouts) he had remarkable acceleration for someone without long legs, and I still believe him to be the toughest footballer I've ever seen, hardly ever missing a game through injury, though forwards would give him a terrible pasting when they caught and dumped him. He once disposed of the colossal (18 stone) Frank Whitcombe in amazing fashion when only he stood between the prop and a Bradford try. As he bore down on the line, Whitcombe made to hand off this minor obstacle in his path; but in one swift movement, Mountford had him by the wrist with both hands, while digging his right heel into the turf as a pivot. It was like watching the hammer being thrown at a Highland Games, Mountford swinging Whitcombe right off his feet before letting that mighty figure go sailing a dozen yards through the air straight into touch. He didn't get up at once, either. Together with speed, durability and an elusiveness that kept him from being damaged more often than he was, Mountford also had a sharp footballing brain, which was behind many of those moves that turned Wigan's defence into slashing attack by a sudden and totally unexpected change of direction.

His partner, Bradshaw, more delicately built except in the lungs (which enabled him to talk almost non-stop through a game), divided his own considerable talents between servicing Mountford from the scrums, and switching position deftly with Martin Ryan at the back. Most dashing of full backs, Ryan was not among the great kickers in his position, like Fred Miller, and Denis Chalkley of Halifax, and Martin's great rival for the England and Great Britain shirts, Jimmy Ledgard of Dewsbury and Leigh. He was, however, a splendid tackler and incomparably the finest attacking full back in the British game, with Clive Churchill and Puig-Aubert the only men offering him competition in this respect abroad. Let any opponent boot the ball down to him and Ryan was off up the field, elbows splayed, ball held with both hands over his diaphragm, ready to die with it if need be, but looking for the gap through which he might send Mountford and the three-quarters away. The moment Ryan began to run, Bradshaw trickled back to watch the line, from wherever he might have been, and I do not recall a single occasion when – if Ryan's skirmish went amiss – this tactic cost Wigan so much as a yard of lost ground.

It was a powerful three-quarter line, however it might be composed; for in this department, above all, Wigan had talent to spare. There were four fast and strong wingers to choose from in Nordgren, Ratcliffe, Hilton and Lawrenson, three of whom played for Great Britain, one for Other Nationalities (as the expatriate international team, mostly of Anzacs, was called). For myself, there was no more thrilling sight on a rugby field than that of Nordgren – Noggie, as they used to hail him on the terraces – in full pelt for the corner from somewhere near halfway. His very walk was athletic, wide shoulders swinging confidently, blond head held high, skin still honeyed from the antipodean sun. With the ball under his arm, knees pounding high, shoulders hunched belligerently, he was swiftness and power incarnate, all the things an adolescent would wish himself to be. In my mind's eye, the Greek gods we were discovering in the Classical Fifth must have been something like this. Nordgren was my Achilles; and as soon as I started to shave, I shaped my sideburns in imitation of his.

When he played on the right wing, his centre was usually the very Welsh, very shrewd Ted Ward, who looked ponderous for a three-quarter, but had great speed for such a heavily-built man, and a devastating swerve. Playing on the left, Nordgren would normally be partnered by the fiercely strong Ashcroft, who every season scored nearly as many tries as his winger by using him as a decoy, dummying to him in that one split second which will almost always draw the solitary defender, then cutting sharply in to the line himself.

'Normally' was a relative expression in that Wigan attack, for there was a surplus of others besides four international wingers where only two at a time could be played. Above all there was Cunliffe, one of the game's great all-rounders, who occupied every position in the backs at various times and never let anybody down (continuing to do so at this level, what's more, until he was thirty-seven and almost in the Gus Risman class). Before long, too, there was young Roughley and young Broome, ready and competent to step into the first team when one of the regulars got crocked. The wonder is that, with such an abundance of skill in the backs, men who were in and out of the side were content to stay with that club. Not until Johnny Lawrenson was transferred to Workington in the summer of 1949 were those permutations disturbed.

The season after they had come so close to winning all four cups, Wigan strengthened their forwards by acquiring a couple of Yorkshiremen, Les White from York and Bill Hudson from Batley, to join Banks as aliens in an otherwise home-grown pack. White had been one of the successes in Risman's touring side, a swift and craggy man, dangerous near the line; while Hudson had been known as a robust attacking forward with the Gallant Youths since the early thirties. Together with the rangy Billy Blan they now made up a highly mobile and incisive back three at Central Park. The two imports both scored more frequently in their first season there than anyone outside the three-quarters, while Blan set a loose-forward's record with thirty-four tries in 1948–9. I can still see the blond Hudson flinging himself in a swallow-dive through the air to score, even when he could have strolled over to touch down, and I can hear the crowd's roar of pleasure at a form of exhibitionism hardly anyone else went in for in those days. That he had got within striking distance of the line was very often the result of sterling work done by the Wigan front row in the scrums; or by their captain/hooker's great tactical skill at play the ball.

Once Wigan's tourists returned from Down Under, Barton and Banks became competitors for the job of blind-side prop, because the No. 8 shirt belonged to Ken Gee alone when he was fit; and he did not often miss a match. At close on 16 stone he was easily the heaviest player in the side, a barrel of a man in spite of a working week spent down the pit. A fine goal-kicker, he also had a surprising turn of speed over fifteen yards, by which time his momentum might take him and any tacklers another ten. But what made his selection for Wigan, England and Great Britain a certainty for season after season was his footballing relationship with Joe Egan. Prop and hooker, Gee cauliflowered in the right ear, Egan in the left, Gee's bald pate luminous under a scrum cap, Egan's thatch slicked down with cream, they made a rare double act in the scrum and out of it. That Egan was unchallenged as our international hooker for so long was, as much as anything, because he could depend on Gee's steadfastness and perfectly timed shove: and in the loose they smuggled the ball back and forth to the endless frustration of all adversaries.

Almost invariably out-hooking his opponent when the match tally was counted, Egan was an outstanding dummy half-back at play the ball, too, feeding his team with an eye for the slightest opening before anyone else appeared to have spotted it. Now and then he would simply turn to face his own goal and amble backwards on those sturdy, bandy legs, shifting the ball's weight from one hand to the other, implicitly taunting the opposition with his delayed choice from among maybe four men he might pass it to – and the moment a finger was laid upon him, the ball was gone with a flick of powerful wrists. At times Egan would gain several yards in this fashion before he passed, while the enemy watched him backing into them, mesmerised.

The captain and his chief henchman and the others, it must be remembered, were playing a form of rugby in which tight possession was seen as a cardinal virtue at all times, when there was no automatic turnover after the sixth or any other tackle; and in retrospect, given also the much greater emphasis on scrummaging in those days, I am slightly surprised that so much *running* football was played by Wigan and other leading teams. Nor is my recollection – of backs and forwards alike streaming vividly down the field, passing and interchanging in breathtaking style – an example of the years distorting reality.

The most credible witness to the Wigan side of that era, as it happens, was a celebrated writer on Rugby Union – no less a figure than Larry Montague, son of the great C.E. and therefore born to the

purple among the great *Manchester Guardian* dynasties. He covered athletics for the paper in summer, Union in the winter, and managed to be
sports editor as well in the *Guardian*'s own gloriously semi-professional
days. Larry was far too intelligent a man to be dismissed as Homo
Twickiens, though he occasionally gave the impression that only his
northern breeding stood between him and a patronising attitude to
Rugby League. Our brand of football was covered by Swinton's
own Harold Mather, whose formal education had stopped short of
grammar school, whereas Larry had finally fetched up (via Rugby,
I think) at Balliol.

Much later in my life, when I was a colleague of both, I discovered
how Larry had taken it upon himself to foster Harold's career in Cross
Street, though he did him no service by trying to drill into him a form of
English composition based on rigidly Latin syntax, which meant that
Harold's prose style was thereafter notable for its determined efforts at
all costs to avoid the split infinitive. No one knew his Rugby League
better, and he cared passionately for the game, enough to be nettled
by Larry's somewhat Olympian regard for it. It says much about their
relationship that Montague allowed Mather to conduct him to Central
Park one Saturday, there to see his first match in the plebeian code.
It says even more that Larry insisted on himself, rather than Harold,
writing the piece that appeared in Monday morning's paper.

I cannot now remember all he said of the match, or the exact
words he used, but I have never forgotten the gist of his report.
This was that, like most Rugby Union people, he had entertained a
number of prejudices against Rugby League, some of which he had
now seen to be ill-founded, for he had just watched a game played
in a spirit wholly to be admired, with high technical skill abundantly
displayed. Of Wigan he said he had no doubt that this XIII could, on
its best days, beat any rugby side in the world, at Union or League.
He thought its brilliance depended chiefly on two things: the speed
with which every footballing skill was performed; and the fact that
any man in that side could throw the ball in any direction and any
distance he chose, without even looking, in the certain knowledge
that a team-mate would be there to take the pass.

It is a fact of sporting life, on the whole, that great sides in any
version of football only stay together unchanged for a season or two,
because injuries – let alone other factors – take too great a toll for
it to be otherwise. Club politics, in fact, were mostly responsible
for breaking up my first Wigan side, starting with Lawrenson's

departure in 1949, which was followed (unthinkably, it seemed at the time) by that of Joe Egan and Ces Mountford in consecutive years. Within half a dozen seasons only the evergreen Cunliffe and Ashcroft remained as tokens of what had been, and by then another fine side was taking shape, with Boston, Ashton and Bolton heading for international honours in the backs, and Brian McTigue assuming Ken Gee's old mantle in the engine-room. By the fifties, it was clear, a star-spangled era had come to an end, and although some splendid teams have worn the cherry and white in the period since, nothing quite as remarkable as the side Egan captained came along again until Graham Lowe coached another team that very nearly cleaned up every available trophy in season 1986–7.

My first Wiganers may not have been the greatest club side ever produced in this country; by any sensible computation that title can only be shared by Albert Goldthorpe's Hunslet, which won all four cups in 1907–8, by Harold Wagstaff's Huddersfield, which did likewise in 1914–15, and by Hector Halsall's Swinton, which repeated the feat in 1927–8. Wigan's burning ambition ever since has been to join that triumvirate, and on half a dozen occasions it has narrowly failed to achieve the crown that the entire town, as near as makes no matter, has been hungry for across nearly a hundred years. Such failures, though, are statistical and secondary to the real worth of a team taking the field. The fact is that, of all the club sides I have seen at both ends of the earth in four decades of watching rugby football, the one Joe Egan led between the autumn of 1947 and the spring of 1950 is the team I would choose to play for me, against any of its contemporaries, if my life depended on the outcome. I salute them, my champions, across the years.

Three

Grounds for Reassurance

In a world where sheer size and showiness are too highly regarded for my taste, the Rugby League grounds of northern England are enormously reassuring. This is not to say that I'm happy with the way things sometimes are there these days, and I'll come to that in a moment. What it does mean, however, is that these particular football grounds encourage you to have a relationship with them, which doesn't happen so easily in something much grander. Has anyone ever felt the slightest warmth or sadness or joy or compassion when contemplating the fabric, the appearance, the story of Wembley Stadium? If not, the reason may very well be that while it has long been a magnificent location for the staging of important events, it has never been the focal point of any community's sense of identity, where local hopes and fears and triumphs and disasters – in one of their manifestations – occur. I suspect that Wembley does not deeply belong to that outskirt of London where it was built. It is something used almost entirely by strangers throughout the year. And it feels like it.

Run down the list of clubs in the two divisions of the Rugby Football League and one thing is immediately striking about the places where they play. This is the high proportion of grounds that, judging by their names, could not possibly be anywhere but in the English North. We have our share of conventional Parks, to be sure, which might be anywhere at all: Craven, Derwent, Central, Naughton and so on. A number of others are stuck with the name of the road in which they were sited during some Victorian building spree: Wheldon, Post Office, Knowsley and one or two more. But there are also grounds whose names belong quite exclusively to their local turf, sometimes mysteriously so, inviting further speculation on their origins. Where on earth, other than Halifax, could Thrum Hall possibly be? Nowhere but in some place where weaving was the local trade, at any rate, because thrums were the untidy fringes left on a loom when the finished cloth was cut away. Thrum Hall, in fact, was a farm on the edge of town when the Halifax Cricket, Football and Athletic Club moved there in 1886, and it is quite possible that a farmer's wife much earlier had worked a hand-loom in the attic of her house, giving rise to a name, well understood locally, that would distinguish it from Spring Hall, Sand Hall, Hardwick Hall and other farms nearby.

There is a small thesis to be written by some local historian on these derivations. At Dewsbury, Crown Flatt sounds adamantly right for a pitch situated on a bit of level ground high above the town whose business has been to do with blankets and shoddy ever since the Industrial Revolution began, if not before. But how did it come to be parted from the final 's' that is a more normal spelling (as in Crossflatts, near Keighley) in the West Riding of Yorkshire? Not much guesswork required for Watersheddings, once you realise that at 820 feet above sea-level this is the highest ground in the championship, where Oldham is beginning to give way to one of the bleakest stretches of the Pennines, from which rain comes down in swathes across many a promising three-quarter movement. But is there some Viking saga to account for the sturdiness of Odsal, where Bradford Northern have played since 1934, or does it derive from some arcane procedure in municipal waste disposal, which is what used to happen there until the football club moved over from Birch Lane? And what, in Warrington's ancient past, happened at Wilderspool long before the rugby footballers arrived over a century ago?

The history of the North, you see, is forever cropping up in the background of this game. Long before pits were sunk at the Glasshoughton and Wheldale collieries, Castleford was a Roman settlement, with a fort standing guard over a crossing of the Aire, on high ground above the land now occupied by the football club in Wheldon Road. The most unappetising river in Lancashire since the Irwell was cleaned up, the Douglas, which trickles past the grandstand bearing its name at Wigan RLFC, once flowed with blood after a Civil War battle near by, in which Lord Derby and his Royalists were seen off by one of Cromwell's commanders.

There are a few oddities in the lists. If I were a Bramley supporter,

I'd be wistful for the days when the ground used to be known by the name of the pub in which the players changed, the Barley Mow. But a benefaction in 1966 caused the pitch to be somewhat realigned a bit farther from the pub, and one of the neatest and most pleasant grounds I know was simultaneously translated into McLaren Field – which sounds as if John Wayne or some other celluloid hero of the old Army Air Corps might be bringing his crippled biplane in to land any minute now (having taken off, perhaps, from Tatters Field down at Doncaster). These titles don't tease me as much as a couple of others, though. What French connection resulted in Wakefield Trinity being located at Belle Vue, where the most conspicuous things in sight are the power station cooling towers half a mile away, and the nearest things of natural beauty the fields of rhubarb that flourish beside the London to Leeds railway line: why, moreover, is Trinity's emblem the fleur-de-lis? And how came Hull FC to call their premises The Boulevard, which also has a Gallic ring, though they were known as the Athletic Grounds up to the moment of purchase in 1899? It is a curious title for a club to use when it is so firmly anchored amid fishermen's terraces on Humberside.

The Airlie Birds are not the only Rugby League players hemmed in on all sides by mass-produced housing or industry. Yet while this is the rule, there are some notable exceptions. There is something aesthetically pleasing about a visit to Keighley where, if you stand at one end of the Lawkholme Lane ground, you can watch rugby against the panorama of a hillside which becomes Ilkley Moor beyond its summit, at the threshold of the Yorkshire Dales. Homes have been built on that slope in the past generation, softening its former wildness; yet still there clings to it a ghostly presence which speaks of the Brontës, of Cathy and Heathcliffe, who haunt all the heights surrounding the little mill town.

For tremendous wildness that will never be softened, there is nothing to touch the journey that must be made to reach the football at Workington or Whitehaven, which necessitates breaching the great mountains of Cumbria, driving beneath the crags of Blencathra and the long whaleback of Skiddaw, within sight of Great Gable and Scafell, before winding down to the harbours of the rugby towns beside the Irish Sea. A fixture at Barrow takes you across gentler but no less pleasing country, between the highlands of the Lake District and the shoreline of Morecambe Bay, and then down some of the widest main streets in England, because Barrow-in-Furness was that rarity, a planned town in the middle of the nineteenth century.

All the long journeys to the extremities of our game have their compensations if you are prepared to keep your eyes open en route. Go to Carlisle and you are in hill country again (the shapely humps of the Howgills, just before Shap) before crossing the Eden Valley, which is as tranquil and beautiful as anywhere in the land. Strike due east along the main axis of Rugby League, and after running out of the industrial belt past Castleford and Featherstone, you are in the prosperous farmlands of what ought still to be the East Riding, including the curiosity of Selby just to port, with its old abbey miles from the sea, yet where they still build ships and launch them sideways into the River Ouse. When you have almost given up hope of reaching it the Humber itself appears, majestic and broad, and now crossed by one of the most breathtaking bridges in the world.

Even the rugby grounds in the thick of the industrial North can know visual drama. From the plateau of Mount Pleasant, where Batley play, it is almost possible to see Crown Flatt similarly perched not far away across one of the deep gullies that separate the various segments of the Heavy Woollen District. It probably was very pleasant when the Victorians began to build up there, away from the muck and misery they had created along the bottoms, and it is not so bad today, now that smoke abatement policies have given everybody a view again; not only of houses and churches and factories distantly filing up hillsides, but also of fields where crops are grown and hay is mown.

Another second division side does just as well in a grittier way. Runcorn Highfield is the latest manifestation of that nomadic club which started life in 1922 as Wigan Highfield, and reached its present shape by way of previous existences as London Highfield, Liverpool Stanley, Liverpool City and Huyton. By a strange historical quirk it has come to rest – permanently, it would be nice to think – on the ground that was inhabited by the Runcorn club which was one of the Northern Union's first members in season 1895–6, but which failed to survive the First World War. The sloping pitch at Canal Street subsequently served an Association football club, which now shares it with the men of Rugby League.

Just above the ground is the final stretch of the Bridgewater Canal, along which genuine narrow boats – working craft carrying cargo, not conversions pressed into the holiday trade – go pop-pop-poppety-pop-popping along. Below the football field is the wide sweep of the Mersey in all its humdrum grandeur, with the silver curve of the late-lamented transporter bridge's successor traversing the water to Widnes, where cooling towers and factory chimneys plume smoke and steam into frequently leaden skies. It isn't pretty, but it is unforgettable.

Almost without exception, the grounds are in scale with their immediate surroundings. They do not dominate so much that they are in danger of seeming to crush whatever has been built around them, especially the dwellings. They have developed bit by bit and higgledy-piggledy over many years to achieve their present condition, and in this they have something in common with almost all our cathedrals. The relationship with their surroundings is often homely; never more so than at Featherstone, where the people who live in the terrace which runs down one side of the little ground habitually tether the ends of their washing lines to the football club's boundary wall. This is one place where it is possible to see quite clearly the ground's growth across a hundred years or so, in the different stages of building. The basic shape of Post Office Road was settled in 1898, when the first game under Northern Union rules was played on the 'new sports ground near the railway station'; and the shed sheltering those standing on the eastern terrace will not be much later than that, I imagine. After entering the ground you pass a more recent memento, the gateway presented to the club a quarter of a century ago by the Knottingley branch of the supporters' club 'In memory of Freddie Miller. A great player and a gentleman.' More recent still is the smart prefabricated stand with its attractive pattern of cobblestones at the back, all of which arose from the ashes of the fire that destroyed its predecessor a few years ago.

At many other grounds, too, it is possible to read something of a club's history with the curiosity of an archaeologist. Nowhere is much more rewarding than Wilderspool, where Warrington have played rugby since 1883, the fourth ground the club by then had occupied. It is snugged down in its neighbourhood more tightly than any other, perhaps, so that anyone who goes in search of it for the first time without the march of crowds to point him in the right direction, can easily miss the way down a narrow side street. It isn't the same ground I knew when I first went there forty years ago, when the Wire normally played in primrose and blue hoops. For one thing, the grandstand has been reroofed and they regrettably failed to reproduce the old pedimented gable in the middle, with its flagstaff and its bold announcement that this was the home of Warrington Rugby League

Club. For another, the arrangements along the opposite touchline have changed out of all recognition.

I can't for the life of me remember what was there in 1947, when I stood by the corner flag in one of the densest crowds I've ever known, and watched Brian Bevan score the most remarkable try I shall ever see. Wigan had been in the Warrington 25 for several minutes, and had succeeded in pushing the home side back to their goal-line. Bevan, so close to me that I might almost have touched him if I had reached out, was actually in goal when Gerry Helme slung him the ball in what must surely have been a desperate move, with the Australian so tightly placed. But at once those spindly, heavily-bandaged shanks began to revolve, the tongue came purposefully out of the sucked-in cheeks and the toothless gums, and this bald-headed wreck of a man who just happened to be one of the greatest athletes in the history of any sport anywhere, proceeded to show us why this was incontestably the case. It was a shimmying side-step or two which took Bev past the first three Wigan players before he was off, swerving across the field towards the grandstand to beat two more, before straightening out and, by what devices I couldn't see, crossing at the far corner before any more defenders could catch up with him. He had run much farther than the length of the field, for he had swept from one end of it to the other in a diagonal; and he had gone through the entire Wigan team in doing so.

On the side from which Bevan took off there is now a product wholly of our times, not his; a looming social centre with a posh-looking restaurant which oversees the pitch and a name, Snookers, that sounds as if it is intended to entice the trendy from the arable depths of Cheshire. It has been grafted on to a low little stand, only a few rows deep, that goes back much earlier in the history of Wilderspool. Elsewhere, too, Warrington's past has pretty well managed to hold its own. At one end of the ground a shed runs the full width of the pitch. But at the other end are two small sheds, built at different times, one with a chamfered corner to its roof; and they are still awaiting the third that would complete the composition and make it symmetrical. But then they'd have to shift the score-board which occupies some of the open space.

The Craven Park belonging to Hull Kingston Rovers is another which bears all the marks of gradual expansion, in bits and pieces over many years, an effect heightened by compromises between its function as a rugby ground and its alternative use as a greyhound track. At Naughton Park, where everything seems always to have been just given a fresh lick of paint (in the black and white which, I trust, Widnes will return to in their playing strip before too long) there are no fewer than six different versions of grandstand or terrace shed deployed around the most compact ground in the championship. This is the hallmark of organic growth, the factor that makes it easy for people to relate to their surroundings, the antithesis of alienation or indifference. The oldest supporters of the Chemics, after all, can probably remember some of those stands being built.

There are grounds one remembers as much as anything because of some external feature, like the cooling towers near Belle Vue. At Castleford it is the trains rumbling past the embankment during the course of a match. At Workington it is the red sandstone of St Michael's church behind one of the goals, with its tower built low to dodge the worst of the weather coming in from the sea. At Whitehaven it is the immensely hospitable Miners' Welfare beside the main entrance, which signifies a particularly close relationship here, because the football club leases the Recreation Ground from the local colliers. At Leigh it is the mill at one end and the winding gear of the nearby Parsonage pit (but nowhere can I find a trace of the improvisations that allowed the club to resume football on this new site after the war, when Hilton Park was Kirkhall Lane, and its outworks consisted of corrugated iron sheets bolted together, surplus to the wartime demand for Anderson air-raid shelters).

There are grounds one remembers because of some internal aspect. Salford's cantilevered North Stand, fringed at the back by the willows that give the club's home its name, is one of the best places to sit in the whole of the two divisions, especially when the action is at that end of the field, for then it is possible to see quite clearly every step a player takes, and where it fits into the pattern of the game. Its only rival for such a view is the G. F. Hutchins Stand at Oldham (once known as the Penny Rush), this being so close to events that a successful goal-kick is liable to put the ball straight into your lap. Barrow's Craven Park is the only ground, apart from Wilderspool, with almost continuous cover on all four sides, and I can think of no other with a statue standing unexpectedly beside one set of its turnstiles (it is to Lord Frederick Cavendish, one of those entrepreneurs who gave the town its uncommonly wide thoroughfares). At Thrum Hall, nearly as compact as Naughton Park and with a moorland view to rival that from Lawkholme Lane, Halifax have their pavilion faced with glazed tiles in blue and white, just like one of those gin palaces the breweries used to build. At Mount Pleasant, handsomely approached by way of a cricket field, with a greater sense of surrounding space than most grounds know, Batley have a grassy bank for spectators to sprawl on when it isn't too damp, as do Bramley at McLaren Field. This is what, in Australia, they call The Hill.

There are some grounds, alas, in such a state that one's first and lasting response to them is dismay, especially if you have known them in much better days. To visit Huddersfield now is to be numbed by the catastrophic decline in the fortunes of a club which used to be such a matter of civic pride that the elders of the town competed strenuously to be seen there in positions of authority. Here Wagstaff, Rosenfeld, Cooper, Hunter and many more giants played football; and on the other side of the Fartown grandstand, Hirst, Rhodes, Sutcliffe, Hutton and a host of other doughty Yorkshiremen played county cricket once upon a time. The humiliations of the once mighty rugby team in the past few years have included the infliction of synthetic names (Barracudas, Arena 84) as well as crushing defeats and the owner's offer to give the club away.

Fartown these days looks as if it has hit rock bottom indeed, with its grandstand – once one of the most commodious in the championship – and its shed both deemed too unsafe to use, with vegetation growing out of the steep terracing opposite the stand, and with a raggle of barbed-wire entanglement at the score-board end; where, if you look hard, you will discover a tablet in memory of the late and great David Valentine, who must be turning in his grave, along with all the other magnificent Huddersfield ghosts.

If it comes to that, there will be other shades of the past not best pleased with the transformation of Station Road, Swinton, either. Here, where I first set eyes on Clive Churchill, Reg Gasnier, Keith Barnes, Brian Clay and a score of other illustrious Kangaroos, was one of the major Test match grounds up to twenty years ago, with grandstands running down both touch-lines and a marvellous atmosphere for international games, which invariably commanded a full house. Now one of the stands has been pulled down, an end has been almost blocked off by encroaching squash courts, and a dilapidated Station Road echoes half-emptily to the cheers of those faithful Mancunians who come to watch the Lions yo-yo between first and second divisions yet again.

Rugby League was bound to be hit hard by the stringent new

regulations imposed on all sporting venues after the disastrous fire at the Bradford City soccer ground in May 1985. Too many of the less successful clubs had been struggling to make ends meet for too long, with scarcely enough income to settle the weekly overheads, let alone to maintain their grounds in tiptop condition; and the local authorities were demanding much more than this in their peremptory new mood. Big fish like Wigan (extensive replacement of crush barriers) and Hull (the famous old Threepenny Stand condemned) were penalised as well, but it was the smaller fry which bore the brunt of the new zeal to make sure that the buck stopped anywhere but on the desk of local government officers. No ground had been kept in better shape than Mount Pleasant, within its modest limitations, but the fact that its little grandstand was a beautiful piece of old-fashioned carpentering, carefully repainted every few years, counted for nothing now; Batley were told it no longer passed muster and could not be used. Blackpool Borough had a perfectly good ground, custom-built for the game as recently as 1962, almost within a drop-kick of the celebrated seaside Tower, but such was the order of alterations demanded by the safety officers that the club had to abandon it, and wandered off elsewhere in search of a permissible home.

They were not the only one. A long era, stretching back to 1003, came to an end at York, whose directors decided there was nothing for it but to relinquish the old ground in Clarence Street, from which it had been a pleasure to watch rugby with a view of the Minster's towers beyond the municipal bowling green and its trees next door. Rochdale Hornets turned their backs on their Athletic Grounds in 1988, and it was indeed time to go, for it was in a sorry state by then, a forlorn shadow of the place whose Hill 60 – the embankment named after a First World War battle in which the local Lancashire Fusiliers took part – used to be packed at all home games. This was another ground, like the Watersheddings, lying beside the backbone of England and therefore exposed to ferocious weather at times. There was something attractive in the distant sight of headlights winding spectrally down the M62 through the Pennine mists late on a winter's afternoon, with the prospect of a good tea in front of the fire after the match, but sometimes the elements were rougher than that. During the bitter winter of 1946–7, snow lay so thickly hereabouts that a man crossing the Hornets' pitch was able to touch the goalpost crossbars with ease.

It was a misfortune for all these clubs that someone else's tragedy should cost them so dear. But for really rotten luck there was nobody worse off than Dewsbury. Crown Flatt had seen much better days by 1985: February 1890, for example, when Wales defeated England in a Rugby Union international for the first time, by a try to nothing, when 'a sleeting snowstorm, which continued throughout the game, rendered the ground a veritable quagmire'; and in those wartime seasons when Eddie Waring collected such a team of guest players as to make Dewsbury all but unbeatable. The moment the Popplewell Report's recommendations were enacted, Crown Flatt became decorated with Day-Glo orange tapes to warn people off areas reckoned unsafe, as happened on many grounds. The club was told it would have to spend at least £25,000 to bring its solitary stand up to scratch; and by a huge effort of local sweat and goodwill it had accomplished this when vandals broke in and set fire to it. Not only was one of the few remaining barrel-roofed stands in the Rugby Football League destroyed, but with it went all Dewsbury's equipment, its records going back to 1875, the trophies it had occasionally won, and other mementoes of its not undistinguished history.

The major Rugby League grounds survived the new strictures without much trouble. Odsal ought to be counted as one of these, for here is the natural amphitheatre that made the late Stanley Chadwick never cease to campaign for its development as the Wembley of the North. And one can see why, when it accommodated over 102,000 spectators for that 1954 Cup Final replay, with terracing made of nothing more substantial than railway sleepers, and the players reaching the field through the crowds, down a long cascade of steps from their dressing-rooms on the amphitheatre's rim, so that Bradford Northern and Great Britain sides, with their predominantly white strips, always looked like slowly descending waterfalls. Now the players emerge from a tunnel at the edge of the pitch, and terracing and crush-barriers are made of heavy-duty materials to the highest specifications. There is also a considerable stand with individual plastic tip-up seats.

But that's about as far as ambition has gone. The club offices and hospitality lounges are still on that ledge high above the arena, and there are a few necessities closer to the people watching the game. But the feeling one mostly has at Odsal is that somebody hasn't been able to make up his mind what to do with this overwhelming place. It is part rugby ground, part speedway track, but mostly it is still just a highly promising cavity on the edge of the city, so

35

deep and wide that it can have a climate of its own. That's what caused the Third Test against the 1948 Kangaroos to be postponed from December until January 1949. The original fixture could have been played anywhere in the North of England that afternoon, for a foggy morning had turned brilliantly sharp and sunny, the perfect English winter's day: anywhere except in the amphitheatre at Odsal, that is. For there the fog bank had become trapped and could not be dispersed. It was impossible to see more than a few yards from anywhere along the touch-lines.

Odsal is, for me, one of two Rugby League irregulars, Elland Road being the other one, though the reasons are not at all the same. Elland Road, which belonged to Leeds United alone until Hunslet became a junior partner under municipal patronage a few years ago, is a classic example of what Mr Justice Popplewell had in mind when he remarked that soccer grounds nowadays are 'built like medieval fortresses'. I was within earshot when that point was made more forcefully before a match in which Wigan played Hunslet at this stadium. An elderly couple with Platt Bridge written all over them, the sort of people who have helped to give Rugby League its reputation for civilised spectating, having negotiated the various forms of obstacle with which Elland Road is well endowed, finally made it to the terraces, and stood speechless for a moment or two while they looked around at the impregnable fences, the iron gates and all the other evidence that Elland Road is as much penal as sporting nowadays.

'Well, Mother,' he finally exclaimed, 'have you ever seen owt like this before?' He sucked his teeth disparagingly. 'Call this a football ground? Looks more like a bloody concentration camp to me!'

Because it has all the apparatus required to handle massive crowds with security, and would, indeed, be a great place to watch rugby in were it not for those awful fences, Elland Road is now numbered among those venues that can be used for the big occasion. But I wouldn't mind betting that there isn't a Hunslet fan able to recall the club's more natural home in South Leeds before the building developers got hold of it, who wouldn't trade all the opulence of this stadium for the old Parkside ground, which was the antithesis of this, as nearly rural as you could be on the outskirts of the city, with a pair of ancient cottages lying picturesquely behind the Middleton end goal.

That elderly couple's own home patch has been steadily modernised in recent years, and there are ambitions to go even further. By the time these words are read it may well be that Wigan will have an additional stand on the popular side, with hospitality boxes in the grand and fashionable mode of our day. Central Park hasn't quite changed out of all recognition since I first knew it, but you no longer need get wet on the Kop, and it is not quite as draughty in the Popular Stand as it was in its predecessor, the old Dutch barn. All the railway sleepers have been banished, though they once provided terracing and crush-barriers; and with undersoil heating as well as powerful floodlights, Central Park might well be envied by some clubs in the First Division of the Association Football League.

Here is a ground that has distinctly kept up with the times. Yet in one small but vastly important way, it still proclaims its allegiance to its past. The traditional approach to Central Park, along Hilton Street, is now dominated by the Riverside Cabaret, which brings welcome income to the football club. Yet beside this remain the old club offices, with the honours boards arranged along the front, and the original sign in bold cherry lettering on a white ground above the upper row of windows – Central Park A1909D Wigan Football Club. This quite small and now decidedly old-fashioned brick building is still at the heart of the whole successful enterprise, in spite of expansion and modernity all around. I hope it stays that way, as long as it will stand up, to serve the same purpose in times to come as the curtain ring which Maggie Mossop wore on her wedding finger and which, she swore, she would never exchange for a proper gold band, however prosperous she and Willie might become; 'To stop us,' she explained, 'from getting too proud.'

Our sporting archaeologist would note that as a consequence of that old building being retained, the players here still come on to the pitch from the clubhouse directly behind one of the goals. This seems to be a peculiarity of South-West Lancashire, for it also happens at Widnes and Runcorn and at Knowsley Road, St Helens, but nowhere else. At Knowsley Road, again, it is a link with the more modest beginnings of a club that now possesses one of the ampler grounds in the game, where county cup finals and Challenge Cup semis are frequently played. You can find its token equivalent at all the major grounds of Rugby League, even at Headingley, which has an atmosphere quite unmatched anywhere else.

This derives, above all, from the fact that here, as a notice near one of the main entrances says, is the 'Home of Yorkshire Cricket and Leeds Rugby League'. The relationship between the two games has often been close in the North of England, and there are cricket pitches immediately adjacent to the grounds at Keighley and Halifax, as well as at Batley, Huddersfield and Leeds. What separates the cricket from the football at Headingley is a grandstand which, as far as I'm aware, is unique in the whole of British sport, for it faces both ways at once.* What might be the back of the stand to supporters of Leeds RLFC is its front to those who come to watch Yorkshire County Cricket Club at work in the summer months; and vice versa. As a result, Headingley has seen many magnificent Test matches of both kinds over the years. It was here that Don Bradman scored 334 against England in 1930, here that Ian Botham transformed a Test with his phenomenal slog of 149 not out against Australia in 1981: it was here, in 1948, that Ernest Ward and his men just shaded the Kangaroos 23–21 in one of the most thrilling rugby matches ever played, and here in 1982 that Max Krilich's Invincibles devastated Great Britain 32–8 in the last fixture of their tour, having won every match they had played and demonstrated a superiority that had never been seen in the northern hemisphere before.

Just once was Rugby League played on that cricket pitch, when the football ground was too frozen to use in December 1938, and the goalposts were shifted to the other side of the stand for a fixture between Leeds and Salford, enabling Vic Hey to score the only try ever registered on the turf of the summer game. But no spectator at any season of the year, who uses Headingley's bars and tea-rooms, can fail to be aware that football and cricket go hand in hand round here, with Vanity Fair prints and team photographs of Yorkshire CCC hanging alongside mementoes of Lions touring sides composed by Melba Studios of Sydney, and of Loiners' teams that have brought trophies home to the boardroom at Headingley.

There is no more agreeable preliminary to a game of rugby than to have a drink or simply to eat your sandwiches amid those pictures at the top of the stand, before passing through to the football side and taking your seat in time for the kick-off. No vision of elms here, which the cricketers enjoyed at the Kirkstall Lane end of the ground till disease destroyed many of the trees; instead, a vista of central Leeds distantly beyond one of the embankments, and

---

* The nearest thing to it is at Cardiff, where the major stand in the National Stadium is backed by a smaller version for those watching club games. In Leeds the two stands are virtually identical, with 3,800 seats on one side and 3,600 on the other.

at the other end an array of semi-detached roof-tops and upstairs windows through which the impecunious or the miserly can watch some football free. It was from that direction a few seasons ago, while we were all waiting for a match with Hull Kingston Rovers to begin, that a suburban fox suddenly ran down the embankment, leapt a wall on to the field and, after trying unsuccessfully to make his exit through the crowd assembling in the south stand, finally made off across the embankment at the city end. That south stand contains the curiosity linking Headingley with its origins in 1890: the quaint cast-iron spiral staircase which winds round one of the pillars upholding the roof, and which will have given many a cameraman vertigo as he makes his way to the observation platform at the top.

There is nothing in this catalogue remotely resembling that enormously gaunt stadium at Twickenham, which was once sharply described (by Ivor Brown) as 'the last fortress of the Forsytes'. Even the grandest of our grounds differs from the English Rugby Union's headquarters by a great deal more than structure and scale and some obvious social and regional characteristics which, to some extent, are at long last beginning to budge. What every Rugby League club without exception has in common with the rest is a relationship with its local community, sometimes (as at Bramley and Hunslet, for example) an intensely parochial one.

The circumstances which produced the stadium at Twickenham in 1910 – the RFU wanting a ground of its own for big matches and the prestige that would result – had nothing at all to do with an attachment to that previously empty corner of Middlesex; and even though the Harlequins have a tenancy there, they divide their time between the field at headquarters and the Stoop Memorial Ground. In the Rugby Football League, the relationship with a local community may no longer be as profound as it once was in some cases, but it has remained strong enough almost certainly to have made the difference, these past few hard-pressed years, between some of the smaller clubs surviving and going under. The grounds are where you cannot fail to be aware of this, where you can feel the passion of local identity, where you may take note of local idiosyncrasy. I hope one day to find out why Barrow start their matches at 2.30 p.m. instead of the customary three o'clock, even when it doesn't get dark till nine; and why, at Wakefield and one or two other grounds near by, they delay their kick-off till 3.30 p.m. Could this be because of long sermons in chapel on Sunday mornings? Or do they have more sluggish digestions than elsewhere?

My unhappiness at Elland Road is not only because its fortifications remind me how nasty some people can be at a football match. At bottom it is because those cages are a repudiation of civilised communal relationship: they prevent football followers from mixing with each other irrespective of their rivalries. At no other Rugby League ground do we see anything of the sort, and I pray we never shall. For the most part the grounds are not obviously the abode of super-stardom and glitzy success, big television deals and players strong-arming everyone in sight with their lawyers in tow; and some will see this as a deficiency in our game. But they are companionable places, where you can be easy with your neighbour, and this is a more precious thing.

Four

Cloth Caps and Other Images

Nothing lately has exercised the Rugby League authorities in England, and many commentators, too, much more than the image of the game. How does it look to outsiders? Is it presented glamorously enough to attract new fans? These and kindred questions have begun to obsess the administrators as they have contemplated their position in an increasingly crowded market-place. As long as I have been watching the game, those whose lives revolve round Rugby League, in one way and another, have been keen to see it played professionally throughout the land; but I do not recall any other period when there has been such an ardent desire in these quarters to see it become one of our indisputably national winter sports. This passion has been heightened, I suspect, by the truly remarkable selling of American football in Britain, which may well have produced feelings of envy and resentment, such as only the complete outsider can provoke when he walks off with the prize the homespun contender has set his heart on. I myself do not believe that the prize has, in fact, been won yet. I think we have been witnessing an unprecedented infatuation which will cool when those people who are at present enthralled by what they *perceive* to be American football, realise that they have been admiring a spectacular confidence trick. This needs some explanation, but I will try to be brief.

The popular perception of the game over here is that which has been promoted on Channel 4 television every Sunday night, and at sundry other times, in highlights from the previous week's matches across the Atlantic. Filmed and produced, edited and cut with great expertise, the programmes show almost nothing but high-speed action, concentrating especially, over and over again, on that compelling moment

41

when the quarter-back receives the ball, must decide quickly what to do with it, and then, more often than not, throws it to where he hopes a team-mate will catch it and score. The quarter-back's throwing of the ball, often over considerable distances with remarkable accuracy, is an extremely difficult feat, and I would not argue much with anyone who suggested that it transcends – for sheer skill under fire – any single act that any other form of football has to offer (though the placing of a soccer ball precisely on to the head of a player 30 yards away, so that he can nod it into the net, is perfectly comparable for skill alone). But nothing else in American football even begins to approach the quarter-back's craft.

For the most part, this is a sport in which grotesquely overdressed and often grossly overweight men run very short distances before thudding and blundering into each other en masse; whereupon the game stops dead, sometimes for minutes at a time. So relatively uneventful is it, so repetitive are the crashing mauls, that it can leave sports writers badly in the lurch when they try to describe what went on. Many British newspapers, highly susceptible to the infatuations of their readers, sent their own men to San Diego in January 1988 to cover Super Bowl XXII, the climax to the American season, and the correspondents were given plenty of space by their editors in which to do so. The most striking thing about their reports was that most of their column inches were spent on what people *said* about the match after it had been played, not about the activity on the field. But, then – to pick a random example which typifies most of what goes on – how do you make a goal-kick sound exciting when it is always taken from right in front of the posts? And how do you curb your sense of the ridiculous when the man who has kicked it promptly leaves the field in order to recover, so that he'll be in mint condition again if he's required to take another kick at goal?

The interminable stoppages are part of the confidence trick perpe-trated upon the viewer of television highlights. The statutory playing time of a match is sixty minutes, divided into four quarters. The professional match which has dragged on for less than two and a half hours has probably never been played; and some have been known to last three times the active length. Much of the excess is occupied by the elaborate preparations of the players before the next tactic is tried; some of it by the time needed for the attackers and defenders on both sides to swap places in the middle when possession changes hands. But in professional football the television factor is paramount –

the break every five or ten minutes so that commercials can be slotted in for the people viewing at home, the referee watching for the signal that tells him to stop the action now, as closely as he watches anything on the field of play.

'Selling the product has priority as far as TV sport is concerned,' an American handbook to their football pointed out a few years ago. 'In one Super Bowl game a kick-off was actually replayed because TV wasn't ready and missed filming it.' Candour of that order has not, unfortunately, been exported across the ocean along with the alien game. And yet it is very clear to anyone who keeps his eyes open, that the enormous effort the Americans have put into capturing a British audience for their football, is directed towards an end much more tangible than merely securing our applause and enthusiasm. It is bent, more than anything else, on selling merchandise.

The National Football League shops which have sprung up across our country, stocked with their expensive football gear and other material, are a prime example of this. So are the plethora of publications prominently displayed in bookshops and newsagents. More than fifty British companies have been recruited by the Americans to make things for sale over here, all of it under licence from the NFL, which stipulates all terms of trade and takes a rake-off from every purchase. It's our money they're after, as well as our approval of the American way of life; and this should surprise no one. The British, after all, conducted themselves in much the same fashion during their own imperial heyday.

Because the Americans are without rivals when it comes to what they call pree-sentation, the image of their football and everything to do with it has been very seductive over here. Admiration is the only decent response anyone can make to a carefully planned strategy of propaganda which results, on the occasion of the Super Bowl, in significant numbers of our population staying up until nearly four o'clock in the morning to watch a foreigner's sport unfold cumbersomely for hour after hour, six and a half thousand miles away, the commentators being hard pressed to find something to say during the interminable interludes when the play has stopped, while the American TV audience (but not ours, well out of prime time) are force-fed the commercials that pay for the whole bonanza. It is as though the Wembley Cup Final (FA or RL, it doesn't matter which) had thousands in Pittsburgh, Miami, Houston, Denver and points west, arising with the dawn in order to goggle at the action from

London. The average American would find this idea too ludicrous for words. He doesn't want to know about other people's games except, conceivably, as quaint events he might spend a few minutes on while doing Yurrup on a package tour.

The image of his own brand of football, which doesn't quite coincide with the reality, is chiefly one of slickness and smartness, an operation in which everyone is well-groomed, wherein all useful forms of technology are employed without hesitation, with a distinct impression that no expense has been spared to make this whole happening a marvellous, a magnificent, a stoopendous event. It is a beguiling prescription, and people of my generation were initially exposed to it as children during the war, when we became aware of the American servicemen stationed near Warrington and elsewhere.

The first thing I noticed about them was how splendidly they were turned out, with gleaming white teeth, sparklingly gold-framed and rimless spectacles, caps peaked with real leather and protected from our rain by opaquely olive plastic covers. Their immaculate uniforms were made of the finest cloth, and these soldiers were altogether several cuts above their British counterparts, who looked as though they were clad in surplus Army blankets dyed khaki and miserably ill-fitting. It is contrasts at this level, I think, that have caused the administrators of our Rugby League to be uneasy with the image that our game presents to the world at large, for the contrasts are part of the Rugby League package; and packaging has never been more important in successfully selling than it has become nowadays. Certainly, there could scarcely be a bigger difference – off the field as much as on it – between the game of football authorised by Chapeltown Road in Leeds, and that manipulated from Park Avenue in New York.

Nor are the administrators alone anxious, judging by the number of people who write letters to our periodicals, complaining about some of the men hired as commentators by the BBC whenever Rugby League is televised. These do not, in truth, much resemble the earnest fellows who perform a similar service for American football, nor are they equipped with a paraphernalia of electronic diagrams to make an essentially crude and simple activity look subtle and sophisticated.

Latterly the domestic fire has been concentrated on Ray French and Alex Murphy, men steeped in their rugby, fine players in their day, but neither of them trained for broadcasting, which is not something that everyone can handle. Before them the target was Eddie Waring, whose reputation in the game was made during the war, when he managed Dewsbury and turned a very average side into a team of stars who won more trophies and contested more finals than at any other time in the club's history. It has become almost fashionable to belittle his performances with the microphone, on the grounds that he invited Southern audiences to guffaw at our game, with his eventually predictable humour ('If that thing in the mud moves, it'll be 'is 'ead, not the ball') and his refusal to make his act more stylish. He was probably incapable of doing that.

Although there were reasons to deplore something of Eddie Waring as a commentator on Rugby League, they had nothing to do with his near-caricature of Northern man. The trouble with him was, I think, that in the end he had become more intent on his own performance than upon the game he was describing, having been made well aware (and it must have astonished as well as gratified him when this dawned) that the BBC producers in London regarded him as more of an entertainment than the football; just as they seem to have done again with Brian Johnston in relation to cricket.

The image Waring conveyed to most people, the one widely attached to British Rugby League, and a sensitive matter to some, is loaded with attributes which many outsiders seem to think peculiar to the English North; at least, many outsiders appear to give many Northerners that impression. A number of words and phrases are well known for suggesting the image without the need for saying more: *flat vowels, ee bah gum, where there's muck there's brass, whippets, fish and chips, tripe and trotters, dark satanic mills, clogs and shawls* and several more (the sound of the belly laugh when someone has cheerfully farted in public is part of it, too). Nothing, however, is more evocative than a reference to cloth caps, which instantly conjures a picture of someone who is short rather than tall, muffled at the throat with a scarf that's probably white, with a gasper jutting from the corner of his mouth and hands in trouser pockets; or, alternatively, of someone propping up a bar with a pint at his elbow or in his fist. That, according to the mythology, is typical Northern working man; therefore Rugby League. This figure has never been portrayed more eloquently, with greater feeling for locality, than he was by J. B. Priestley some sixty years ago, in an essay about the Northern rugby game:

> I simply followed a grey-green tide of cloth caps, which swept me down streets that grew meaner at every turn, past canals and gas works, until finally we came to the edge of the town. In that part

of the West Riding, the Bruddersford district, there is a not very marked difference between town and country. When the last street brings you to a field, you are not aware of any dramatic contrast, simply because the field is not one of your pretty lush meadows, peeping and smiling, but is a dour slab of earth that keeps its grass as short as a wool merchant keeps his hair. This countryside, an angry spur or two of the Pennines, valleys full of black rock, does not regard the local handiwork of man with disfavour. If there must be men about, it says, then let them build factories and railway sidings and gas-works: and so all these things seem to flower naturally out of that grim country . . . It is a country, whether it expresses itself in fields or streets, moors or mills, that puts man on his mettle. It defies him to live there, and so it has bred a special race that can live there, stocky men with short upper lips and jutting long chins, men who roll a little in their walk and carry their heads stiffly, twelve stones of combative instinct.

Here is a people rooted in their environment, belonging to it organically; unlike the middle classes of the Home Counties, say, who are mobile opportunists almost to a man, uncertain of any allegiance beyond that to hearth and home.

The cloth-cap image has had a very good run for its money, and it would perhaps be an unusual Northerner – male Northerner, that is – who did not find himself responding to it from time to time with pride as much as anything, whenever he contemplates his lineage, for it describes his kind in terms of strength, speaking of 'mettle' and 'combative' and the defiance of 'a special race'. Yet it never did – nor was it meant to, I think – more than correspond broadly to the truth in any sense. Those inclined to take things literally, word for word, should know that Priestley's tide of cloth caps would in reality have been relieved somewhat by bowler hats and trilbies. There is a photograph, taken at the first Wembley final in 1929, with the visitors from Wigan and Dewsbury standing side by side on the terraces, in which the chaps wearing 'nebbers' are clearly balanced, possibly outnumbered, by the combination of the other two. Surprisingly few have nothing on their heads. Trilbies and billycocks have vanished from the football grounds of today, while the peaked cap has persisted and has been joined by varieties of headgear made from the colours of the different teams; and the most notable article of clothing everywhere seems to have become the replica team shirt, with which the supporters of both sexes, up to middle age, colourfully proclaim themselves. Sheepskin coats and officers' warms are less often on show, but they, too, can be spotted, along with Barbours and other garments designed for the well-to-do; some small evidence of a deviation from the popular model of Rugby League support.

What else is there to be said about us? Well, unlike the crowds who turn up to watch cricket matches in the North, we have no great reputation for provoking laughter among ourselves, though very often we are one and the same folk. The reason for this omission is obvious enough. In the relative quietness of a county fixture at Old Trafford or Headingley in summer, the well-turned quip which has been loosed with half an eye to the widest possible circulation, can be sure of reaching an appreciative audience in at least a segment of the ground. The pandemonium of a football match means that you hear nothing uttered more than a few yards away unless you frequent the sparser second division attendances, where you suddenly become aware of how much the players shout throughout a game. The muffling effect of crowd noise at a first division match perhaps deters the natural exhibitionist, too. A long, raking kick puts the ball behind the full back, who has been lying up too far, and he has to turn to collect it to generally derisive cheers. 'Nobody at home', your neighbour muses cryptically, as the ball lands in the empty space; and he doesn't intend to be overheard. Now and then someone does, and is, and the caustic remark bellowed across the touch-line begins to circulate in the drinking sessions after the match, and eventually enters the general lore of the game.

Sooner or later, therefore, everyone hears about the day when David Watkins made his home début at Weaste, following his arrival from Rugby Union for a substantial sum. He was having trouble bringing down some of the visiting forwards, much bigger men than he, and after yet another struggle heard an impatient Salfordian shout, 'For God's sake Watkins, 'it 'im wi' yer wallet!' Another great Welshman, Lewis Jones, appeared at Knowsley Road on the wing in a match where play was so tight that whenever he received the ball he was already almost crowded into touch.

'Give 'im *room!*' howled an anguished Leeds fan, as the pass came too late again. 'What does 'e want,' echoed a St Helens voice, 'board and bloody lodgin'?'

This was the thrust of someone with an ear finely tuned to the cadences of the language: put the expletive elsewhere in that phrase and it hasn't half the rhythmic appeal. For the most part, though, the wit and humour of our crowds is lost in their collective noise, which has more in common with the noise of a soccer crowd than that of the other rugby game. There is nothing comparable to the tribal sound of Twickenham as a scrum packs down near the line, the baying of ten thousand hearties as they urge the forwards to 'Heeeeeeeave!'

Often enough, the noise of a well-filled Rugby League ground contains a distinctly soprano note, for the mixture of sexes among our spectators is significant. In that 1929 shot of the Wembley crowd there are perhaps a score of women within camera range, among several hundred men, much more uniformly dressed in their best than the chaps, all wearing the fashionable cloche. They are much, much more numerous today, and they seem to span the years, from the adolescent to the elderly. Teenagers abound in equal proportion to the lads on many grounds. Women lately or about to be wed turn up in quantity beside their partners. Matrons sit with their hubbies, now that Rugby League has largely distanced itself from the Saturday counter-attraction of the supermarket. Really frail-looking old ladies watch this game, and one of them sits near me in the Douglas Stand at Wigan every other week. Another grannie figure, not so fragile, who might very well have been in that crowd at the first Wembley, never misses a game at Crown Flatt. She doesn't have a season ticket but, by acknowledged custom and right, she occupies a front-row seat to the left of the directors' enclosure, and keeps warm the one next to it for her husband, who is a gateman and therefore can't join her until the match is well under way. Let some ignorant stranger arrive early and sit himself in her place, and he will know about it when she turns up shortly before the kick-off. 'Beaten to it, today,' she says meaningfully to some familiar, sitting further back; and unless the stranger is very obtuse he takes himself elsewhere without complaint, to watch the match.

Of the same vintage, but belligerent with it, too, is the old harridan who follows Leeds wherever they go, and spares not the referee nor the touch-judges, the opposing players, their coach, physio or other auxiliaries, and most especially not one of their supporters who dares to cross her with a contrary opinion; lashing out with a tongue that might earn her something more than angry backchat if she were a man. She must be the only person to have sat in the stand at Wheldon Road, to have denounced the entire Castleford crowd as 'pit scum', and to have emerged in one piece. Even now, several seasons after I heard her at it, I marvel a little at their self-control.

It is not at all uncommon to see three generations of the same family, half a dozen of them, tricked out in club colours, from grandma and grandad downwards, at a match; while many a young mum and dad will take a pair of toddlers along even to the most tightly-packed crowds. And this family element, this companionable leavening of the potential roughnecks in our midst, has had a powerful effect on the behaviour of RL followers in the mass, which outsiders note with pleasurable surprise. Mr Justice Popplewell, preparing his report into all aspects of safety at sports grounds in the wake of the Bradford fire in 1985, went to watch Salford play at Central Park one Sunday and there found himself among 12,500 regulars.

'There were no perimeter fences,' he noted. 'There was no form of segregation. There were no incidents. Only some twenty police officers were on hand. There were large numbers of women and children present; the afternoon was an enjoyable day out for everyone.'

He was, of course, making the point that all of this was a striking contrast to the contemporary experience throughout the English Football League. So was a senior official of the Wasps Rugby Union Club, who in 1988 wrote that 'The recent Rugby League Challenge Cup Final offers a clear example of how a semi-professional competitive sport can be played in an atmosphere of cordiality, good humour and sportsmanship.'

It happens to be a sorry historical fact that large crowds massing for entertainments of one sort and another have been known to get out of control since the year dot. Riots have afflicted the circus in ancient Rome, Test cricket in British Guyana, ice hockey in Montreal, American football in Massachusetts. English football has known such turbulence since the seventeenth century, if not earlier, though it may never before have known the deplorable behaviour that is now common, week after week, on soccer grounds all over the country, and wherever else rival soccer fans are liable to meet. A lot of sociologists, (not to mention the inevitable Dr Desmond Morris, whose speciality is animals), have spent much time, thought and paper in analysing and pontificating on this phenomenon. Any number of reasons have been put forward for soccer hooliganism, some of them contradictory, and the poet Tony Harrison may have come as near to the truth of it as anyone. Shocked by the graffiti he one day found disfiguring the grave of his parents in the cemetery on Beeston Hill, he contemplated

. . . the ground where Leeds United play
but disappoint their fans week after week,

which makes them lose their sense of self-esteem
and taking a short cut home through these graves here
they reassert the glory of their team
by spraying words on tombstones, pissed on beer.

The record of Rugby League crowds is not exactly immaculate, and the biggest disservice the game's normal followers could do is to assume that it is. In the 1947–8 season, referees had to be given police escorts after the final whistle on three occasions because of hostility from the terraces – once at Oldham and twice at The Boulevard, Hull. The following year Eddie Waring, writing in *Rugby League Review*, found it necessary to bemoan the behaviour of St Helens fans during their club's match against the Australian touring side.

During the first half, when Hand was injured and collapsed before he could take his hooking position, his fall to the ground was greeted with a resounding cheer. Keith Froome, a grand little sportsman from Sydney, turned to me and said 'Did you ever hear that in Australia, Eddie?' I just looked at him and mumbled something, for I felt sorry that such an outburst was forthcoming when a player was injured. At half-time the loudspeaker announcer asked the boys to behave in a sportsmanlike manner, and to remember the Australians were their visitors. The groans and derisive laughter which greeted this request were completely unfair and out of tune. Our youngsters must be encouraged to be good sportsmen, but such behaviour on the part of adults is a very poor example for them to emulate.

Some years ago, a number of yobs following Hull Kingston Rovers across the North made everyone else wary of them. If there is some place more alarming than anywhere else today it will be Wilderspool, where a small group of louts lurk behind the otherwise decent Warrington supporters, the only gang in the Rugby League to compare with organised soccer hooligans, having been caught wounding individuals with knives and, once, damaging a train.

A couple of semifinals played at Wigan in recent years have produced more spontaneous combustion, with fighting between Leeds and St Helens fans on one occasion, between toughs from Castleford and Oldham on another. So convinced were the police that neither of these punch-ups would have happened if the combatants had been able to hold their ale, being already intoxicated enough by the 'big' occasion, that they persuaded the host club to close the bars at any future Central Park semifinals – in which, of course, the Wigan team never plays.

The reasoning seems plausible. Regularly, Castleford, Oldham, Leeds and St Helens have played the home side on that ground without a sign of trouble. If there ever had been such a risk, it might have spoiled the Challenge Cup third round in March 1986, when the Glassblowers came to Central Park and defeated a Wigan team that had been expected not only to win that match, but possibly to take every trophy that year. The crowds departed after the game, variously joyful and stunned, without fighting each other. They also behaved properly during the cup-tie itself, though they stood shoulder to shoulder throughout, a large wedge of Castleford lads who had taken station on the Kop in the first half, switching ends for the second period, when they continued to wave their banners and make much noise without being challenged by the increasingly disconcerted fans flaunting cherry and white; and the game's end was signalled not only by the hooter, but by a gratifying salute from the hosts on their electronic scoreboard – 'Well done, Cas. Good luck'.

Sociologists fascinated by the subject of crowd violence might find Castleford a rewarding field for research. A fair proportion of the club's support – like that of Featherstone and Wakefield – comes from miners who manned the picket-lines during the long strike of 1985, when they were known as Scargill's army and were conspicuously hostile to the police. They give no trouble on the terraces of Wheldon Road, though. What is it that makes for such contrasts in the behaviour of the same people? We need to know; and while they are about it, the sociologists might ask another question, this time at Central Park. How many of those families who support Wigan every Sunday afternoon in such numbers have been to church a few hours before? The bond between Wigan RLFC and the Catholic schools of the town, where so many of their players have traditionally been first tutored in the game, is a long and powerful one. Is there also a link between religious observance and civilised football-watching; an influence, however indirect, of the first upon the second?

It so happens that the behaviour of the game's followers is measurable. Police forces throughout the North of England know that if there is a soccer match and a Rugby League match in their area, each with the same size of crowd, they will need between four and five times as many men on duty at the first ground as at the second. And this is one area of society where the old familiarity between constabulary and populace lingers on, with the bobbies still able to chat and joke with those they are invigilating. The police in Leeds, anxious that this game shall never go the way of their local soccer, have made a novel pitch to gain the confidence and co-operation of youngsters who regularly turn up at Headingley.

Helped by some NatWest money, they have produced an attractive series of photo-cards picturing Leeds Rugby League players, with Loiners' Tips on the back of each, covering both rugby tactics and decent behaviour; and these they distribute as part of a wider public-relations exercise at each home match. This is an imaginative way of trying to ensure that our people in future maintain their present reputation. It is perfectly true that, year after year, the Metropolitan Police in London are so impressed by the crowds attending the Rugby League Cup Final at Wembley that they afterwards write to the two clubs involved, thanking them for the behaviour of their supporters. We tend to plaster the capital with a lot of amiably rowdy drunks on Cup Final day, but there's rarely anything worse to complain about.

Among various theories to account for all this, two especially seem to carry a lot of weight. One concerns the behaviour of the players, who set a far better example to impressionable adolescents in the crowd than do many of today's professional soccer players. To some extent they are held on a tight rein by our referees, who generally make it very plain indeed that they will not countenance any cheek or worse from the two sides in their charge. But beyond that there is a self-control among players who, although they are quite capable of behaving badly in some ways (occasionally slugging it out in a full-scale team brawl), draw the line themselves at other forms of offensiveness.

A policeman of my acquaintance who watches the game week after week, on duty in his home town and often for pleasure by following his team away, tells me that not once has he ever seen a Rugby League footballer gesture obscenely to a crowd, though it happens every now and then at soccer matches. Nor have I. I'm not quite sure what would happen if somebody bared his backside at the terraces, or gave them the finger, but I imagine he'd quickly be on his way to the sin-bin. I'm fairly sure the crowd would not communicate admiration at that point. My policeman thinks that the players have a better relationship with those who watch them because several in every team have a local loyalty and pride, rooted in the towns they represent. They are local lads, and a lot of the people watching them are workmates, friends, neighbours of theirs, to whom they must answer throughout the week. I think he's right in this. What's more, no great distance separates the average Rugby League player economically from his fans. He may be their hero; but he is also, in this as in neighbourly ways, still one of them.

The other great force for discipline in the crowd may well be the crowd's own sense of responsibility, which follows from its usual composition. The only time within memory that there has been notable misbehaviour at Wigan's home matches was during the 1980–1 season, when the team had dropped into the second division, and when the attendances were much smaller than they are now – on average no more than 4,000 or so. Not only did the customers rattle like peas on a drum in the great spaces of Central Park, but those empty terraces were an open invitation to running scraps between unruly young supporters. The most notable absentees that year were precisely those people whose presence normally inhibits the hooligans in our midst: there were not nearly so many family groups and mature couples as are commonly to be seen when the team is doing well. With them around in some quantity, our crowds do a fair amount of self-policing on every ground, not hesitating to point out ruffians to the nearest constable when trouble threatens: and it is not unknown for women to lay about them with umbrellas to stop yobs spoiling everybody else's day.

At Thrum Hall a few seasons ago, I found myself close to another form of crowd self-control after Ellery Hanley, with a fierce but perfectly fair hand-off, had flattened one of the Halifax players; at which a middle-aged fellow – who, judging by his appearance, might have been anything from a shopkeeper to a factory worker – roared furiously, 'Yer black bastard!' At once a man of about the same age, a couple of rows in front, swivelled, aimed a menacing finger at his head and ordered him to 'cut that out right now, sunshine. Right now!' Two or three others, wearing the colours of either side, made it plain that they thought little of the outburst, too. It didn't happen again.

All this is part of the cloth-cap image, and if a slightly old-fashioned impression is inseparable from the decencies then I, for one, would not have it otherwise. I am glad that at Wembley our people still sing *Abide With Me* or else stay silent out of deference to those who do, not because of its religious overtones, but from a sense of propriety; for although the singing is in many ways an anachronism, a self-conscious genuflection to the past which comes awkwardly to some, it is not unconnected with those habits that compel the admiration of the Metropolitan Police. The blandishments of change are not always to be trusted, as I think cricket has found out by certain deteriorations there since the Packer revolution. A more garish form of the summer game since then may have been more attractive to some and may have enticed others who would not have watched it in its traditional form: but with jazzed-up international cricket has come player power and player offensiveness, as in soccer. Having spent good money to watch a Test match, I do not care to sit unrewarded on a fine day largely because arrogant and well-paid young men are no longer prepared to turn out unless the turf under their feet is all but bone dry. Nor would I have wished to sit within earshot of Master Dilley's loud-mouthed gutter-speech at Lancaster Park in 1988, and then to learn that his reprimand from the management was derisory (in the context of cricket, where sound carries, his offence was the equivalent of gestures at a football match).

Yet things do change, inevitably, with the passage of time: there is no such thing as human stasis. I and my children stand four-square where our forefathers stood in many respects, in my case determined not to budge. But we are the first generations of our family to own motor-cars; and no one before me ever signed the mortgage for his own home. There was a time when the vast majority of Rugby League enthusiasts, following their teams away from home, did so by train excursion – 1s. 2d. return from Bradford (Forster Square) to Keighley (Midland) for a Yorkshire Senior Cup match in 1924 – or by motor coach. So much did I associate Wallace Arnold exclusively in the immediate post-war years with conveying Yorkshire RL supporters across the Pennines to the Lancashire grounds, that when I first saw one of those coaches full of holidaymakers in France several years later I was briefly confused, as if it had strayed badly off course. The coaches still roll back and forth across the hill (no fewer than fifty-three came from Leeds to Wigan for the Challenge Cup tie in 1988), but nowadays I imagine at least as many people travel under their own steam.

The Americanisation of international one-day cricket (for that, effectively, has been the result of Kerry Packer's intervention), is not something I want to see imitated in our Rugby League, though already I detect some straws in the wind. Where clubs not content with announcing themselves under the name of their town or district once hoisted traditional English football suffixes, like Town or Rovers, we have lately been invited to applaud Barracudas and Eagles, neither of which ought to evoke more than a sniff in places as utterly Yorkshire as Huddersfield and Sheffield. If Bradford (Northern Union) were ever to lose sight of its origins by mucking about like this, I hope there would be such an outcry on the terraces of Odsal, or wherever they may be playing by then, as to cause those responsible to desist, with apologies all round.

It should not be thought that I have an aversion to Americans being associated with Rugby League as, in a very small way, they already are. But if their association is to be enlarged it must be on our terms, starting from our traditions, not theirs; from which they may develop, as the Australians, the New Zealanders, the French and the Papuans have developed, in their own distinctive fashion. I can see that, faced with the deceptive glitz of American football, our authorities might be tempted to compromise on this; not only to repackage but to restructure the product, so as to attract a wider audience. I beg them not to. Even when, if, I am in Another Place, I shall not wish to contemplate a bastard game played by men wearing padded knickerbockers, broken up by time-outs and garnished with goose-pimpled cheer-leaders on the touch-line, between the likes of Wigan Wildcats and Batley Braves. I shall not be happy. I shall haunt Chapeltown Road through all eternity.

Five

Tribal Warfare in Post Office Road

When the footballers of Papua New Guinea opened their first English professional tour against Featherstone Rovers in October 1987, they revealed to all doubters the boundless possibilities of Rugby League. Who on earth, forty years ago, could have dreamt of such a fixture, when the most exotic encounter the game had to offer would have been a match between the likes of Wigan or Leeds with Frenchmen from Perpignan, Carcassonne or some other medieval town in the shadow of the Pyrenees? It would have strained credulity to forecast a day when this Yorkshire pit village might play host to a team from the tropical land of pidgin English, crocodile farms and cargo cults.

The usual extent of Featherstone's horizons even today were suggested by an advert in the window of a travel agency on Station Lane. 'Boulogne Christmas Shopper 4th December', it said. 'Adults £24. Deposit of £1 secures seat.' Another clue to local priorities was inscribed upon the tattered old election poster still adhering to a wall in Post Office Road, where the Rovers' ground lies. 'East Ward. Traditional Labour', this one announced. 'Vote Brooks, David'.

Life round here has generally meant keeping an eye open for bargains, especially come Christmas time, and the need lately had been great, for Featherstone had been deeply committed to the long miners' strike of 1985, from which some families were still trying to recover two years afterwards. Station Lane and its hinterland does not look as if it has ever been in the thick of where the real money-making goes on. The brick walls are discoloured with grime, and most premises have not obviously known the day when they wouldn't have benefited from a fresh lick of paint.

Such a street would be quite anonymous in many a fair-sized

56

Northern town, where it would be merely one among hundreds more, all virtually identical. Here it is rivalled only by an adjacent stretch of the main road from Wakefield to Pontefract, which runs through a countryside that has still not been completely despoiled by coal-mines, cooling towers and other detritus of industry. True, the Post Office Road ground stands not far from the winding gear of the Featherstone Colliery; and there are slag heaps in the neighbourhood, and gouts of steam rise from Knottingley power station in the far distance, and behind the covered terrace opposite the grandstand is an untidy collection of hen coops and pigeon lofts. But fields yet harvested for corn slope away to ridges thickly outlined with trees.

As this momentous game began, a school of horse-riders could be seen cantering across open ground towards the railway line. Though in some ways sorely changed by the Industrial Revolution, this is recognisably a village still, legatee of the Domesday Ferestane, where King William's commissioners noted that 'Ligulfr had 16 carucates of land taxable; 6 ploughs possible there.' Post Office Road is a long, long way from the steaming rain forests which surround Port Moresby, Rabaul and Wewak.

Conscious that yet more history was being made, Featherstone had invited as many luminaries as they could entice to their attractive little ground. The General Secretary of the Rugby Football League was there, of course, as well as a brace of local mayors. So, less predictably, were the chairmen of Wakefield Trinity and Castleford, whose own teams were both playing away that Sunday. So, too, was the Earl of Swinton, patron of the Featherstone club, who had descended from his home in the wholly rural North Riding, where they never vote Labour under any circumstances and where they are somewhat more familiar with sheepdog trials than Rugby League, with farming subsidies than with strike pay. In less exalted company on the terraces a couple of parsons were in the crowd, which had grown to 3,300 or so by kick-off, several hundred more than Rovers' average gate the previous season, which saw them relegated to the second division.

It was a perfect autumn day for football, with streaks and puffs of high cloud relieving the blue sky and enough crispness in the sunshine to let us know which month we were in. It is perfectly possible that neither Matthias Kitimun, Dairi Kovae, Arebo Taumaku nor any other member of the visiting side had been so nearly frozen stiff in their lives as they were when their captain, Bal Numapo, led them out. Each man walked alongside his opposite number in the Featherstone team, which was the occasion of a pleasing little ceremony when both files were lined up in the middle of the pitch. For every Collier was carrying a gift-wrapped team jersey, which he then handed to his opponent with a shake of the hand, to great applause. Then the visitors, in their vivid, almost Day-Glo strip of scarlet and gold, peeled off from the line as one player after another was identified by loudspeaker to the crowd. They seemed every bit as colourful as Yorkshiremen might assume the native birds-of-paradise to be, from which they take their nickname. After the Lions, the Kangaroos, the Kiwis and the Chanticleers, the Kumuls are the most recent Rugby League footballers to be incorporated into the highest levels of the game.

And they quickly showed the flair that had been rumoured for some years out of the southern hemisphere, getting points on the board early by elusively swift running and ball-handling that approached the dexterity of the basketball court, while Featherstone appeared to be weighing them up still, relying for their own progress on forward rushes and Deryck Fox's probing kicks. It was clear from the outset that these Kumuls were simply not built for that form of football which has more in common with siege warfare than the cavalry charge. Not one man in a touring party of twenty-six weighed in at fourteen stone, and only a couple made six feet, which was to be an obvious hindrance on this tour against English packs loaded with long-limbed beef. But playing the game they are cut out for can overcome disadvantages of substance, as they demonstrated in 1986, when they defeated a powerful New Zealand side in a World Cup match.

Some of the Rovers' set pieces had the Kumuls groping, and once or twice their men bought dummies that could be seen coming even by people in the back of the stand. Nor was their tackling the most robust ever witnessed at Post Office Road, doubtless another consequence of slightness rather than a failure of nerve. Yet only once, for ten minutes of the second half, were Featherstone in the lead, and they eventually went down 22–16, having scored only three tries to the visitors' four. The Kumuls had the character to come back from 16–12 behind, though it wasn't that which had the crowd applauding them as much as it did the home team before the end. The spectators were simply pleased to be watching footballers whose primary instinct was to whip the ball out to the wings, and then to flash it back again if the way was blocked there. They were moved to laughter when, more than once, a Papuan ducked and bobbed and weaved and side-stepped while multiple Featherstone hands clutched frantically at thin air. Such passages unfailingly earned the visitor an encouraging cheer, for this was a generous Yorkshire crowd, which may have been warmed by another incident which in its way reciprocated their friendliness. When Peter Smith was slightly concussed in a multiple tackle and matters came to a halt because he still had the ball, the Papuan players responsible bent over the semi-conscious forward just as solicitously as the Featherstone physio. It was very civilised tribal warfare in Post Office Road.

Yet the most significant thing about that lovely October afternoon was not what was happening out on the pitch, but the historical fact that the visitors were there at all, and playing their national game. Of all the countries where Rugby League is enjoyed, Papua New Guinea is the only one where it is possible to make this claim, and it is relevant to outline the processes by which this remarkable circumstance came about. It was not by any means a sudden conversion, such as some happy souls hope for when they struggle to get this form of football started in a previously unreceptive place.

Its origins in Papua New Guinea go back well over half a century, to the days after gold had been discovered near Wau in 1922. As with every such discovery, prospectors arrived from all points of the compass, including Australia; men from New South Wales and Queensland, who immediately began to play football in whatever time and with whatever energy they had left over from back-breaking toil on the diggings. By the late '30s the gold was effectively finished; and so might Rugby League have been if there hadn't been a Second World War. But for three years or more the Australians fought the Japanese up and down the islands of New Guinea in one of the bitterest theatres of the war and, again, turned to rugby as well as cricket for relaxation whenever they could. With the peace, more Australians arrived to work in the civil administration of the country and in its commerce until, by 1949, enough footballers were living there to start a regular competition in Port Moresby. This was white man's football at first, a by-product of government by Australian mandate. Not until Papua New Guinea was well on the road to independence would the natives be allowed to take part in racially mixed games. But, watching the Australians playing their rugby and their cricket, they acquired a huge appetite for both.

The Papua New Guinea Rugby Football League was not founded until a few months before full independence came in 1975, but local enthusiasm had been running high for nearly a decade by then; at least since 1966, when a team of schoolboys toured Australia and with their bare feet defeated a New South Wales side in a curtain-raiser to the Third Test between Great Britain and Australia on Sydney Cricket Ground. That was the point at which these descendants of head-hunters appear to have decided that, of all the sports bequeathed by colonialism, Rugby League was the one which suited their temperament most of all. So much did its aggressive vigour and range of athletic skills coincide with instincts bred in the bone, that there was a period in the '70s when Rugby League was proscribed in the schools, because too many youngsters were using matches as a pretext to settle old tribal scores. But, since the Kumuls began to play full international matches with their tour of France at the end of that decade, the game has flourished beside the Coral Sea at every level, with twenty-seven separate leagues affiliated to the governing body. Their playing record on the English tour of 1987 was not especially gratifying – they won only three matches out of eight, another being drawn, and were beaten 42–0 in the solitary Test – but no one who watched their exhilarating approach to the game could have doubted that one day, before long, the Kumuls will be a force to reckon with every time they take the field.

They are a reminder that there is no earthly reason why Rugby League football cannot spread to some of the most unlikely corners of the globe, *provided* a progression is right. At the same time they constitute a warning that lasting expansion cannot normally be achieved except by patient spadework at the most junior level of the game over a long period, so that roots will develop strongly enough to sustain permanent growth. In Britain alone, the domestic game is littered with a history of clubs that joined the professional ranks in a burst of optimism but no groundwork, collapsing soon after because there was not enough support to be found in their areas, a miscalculation that ought to have been foreseen.

In the North-East, where working-class men have always gravitated to soccer and just as many of the middle classes have preferred Rugby Union, two such attempts came to nothing: at South Shields shortly after the Boer War, at Newcastle shortly before the Second World War. In the London area, where similar preferences have been a fact of life for a century or so, a most remarkable ambition saw wealthy Mr Sidney Parkes launch two teams simultaneously, with an almost American extravagance, in a brand-new stadium apiece, to begin season 1935–6. Acton and Willesden, whose players became temporarily among the best paid in the League, attracted home crowds of 18,000 at one stage and even briefly topped the championship; but although nine teams finished below them in the final table (including such as Wakefield, St Helens, Hull KR and Featherstone) they did not emerge for the following year, Mr Parkes having evidently found them too much of a burden on his purse without doing enough for his reputation as an impresario. His other creation, Streatham and Mitcham, having enlisted the great George Nepia at full back (not long past his prime as an All Black), pulled in 20,000 for their first home game against Oldham, yet didn't complete their fixtures in their second season, leaving London to get along without professional Rugby League until Fulham tried again in 1980.

As for Wales, it has been the gloomiest repository of misplaced hopes, time after time, with 1908–9 holding the most wretched record of all. That season saw clubs started in Aberdare, Barry, mid-Rhondda and Treherbert, only the last of them surviving for just one more term. The quartet had been launched on a wave of enthusiasm to imitate Ebbw Vale, which came into the league in 1907–8 and lasted five full seasons. No other Welsh side – and eight of them have been started since – has succeeded in hanging on for more than four. Nor could anyone have realistically expected any other outcome than this, when Union occupies in Wales exactly the position held historically by League in the trans-Pennine lands, being primarily the game of men who have worked for wages with their hands. The English game of 13-a-side can therefore too easily be seen as an intruder down there by too many rugby folk. It is another form of encroachment by the alien overlords; and if the intrusion had happened in the mid-Welsh countryside rather than in the southern coal-mining belt, it is odds-on that one of those Rugby League clubhouses or pavilions would have been burnt down in protest.

The history of Featherstone Rovers, as it happens, is a good example of a Rugby League evolution that has produced enduring gain, in good seasons and bad. Only three years after the historic breakaway in Huddersfield, the rugby footballers of Featherstone switched to the Northern Union game, playing in various Yorkshire leagues for ages before being admitted to the semi-professional senior ranks. They first gave some indication of their calibre when, in 1910, while competing in the Wakefield and District League, they won the Yorkshire Junior Cup, which secured them admission to higher company – the Yorkshire Combination of the Northern Union, the level at which the reserve teams of the top sides played.

In the first season after the First World War, Featherstone were good enough to contest the final of the Northern Union Combination Cup with Wigan 'A', and to miss the trophy only by the margin of one try. So outstanding were they among junior teams that not once, between 1913 and 1921, did they fail to reach the first round of the seniors' Challenge Cup; and in the last of those five consecutive appearances they found themselves in the second round against a senior side after trouncing fellow juniors Pendlebury 41–0. They then lost to Dewsbury, in front of 9,000 people who taxed the little Featherstone ground so much that charabancs were parked round the perimeter, as improvised stands.

But for a quarter of a century, Featherstone had demonstrated their ability to make headway – and to stay solvent – in the rebellious new rugby code. That was the pedigree they were able to invoke when they submitted their application in 1921 to join what almost at once was translated from the Northern Union to the Rugby Football League. They were accepted unanimously by the senior clubs; and within a year Featherstone had not only knocked Widnes out of the Challenge Cup, but had gone out of the next round only by a whisker, 14–13, to one of Wigan's most powerful sides.

Castleford, too, played successfully as junior footballers before they were voted into the senior ranks in 1926. They had tried the new code early in its history, joining the Northern Union in 1896, but had dropped out of the big time after ten years, doing nothing for another six. Then they re-formed and eventually entered the Yorkshire Senior Competition, where they soon became a side to watch. In four consecutive seasons, between 1922 and 1926, they played against senior sides in the Yorkshire Cup thrice and the Challenge Cup four times, once holding Bradford Northern to a memorable draw away from home and losing the replay 11–5.

Two other examples of the evolutionary process may be taken from Cumbria, where Workington Town and Whitehaven joined the Rugby Football League in quick succession just after the Second World War. It took Workington but one season to find their feet before they made spectacular assaults on both the Championship and the Challenge Cup. In 1945–6 they finished nineteenth out of twenty-seven clubs, and in the next four seasons were placed eleventh, fifth, eighth, and tenth, before coming third in 1950–1; which meant a place in the Championship play-offs. In the semifinal they defeated Wigan 8–5 at Central Park, the only side to win there that season (and they did so twice) before they took the trophy at Maine Road by licking first-placed Warrington 26–11. The year after, they beat Featherstone for the Challenge Cup in what must still rank as the most romantic of Wembley finals, contested as it was by two unfashionable sides from small communities.

It was doubtless Workington's success on the field as well as the fact that occasionally they were capable of attracting nearly 20,000 to their home games, that encouraged their neighbours just down the coast at Whitehaven to apply for membership of the League in 1948. But the much more relevant fact is that both clubs were able to draw playing strength and spectators from a long tradition of Rugby League in their part of the world. At the very end of the nineteenth century, the Northern Union had been represented there by the Millom club, where Cumberland faced Furness across the Duddon estuary; and though it left senior football within half a dozen seasons, it continued as an amateur team among many others that had started up nearby. Full forty years before their admission to the major championship, Workington had reached the first round of the Challenge Cup as a junior side, as did a team called Whitehaven Recs. In a roll-call of English amateur Rugby League teams, few names have a longer or a more honourable history than those of a dozen clubs to be found on the seaward side of the Lake District. So that when Whitehaven began their first season of big-time football in August 1948, they did so with more than half their playing staff recruited locally, from Risehow-Gillhead, Millom, Ellenboro, Clifton and Kells.

Only in the most exceptional circumstances can the game expect to succeed in the long run without such foundations as these; and it is pertinent to note that such circumstances have so far been confined to the game's inception in Britain and to its adoption in the Antipodes and France. The first, the separation of leading Northern clubs from the Rugby Football Union, was nothing less than a revolutionary act. The affiliation of the Australians, too, was a rebellion initiated by a footballer's hardship and sense of economic grievance: and it is worth noting that as a result of those meetings in Victor Trumper's sports shop after Alex Burdon hurt his shoulder in a Union match and was refused medical expenses, let alone 'broken time' money for being off work, the new code of rugby started in New South Wales in 1908 with eight teams, of which five – Balmain, Eastern Suburbs, North Sydney, South Sydney and Western Suburbs – are still competing in the Sydney League today.

The New Zealanders, whose own switch of allegiance was instrumental in spurring the Australians on, are more difficult to assess, the only certain thing about their new venture being that it followed the tour of the British Isles by Dave Gallaher's first All Blacks in 1905–6, which gave one of the team – the winger George Smith – a chance to see the Northern Union game, after he had been side-lined by breaking his collar-bone halfway through the tour. Whether he was fired mostly by the Northern game as a spectacle, or whether material inducements offered by Northern officials were even more attractive is unclear. At any rate, fired he was, passing on his enthusiasm the moment he reached home to the Wellington forward A. H. Baskerville, with whom he raised a team – derisively labelled the All Golds by their Union compatriots because they were to be paid for their rugby – to tour England and Wales in 1907, with some missionary activity in Australia en route; arriving for their first match, against Bramley, the season after the Northern Union had reduced team numbers from fifteen to thirteen, and at the very moment when it was ordained that a tackled player should henceforth be allowed to get up and play the ball.

As for the French, their adoption of Rugby à Treize came about in the most exceptional circumstances of all, *force majeure*, when the Rugby Union authorities of England, Scotland, Ireland and Wales in 1931 decided their teams would no longer play sides from across the Channel, because 'professionalism' had entered the game there; and no French team took part in Rugby Union's home championship again until 1947 as a result. Aided and abetted by English proselytisers and the 1933 Kangaroos (who interrupted their tour to play an exhibition match against the British in Paris) the enterprising Jean Galia, a centre three-quarter with a score of international caps, seized the opportunity to fill the French rugby vacuum by giving League a go, and persuaded enough frustrated players to join him; so that by 1934 not only had the Frenchmen a championship of a dozen clubs, but were also able to make a short British tour.

It is hard to see where such exceptional circumstances as these can ever occur again. Certainly not in South Africa, where Rugby Union represents Afrikaner nationalism as much as it signifies a sporting obsession, and therefore is likely to command more allegiance, not less, within the laager as the ANC impis prepare for the Armageddon that must surely come to that unhappy land. Surely not in Italy, where nationalism – at least since the Battle of Highbury in 1934 – has similarly identified itself with a particular sport, in this case soccer. Emphatically not in the United States, where the only sports anyone takes seriously are those which come garnished with millions of dollars. Yet in all three countries, the past forty years have seen the missionaries of Rugby League spending time, effort and money in trying to convert the natives; so far, more or less fruitlessly. They show every sign of continuing these unavailing efforts, but little evidence of understanding the nature or the magnitude of the obstacles in their way.

Few things have been more depressingly ludicrous in recent years than the assumptions that went into taking an Australian State of Origin match to California in 1987, the self-congratulation when it was done, and the further ambition it generated. The first and preposterous notion was to stage the game in New York, where it simply was not wanted, and it ended up 3,000 miles away in a stadium about eight times smaller than the one the nearby Los Angeles Raiders fill for every game. Only very local, very small-time newspapers and television stations paid it any attention, and pretty patronising stuff this was. ('About 11,000 spectators showed up at 12,500 seat Veterans' Stadium, with most appearing to be from Australia or Australian expatriates,' the *Long Beach Press-Telegram* reported. 'Beer was flowing freely. By the way, New South Wales routed Queensland 30–18 . . .') This might have been anticipated when Americans, after all, are working very hard and spending immense sums of money to foist upon the rest of the world their own brand of football, in that dubious process known as Cocacolonialism; having been assisted in this country by the coincidental establishment of a new television company – Channel 4 – in search of a distinctive identity, and by a variety of individuals who joined the bandwagon for their own good reasons, ranging from the sports columnist Hugh McIlvanney to the entertainer Max Boyce. Yet the Australian Rugby League administrator responsible for the Californian venture, Mr Arthurson, said that the $A40,000 or so lost on the transplanted State of Origin fixture was money well spent by his people. The English RL Secretary, Mr Oxley, said, 'It is important that another major event is staged fairly soon.' And in the same issue of *Open*

Rugby in which that opinion was expressed, a hint was dropped that the authorities were seriously of a mind to play the 1988 World Cup Final in either the United States or Japan!

They might have done better to ponder the fact that nowhere yet, as Rugby League approaches its centenary, has it been adopted as anybody's principal winter sport, with the sole and improbable exception of Papua New Guinea. In its homeland it rivals soccer for the position only in the North of England, where it began. In Australia it is supreme in New South Wales and Queensland alone, and even there Australian Rules has begun to mount a challenge that has some League people looking nervously over their shoulders. In France they have been in a depression for so many years that some observers have thought it quite possible that League might go under, especially as Rugby Union there is much more profitable to all hands, with neither the English, the Scots, the Irish nor the Welsh authorities any longer giving a damn that this should be so. Only in New Zealand, of the senior nations, has there been sustained advance in the past generation, as the game has spread territorially and as significant numbers of the best players have been able to earn money from it for the first time by obtaining engagements in Australia or England. But no Kiwi will delude himself about the domestic future, when what is always likely to matter more than Rugby League there is the alternative handling code which produces the All Blacks.

The voice of the expansionists has long been heard at home, in chorus with that of the optimists. 'Michael Beale thinks Tyneside will soon be ripe for Rugby League Football and suggests Jarrow could support a club,' was an arresting strapline in the fourth number of *Rugby League Review* back in December 1946. Almost two years later, in the same publication, Eddie Waring's monthly piece was entitled 'Rugby League in Wales. What are our Plans!' He concluded that we didn't appear to have many; none that could be described with precision, anyway. We seemed more than anything to be hoping for the best.

Even now, forty years on, it may not be doing the most ardent expansionists a grave injustice to wonder whether many of them have a clear vision for the future of the game in Great Britain, and what expansion might entail. Let us ignore the matter of hard economics when considering this, for that factor is obvious enough. But if, for example, our game overtook soccer as the undisputed popular winter sport in these islands and, professionally, was played by ninety-two teams arranged in four divisions like the Association Football League, is it expected that the character of the game would stay the same? And if it is conceded that almost certainly its character would be changed, would these changes be acceptable? Is it supposed, for instance, that Rugby League, as the British national football game, would manage to avoid the excrescences that have fouled soccer in the past generation, with rival supporters ghettoed inside steel stockades because they are all too often likely to maim or even kill each other if allowed to mingle freely on a ground? Is it believed that Rugby League players in such elevated circumstances will remain on the same unassuming and affable terms with their supporters as they are now? Or will some of them, like many soccer stars who have believed their own publicity, treat the crowds to a mixture of petulance and arrogance, contemptibly telling small boys who worship them and only want their autographs, to 'Piss off!'

These are negative questions, but they follow from a very positive one, and it is this. Why do we want our professional Rugby League championship to become bigger than it is? Why would someone living in Wigan or Warrington, Leeds or Hull, who can watch top-class football at least every other week, yearn for the day when he could do the same if his home were in Bristol or Southampton, Norwich or Stoke? Would it increase our self-esteem so much to know that we were in the sporting majority between September and May? Are we simply bored by seeing the same old faces year after year, and could do with more teams to permutate? Is it that we merely crave more attention from television and the national press, and this sometimes seems the only way to get it? Why *should* it be thought desirable to expand? The alternative, to anticipate an obvious riposte, is not necessarily to wither and die. Possibly it is to be content: and it's a wise man who recognises when he can be that.

These questions are asked not out of any great hostility to expansion as such; more from a deep dislike of waste, and a reluctance to see decent people unnecessarily making fools of themselves. It was a delight to watch the Kumuls show off their skills in Post Office Road that autumn day in 1987, and I shall hope to see them again before long, but this is one Rugby League follower who cannot honestly thrill to the prospect of some other exotic coming over here for the first time, just for the sake of variety itself.

Rather than fret for the day when the first American or Japanese tourists arrive, I wish for another glimpse of the Australians, the New

Zealanders, the French, with whom we have been bonded in this game – and other matters – across some generations. Rather than assent to domestic resources being sunk into unrewarding missionary work in the benighted parts of this land, I would wish the same efforts to be directed towards the survival of some lame ducks who, nearly a hundred years ago, were the making of this game: the Huddersfields, the Batleys, the Dewsburys of our fraternity, who might be helped with loans for ground improvements necessitated by the legislation the Bradford fire provoked. We shall do well to remember that a people who lose sight of their history, who are heedless of their past, sooner or later too easily lose their way, uncertain of who and what they are, a condition that in crisis can lead to hysteria.

The truth is, of course, that the benighted parts of this land are shrinking almost annually: for the game in Britain is expanding quite remarkably, and in that model fashion which may one day lead to an enlarged professional championship. Nothing is more surprising to those whose only knowledge of Rugby League is what they read in the national newspapers, than the information that there are something like 700 teams of amateurs playing in this country. Their first assumption is that these must obviously be crammed up in the three northern counties of origin, and great is their astonishment when they are told that this is no longer the case; that there is not only a London League and a Welsh League, but that there is another amateur competition involving clubs from Plymouth and Cheltenham, Bath and Hemel Hempstead and elsewhere; not to mention a nationwide tournament of university and college teams. Since the British Amateur Rugby League Association was set up in 1973 to supervise all manifestations of the non-professional game, the expansionists have had good reason for proper optimism, most especially since the Rugby Union has conceded that there can no longer be any justification for treating amateur League players like Untouchables.

A deeply committed expansionist ought, perhaps, to be elated most of all by the annual University match at Headingley. The notion of Oxford v. Cambridge at Rugby *League* may strike some antediluvian examples of Homo Twickiens as a monstrous charade in the name of all that's sacred; yet the match has been played each year since 1981. When the sides met for the seventh time, a most significant thing had already happened before they even took the field. Out of the 34 players selected for the two squads that day, only four men came from traditional Rugby League towns (York, Wakefield and Whitehaven). The rest had been to school in places as notably beyond the pale as Belfast, Hertford, Glasgow, Loughborough, Brighton, Reigate and suchlike. It is far too soon to start fantasising about the conceivable long-term implications of this, but it possibly amounts to the future prosperity of the game, achieved realistically. All we need is the confidence to maintain the course that has at last been set, and patience. And the wit to understand that in this matter there are no short cuts, however spectacular.

Six

Small Worlds

My boyhood conversion to rugby from soccer coincided with a small but significant landmark in the game: the launching of *Rugby League Review*. I remember the sense of luxury when I discovered, at a stall on Wigan market, those twelve stapled pages (there were rarely more than that) devoted exclusively to my new winter pursuit; for until this journal appeared there had been nothing else to read but what the newspapers chose to print. My copies of Stanley Chadwick's creation inevitably appear old-fashioned now, not to say quaint, both typographically and in some of their contents. The fourth number, published in December 1946, was marked by an editorial headed 'A Merry Christmas' in heavy Gothic script. A regular feature was an extensive description of a chosen match of the day by deputy editor Vincent Firth, and this always included a panel entitled 'My Verdict', of peremptory opinions about anything from the refereeing to the ground arrangements and the quality of the programmes. At this distance the quaintest thing of all was the occasional article attributed to 'Edward M. Waring of the *Sunday Pictorial*', which gave Eddie a formality he never achieved in real life. Four decades on, *Rugby League Review* represents an invaluable record for historians wishing to delve into one of the sport's most notable periods. At the time, it was a great stimulus to all its readers, and a unique means of keeping in touch with the game as a whole, at home and abroad. Its importance, on several counts, can scarcely be exaggerated.

Yet there was always something about it that set my teeth on edge, and it was a while before I was clear about the cause of this. Gradually it dawned on me that this otherwise splendid periodical, and most especially its founder, harboured the most terrible grudges.

70

In particular, all forms of authority were sniped at with an asperity that went beyond reasonable criticism. The Huddersfield club once refused a press ticket for covering a match against Hull, and this was not only pointed out most prominently in the *Review*, but the names of the club's football committee were printed ('in response to readers' requests') underneath a quotation from Shakespeare ('A little brief authority . . . as make the angels weep'). It was fairly obvious that Chadwick's greatest satisfaction would not have been unlimited press tickets in future, but the errant committeemen clapped into pillories at Fartown, there to be mocked and abused by an army of his subscribers. Instead of trying to solve his problem with diplomacy, he was indulging in private fantasy. Nor was this his wildest aberration; for it eventually transpired that his self-appointed mission was to rid the Rugby Football League of its secretary, William Fallowfield, who had also offended him.

This was made public in front of Mr Justice Stable at Leeds Assizes in July 1952, when Fallowfield was awarded £300 damages for libel against Chadwick and his publishing company, The Venturers Press, as a result of articles published in *Rugby League Review* between 1948 and 1950. Plaintiff and defendant could without difficulty be represented as natural adversaries. The editor was not only a self-made Rugby League man to his marrow, a printer by trade, but a familiar type of professional Yorkshireman, too: 'In Yorkshire, Mr Veale,' he told plaintiff's counsel, 'we call a spade a spade, not an agricultural implement.' The secretary was as distant from that as it was possible for another Englishman to be: a fairly polished university graduate, an ex-RAF officer, a man who had played Rugby Union not only for Northampton, East Midlands and the RAF, but for England as well in a couple of wartime internationals. Neither man came out of the case very well.

The origin of the quarrel appeared to be a decision by Fallowfield not to let Chadwick publish the Rugby League fixture list for the 1947–8 season, after the League's press and publicity committee had already ruled that he might do so. Even the judge thought this a bit rum, when he was told that Chadwick had evidently been singled out for this prohibition. Thereafter the sniping began, especially in the half-dozen articles which were the subject of the action. Sometimes it took the form of a sneer – 'The functions of the committee must not be usurped or made to look ridiculous by any playboy who blunders on the scene' – and at others it amounted to a blunt call for the

secretary's resignation or dismissal. 'In the name of God, GO!' wrote
the editor one week, quoting Oliver Cromwell instead of Shakespeare
this time. Nothing that Fallowfield could or might do was acceptable
to Chadwick. He was implacably hostile from the moment he was
unreasonably snubbed.

He lost all sense of proportion, and this was nowhere better
illustrated than in his coverage of the case in *Rugby League Review*
after the libel action had been lost and won. He announced on his
front page:

> During the past week, the Labour Party, and in a lesser degree the
> Rugby Football League, have dropped all pretence at being united
> organisations. Mr Attlee and Mr Richard Stokes have fired the first
> shots against the Bevanites, while Mr William Fallowfield, with the
> backing of the RL Council, has taken the gloves off against *Rugby
> League Review* and its associates. In both cases the spectacle has
> been less than edifying and must surely have a damaging effect
> on the respective bodies' prestige and public following.

The air of injured innocence is less pertinent than Stanley Chadwick's
parallel between his own position – even in 'a lesser degree' – and
Aneurin Bevan's. The man had a very large opinion of himself

The episode is worth recalling so long after it happened only because
it exemplifies a cast of mind that is with us still; one which does nothing
to embellish, or even uphold the best traditions of, a great game. The
small and niggling character off the field is the non-combatant version
of the surreptitiously dirty player on it, and both are a plague upon
Rugby League. I'm not sure that either the intricate violence or the
organisation of a rugby match has ever made possible an equivalent
of the batsman 'walking' in cricket – which is sport raised to an
uncommonly attractive level of behaviour – but there can be and
are moments when both League and Union are capable of exhibiting
the decencies of human nature: when both sides fraternise after eighty
minutes of ferocious tackling, when a scrum-half trots a few yards to
pick up the ball and tosses it to his opposite number for the put-in,
when a man helps up an opponent whom he has just flattened on the
ground. For myself, I'm well content if the players do but shake each
others' hands cordially when the final hooter goes; and if Leeds and
Wigan can do this after a match both desperately wanted to win –
as they have done in recent cup-ties – then anybody can.

None of these actions need be inconsistent with the pulverising vigour of, say, an Anglo-Australian Test match, where the occasional punch may be thrown without definitely signalling the end of civilisation; but some things are on and others are not. It must be thirty years or more since a fine Scottish international forward, P. W. Kininmonth, retired prematurely from the Union game, saying that he no longer felt able to participate in a sport where it was thought permissible deliberately to kick or trample on an opponent lying helplessly on the turf. (In much the same spirit Ray Lindwall – who might well have played for his country as a Rugby League full back had he not decided to concentrate on his cricket instead – once said that he wouldn't have thought himself fit to wear an Australian sweater if he had bowled bouncers at any batsman after No. 8). There or thereabouts is the demarcation line which should be observed by all rugby players, to be enforced by their referees, their coaches and their other bosses; also, indirectly, by those who watch and applaud. We are, after all, talking about sport and entertainment, not about open warfare or Roman holidays.

It is the whingeing, embittered character holding on to grudges who concerns me most of all here, however, for he is an unlovely manifestation in our game and we ought to have outgrown him by now; whereas unacceptable violence on the field always has been and always will be a potential hazard needing self- or enforced control, because it is related less to immaturity than to things deep and permanent in the human psyche. I have put that as though I have individuals mostly in mind; and so, perhaps, I have. But the disagreeable sound of collective resentment is often audible if you turn your ear in the wrong direction. There is, for example, a grating sound specifically Australian in its intonation which, with no obvious justification, began to increase in volume at about the time references to 'the Old Country' were falling quite naturally into disuse: it is the noise a people make when they have a chip on their shoulder, and it is not usually expressed with the wit of a television commercial which has been run in Sydney during Test matches between the two old rivals: 'I'm quite partial to Poms – so long as they're well done!'

There is also, I'm sorry to say, a distinctively Wigan sound, a prolonged moan that might be caused by acute belly-ache, directed at whoever may be refereeing that day. Spasms of rage against officials are, as we all know, part of every football supporter's natural exuberance and a sign that he is enjoying himself. But at Central

Park the deep conviction of a sinister and systematic conspiracy to defraud the local team, is vented in a pitiable complaint that 'They never give Wigan owt'. I know of no other ground where the faithful are rallied with such a clarion call.

The roots of these grudges and resentments are often embedded in local history. The most notable of them is entangled in the origins of the game, as well as in the social and economic circumstances which gave it a distinctive character. It is a depressing fact of life that after almost one hundred years, and even after the removal of an official barrier separating amateur players of the two rugby codes, antipathy persists between some people in League and others in Union. I can detect lingering traces of it in myself. I get a satisfaction verging on the malicious whenever I contemplate the results of those two matches played by gracious (almost divine) permission during the war, between Combined Services sides representing the Rugby League versus the Rugby Union. We, it will be recalled, beat Them first of all at Headingley, in 1943, by 18 points to 11; and then, in the following year at Odsal, repeated the medicine to the tune of 15 points to 10. We did so, what's more, by playing them at their own game; that is, at 15-a-side. It satisfies me enormously, childishly, to remember that; and I can scoff quite loudly when I pick up the *Playfair Rugby Football Annual* for the 1948–9 season – a Union publication – and see how they dealt with those fixtures in their retrospective look at what had been happening while the war was on.

The Headingley match they simply didn't notice. Of the Odsal game they remarked cryptically: 'Both sides composed of Service men and not truly representative.' Yes, it must have stung, when it happened not once, but twice: and I suppose it *might* have made a difference to the final score if the games had been truly representative. But we'll never know because, although the secretary of the Rugby League in those days, John Wilson, said at a luncheon before the game in Leeds that he saw no reason why the fixture should not become an annual event, Homo Twickiens would have none of it. His variant at Murrayfield had been even more forbidding, taking the view that Lance-Corporal Ernest Ward, Sergeant Stan Brogden, Sergeant Ike Owens, Sergeant-Instructor Trevor Foster & Co, while quite acceptable as subordinates in hostilities against Hitler, might dangerously pollute the likes of 2nd Lieutenant Bruce-Lockhart, Flight-Lieutenant Weighill and Officer-Cadet Haydn Tanner on a football field. As *Playfair* noted: in November 1939 the 'Scottish

Union announced it saw no reason for departing from its ban on professionals in Services playing for or against amateur sides'.

Narrow little men of inadequate education, constipated with prejudice, continue to regard Rugby League like that even today, and I can spit with fury whenever I find myself downwind of one. I can even rise to the bait put down by a tittering Cliff Morgan in his *Sport on Four* radio programme on the morning of the 1988 John Player Final between St Helens and Leeds, when he had an actor mouthing the preliminary opinions of one Bill Bore, like a caricature of Eddie Waring in *It's a Knockout*. It is at times like these that I am most fully aware how very complex is my allegiance to Rugby League, embodying not only a certain preference in athletic skills, but the way and the where and from what I was reared, the history of the British class system, and persistent cultural differences between North and South.

My position, when I am in that mood, would be more tenable were it not for the indisputable fact that our lot contains its quota of ignoramuses and bigots, too. Some would die rather than admit that in the splendid Rugby Union Varsity match of 1987 there was scrummaging that shamed the incompetent version commonly practised in the first division of the Rugby League championship; that every one of our professional packs could have learned much in this respect from those young Blues, as could some of our grade one referees from the man in charge at Twickenham that day, Roger Quittenton. We include a number who all but wet themselves with mirth whenever they see references to a certain Steele-Bodger, which puts them at the same level as juveniles who crease themselves every time they come across a name ending in '. . . bottom'. There must be legions who are convinced that from the moment of the schism in 1895, nobody associated with Rugby Union has ever treated Rugby League with anything but the disdain of a Brahmin for an Untouchable.

That this has not been the case is clear from a memoir published in 1927 by Sir Wavell Wakefield, who captained England at what he called rugger, and was for ages part of the Twickenham furniture. Looking back to 1919, when football was getting to its feet again after the First World War, he mentions that a special dispensation was made (as it would be again a generation later) enabling the professional rugby footballers to play with the amateurs in inter-Service competitions. It was then that 'W. Seddon, a Northern Union full back who played for Wigan, taught me the secret of spin-kicking. He was a very fine kick himself, and won more than one match for us with his long-range dropped goals.' That's not exactly effusive, but it's more than some would give Wakefield credit for.

Again, if the name Crawshay means anything to the follower of Rugby League, it will probably be associated with a Union invitation side, Captain Crawshay's XV, which has long been part of that code's annual habit of teams touring the land during the Easter holidays. There's a bit more to it than that, though. The Crawshays of Cyfarthfa were important members of the nineteenth-century Welsh squirearchy, whose wealth was multiplied immensely by their investment in coal-mines and iron foundries, and who were therefore partly responsible for the industrialised appearance of the Rhondda and adjacent valleys of South Wales, as well as for the bleak conditions under which many thousands of miners and foundrymen worked and dwelt.

David Watkins begins his autobiography by recalling the grave of Robert Crawshay near Merthyr Tydfil, and its headstone with the carved inscription 'God Forgive Me'. His descendant, Captain Geoffrey Crawshay, was perhaps less in need of absolution, for although his substance was dug out of the earth for him by others, too, his interests were wider than that of most ironmasters, his sympathies a good deal more benevolent than the norm among his contemporaries. He was twice a Liberal parliamentary candidate, a Herald Bard of the National Eisteddfod, a patron of the arts, all things Welsh, and especially its rugby football. He founded the Welsh Guards Choir, the Welsh Guards XV, and the other Union side which bears his name; and at these matches he 'cheered his men on from the touch-line, garbed in a flowing cloak and protected from icy winds by a deerstalker hat'. That makes him sound like a sitting duck for some smouldering League antagonist, but the temptation should be resisted. For Captain Crawshay's XV was founded with the intention, according to the Welsh historians Smith and Williams, of providing 'some individual compensation for many Welsh players whose economic circumstances prevented them from accepting invitations to join the Lions' tours of the inter-war period'. What's more, this ex-Guards officer, dressed eccentrically like Sherlock Holmes in a green cloak and deerstalker, tried in 1927 to start amateur Rugby *League* in Glamorgan 'to play in a competitive spirit where only true sportsmanship was allowed'. It didn't take on, but that wasn't his fault.

The antipathies seem to exist everywhere but in Australia and in Papua New Guinea. The French grievance is that their Rugby Union is professional in all but name, much wealthier than Rugby League, and therefore holds the whip-hand in the recruitment of the best players: also that Union politicians were behind the notorious seizure of League assets and banning of the game itself by the Vichy Government in 1941. In New Zealand, where League is a totally amateur sport, it has been known for a Kiwi side to train on a Union ground before a Test against the Kangaroos, although Graham Lowe has told how, when his Kiwis and Brian Lochore's All Blacks had planned a get-together in an Auckland hotel, as both sides happened to be playing in the city that weekend, the idea was kiboshed by the New Zealand RFU. In Australia alone they appear to have long risen above such pettiness.

In the 1936 symposium of views on Rugby Union entitled *The Game Goes On* – edited by Captain H. B. T. Wakelam and including an article on 'Old Boy Football' by one E. W. Swanton – there is an illuminating piece by E. N. Greatorex, who toured the British Isles in 1927–8 with the Waratahs of New South Wales. He recounted the development of Rugby Union in his country, and made the point that it suffered severely when Rugby League began there, because nearly all the 1908 Wallabies went over to the 13-a-side game. In other words, the older body had as much reason for feeling sore as the English Rugby Union after 1895. He went on: 'The Australian Rugby Union, however, has no quarrel with the League. There is room for both games. Australians are impartial so far as football is concerned. The man who goes out to see a Rugby League international will turn up for a Rugby Union international.' That is as true today as it was half a century ago, producing a climate the rest of us should envy and try to imitate. In such a climate it has been quite natural for the Australian Rugby Union to ask the Queensland Rugby League if they might use Lang Park for a representative match in Brisbane, and for permission to be given. Would that the same civil behaviour were the rule rather than the exception in the northern hemisphere.

It is not beyond the bounds of possibility that we in the British Isles might get there one day; and it says much for the changing circumstances of our times that one can now speculate on a topic that has for too long been petrified in snobbery and recrimination. There are other straws in the wind besides the most substantial advance, the possibility of interchange for amateur players of the two codes; and some of them are to do with social movements in the population as a whole. Most of these can be traced to R. A. Butler's Education Act of 1944, which made university possible for tens of thousands to whose parents it had been forbidden fruit. How else did the Cambridge University rugger side come to be captained for two seasons in the 1980s by Mark Bailey, whose grandfather was a miner and whose father was a former secretary of Featherstone Rovers? An even more striking bridge across troubled waters has been the upward mobility of the Risman family. The legendary Gus had no more than a secondary education in South Wales before coming to Salford as an 18-year-old, but his tremendous success in Rugby League was counterpointed after he had turned professional when, under the wartime dispensation, he captained a Welsh Rugby Union side in internationals. His son Beverly not only went one better in education by getting to college, but also represented his country at both codes in peacetime, one after the other. And while, more recently still, Bev was managing Fulham RLFC, his sons Michael and John were playing Rugby Union for the universities of Cambridge and Oxford.

The logic of this progression is not hard to follow. English Rugby League is at last on its way to becoming a game of the middle classes, as well as of the helots. If it continues along this path it could end up, like rugby in Wales, as a unifying force among people who otherwise have their differences. The very best argument that can be advanced in favour of expansion at home may well be a social one in the widest and most valuable sense; an emergence from the northern ghetto, leading to a broader outlook on life generally, which in its turn might profitably result in northerners appreciating their origins, in terms of Rugby League, from a position of self-confidence rather than one of grievance.

Rugby Union is also at a crossroads, and one at which some painful decisions on which way to go will soon have to be made.* Its traditional autocracy is still going strong, manifested as unpleasantly as anywhere in the preposterous rule which withholds from Lewis Jones – one of the most honourable and excitingly talented players ever to put on football boots in any code – the privilege of a ticket at all international matches on Cardiff Arms Park, which is granted to all who have played for Wales; withheld from him, as from David Watkins and others in a similar position, only because he is tainted

---

* Perhaps, in the surrender to competitive league football, the crucial decision has already been made.

by having played Rugby League professionally. Now there's a mean spirit for you! But how much longer can it be sustained in the face of other happenings in the world of 15-a-side? For it is patently obvious that international rugger in these islands has become as shamelessly shamateur as it always has been in France, and that a day is not far distant when player power will demand that payment for services rendered must be out in the open and pretty substantial.

The New Zealand Rugby Union has already tied itself in knots in trying to pretend that the All Blacks have not been cleaning up dollars and other emoluments rather well in recent years. One of their captains, David Kirk, has even gone into cold print with the following opinion of what will be:

It seems to me that the tide of social and political sentiment in many of the countries in which rugby is played is turning more and more to a belief in a meritocratic way of life. A way of life that provides opportunity and rewards success in due measure. Rugby players are not isolated from this social tide. Is it any wonder then that the world's top players may feel confused and in some senses alienated by a rugby meritocracy that ignores the principal medium of reward the whole world recognises: money? A medium, incidentally, that by its nature acknowledges transitory excellence as deserving of long-term reward.

At this, a snort may be heard coming from the direction of Huddersfield, where a rather less brassy approach was adopted, and condemned, in 1895.

My grandmother would have cackled at Rugby Union's predicament. She knew nothing of rugby, but hard times throughout her life had made her a combative old soul who quite enjoyed the discomfiture of those she identified as her natural enemies. She lived in an industrial Lancashire constituency which, against all likelihood, returned a Conservative to Parliament time after time. She, however, was most vehemently of the other faith, believing to the end of her days that the Gospels were written by Matthew, Mark, Luke, John, George Lansbury and his successors in the editorial chair of the *Daily Herald*. She did not believe that there could be such a thing as a truly decent Tory; and in this she was mistaken, though not in much else. When the 1945 election campaign was warming up, she was discussing with a neighbour the prospects, and working her way towards the conclusion that this time, at last, we might get our man in (she was wrong; the constituency erred again, and we didn't). She was drawing all this conviction from her bright vision of socialism, and the immense benefits that she knew would come from government by Clem Attlee and his team. She was paying no attention to what Winston Churchill and his cronies might have to offer as an alternative. 'But what about the Tories, Mrs Hoyle?' said the neighbour, who lacked her sublime optimism in the face of regular adversity. 'Oh, never mind them!' said Grandma, dismissing the great warlord and his battalions with a wave of her hand.

It is not a bad way of disregarding those with whom you think you have irreconcilable differences. It has dignity. Better by far than griping and grudging whenever they are mentioned.

Seven

Not Cricket

When E. W. Padwick was asked to make a list of all the publications that had ever shared the theme of cricket, it was assumed that the tally would run into several hundreds. When *A Bibliography of Cricket* eventually appeared in 1977, it was found that no fewer than 8,294 different titles were catalogued there, many more than even the most knowing librarians would have guessed. The precise figure is unimportant, the point being that it merely confirmed what lovers of the game had long known in their bones: that cricket has been written about much more extensively than any other sport, ever since the eighteenth century. Even more significantly, it has inspired an amount of writing that meets the most exacting definitions of genuine literature, and in this, too, it will be without a serious competitor.

Novelists, poets and playwrights have all been tempted to practise their craft on it, in much greater numbers than they have ever turned to racing or golf or tennis or boxing or varieties of football. Trollope once wrote a whole chapter entitled 'The Cricket Match', and Dickens was so aware of the game's place in Victorian England that it crops up in no fewer than nine of his works. In our own times alone you could field a couple of cricket teams from among the writers of high repute who have – perhaps only once – described some aspect of the game, seeing in it a form of human activity important or simply attractive enough to be worth recording through the prism of their imagination. People such as V. S. Naipaul and Kingsley Amis, Harold Pinter and Ted Hughes, Gavin Ewart and Simon Gray are to be found among this band. The pity of it is that the only Nobel Prize winner for Literature to get his name into *Wisden* – Samuel Beckett, who is there because in 1926 he opened both the bowling and the batting for Dublin University against Northants – does not yet seem to have committed this particular enthusiasm of his to print.

There are several reasons for cricket enjoying this eminence. One is that it occupies such a position in the evolution of this country that it is scarcely possible to contemplate the essences of *English*ness without some reference to the game and the aura it has acquired: in particular, no record can be made of life in the countryside without at least a genuflection towards the village cricket match. Here is one of the few activities that have always transcended the traditional imperatives of the European class system, the insistence on each group keeping its distance from the other. In cricket the Gents and Players have mingled both on and off the field, We have had the opportunity to settle a few scores with Them in a form of belligerence accepted by everyone, and an agreeable aesthetic has been provided for all manner of tensions to be elaborately worked out, from the widely social to the narrowly domestic. These are compelling reasons for a writer's senses to be engaged by the summer game.

But there is also the very structure of a cricket match, the way it is ordered, its duration, even the techniques it employs. Here is the gladiatorial contest, between a solitary batsman and a single bowler, played within the larger strategy involving twenty other combatants; a double drama unlike any other, with the sole exception of that provided by baseball, America's equivalent sport. Here is an athletic exercise in which the finest subtlety and the crudest battery can marvellously co-exist, wherein a man can excel by sheer skill even when his physique is far from robust (remember Chandrasekhar's Test match googlies, bowled by a polio-withered arm!).

Here, gratifyingly from the writer's point of view, is a game which is not played at breakneck speed from start to finish, and which lasts long enough, even in its shorter forms, for the character of each individual taking part to be displayed. No one can conceal his true nature for six hours unless he is concentrating on the deception above everything else. Anyone who watched Boycott batting, therefore, saw a painstaking fellow preoccupied with self. Observe Botham in the field and you will notice arrogance, boisterous humour and a deep need for companionship, with maybe a glimpse of generosity as well. Cricket offers both ample time and opportunity for the writer to study his cast, to be stimulated by their differences.

No form of football can present so many inducements to the man whose profession is to try to understand, interpret and shed light on the way people are; to tell us stories about ourselves. Though football's origins are even more ancient than cricket's – it is first mentioned in the fifteenth century, cricket a hundred years later – it has never been so closely identified with national characteristics, real or imagined. The very idea of condemning somebody's bad behaviour by pointing out that 'it isn't football' will strike most of us as comical because cricket long ago staked out the moral high ground as its own. Nor has football in these islands formed much of a bridge linking social groups, except in the case of rugby among the Welsh, where it clearly in time became Everyman's game as an expression of nationality in part. Elsewhere, broadly speaking, soccer and Rugby League have been the pastimes of wage earners, Union that of salaried people and the investing class.

The biggest frustration of all to the writer, however, is the nature of the football match, whichever of the different rules it may be played under. It is, quite simply, over and done with far too quickly to exhibit much more than the athletic skills of those involved, and the courage accompanying them. It lacks the slow passages of cricket in which not all the players on the field need to keep their attention riveted wholly on the game. A footballer cannot relax for one moment, and the most obvious thing about him, apart from his ability, is the fact that he is tensely awaiting the next movement that will include him. There is virtually no opportunity for him to display, let us say, the good-natured urchin humour of a Derek Randall on the field of play.

A consequence of this is that most of what has been published about the different codes of football, in whatever form, has been the work of professional sports writers, which means journalists. No one should mistake that for a literary evaluation, for there have always been journalists as capable as any novelist of writing creatively and imaginatively; that is, with an intuitive ability to see possibilities, to perceive connections, to make allusions, to *enlarge* upon the bare bones of the matter to hand; and there are novelists, just as there are journalists, who could not do that to save their lives. The restriction of column inches, however, and the very nature of reporting (which means presenting information as a chief priority) ensure that in practice very few sports writers get the chance to exercise whatever imagination they may possess. A Denzil Batchelor or an Arthur Hopcraft among those who have reported on football has been a very rare bird indeed, like a Neville Cardus, a Matthew Engel or an Alan Ross among the cricketers.

Rugby Union has seen occasional sallies by more generally known literary figures, starting with Thomas Hughes's famous description of the match in *Tom Brown's Schooldays*, and continuing with the likes of Hugh Walpole, P. G. Wodehouse, John Buchan, Richard Llewellyn and Alec Waugh (not to mention a highly professional piece of Sunday newspaper reporting on the 1955 match between Ireland and France from none other than the poet Louis MacNeice).

Yet when it comes to specialised writing between hard covers, there seems to have been little imagination at work, though a number of other literary virtues have appeared from time to time: in the thoughtful *Report on Rugby* which W. John Morgan and Geoffrey Nicholson wrote thirty years ago, and in the superlative history of Welsh rugby, *Fields of Praise*, which David Smith and Gareth Williams produced in 1981 and which may, indeed, be the finest history of any sport.

Otherwise, judging by a recent catalogue circulated by a second-hand dealer in Rugby Union publications, performance has been limited. Of the 200 titles on offer, there were annuals, books on technique, and histories of the game at various levels: but by far the biggest categories were slight biographies of contemporary heroes, and accounts of international tours, usually by newspaper correspondents who had merely rejigged the reports they originally cabled home from day to day. Standing out from the ruck among these was Denis Lalanne's engaging diary of the 1958 French tour of South Africa, *The Great Fight of the French Fifteen*. But there was nothing even approaching Garrie Hutchinson's splendid volume of observations on Australian Rules, *From the Outer*, much less anything in the same league as the writings of C. L. R. James.

All forms of football still await – and badly need – their equivalent of something as wide-minded as James's *Beyond a Boundary*, which is regarded by many connoisseurs as the most important book ever written about cricket, because it illuminates the game by observing it from many related points, and reveals much about West Indian life in particular by perceiving it through the medium of a Caribbean obsession. 'What do they know of cricket, who only cricket know?' is where James begins. A similar question is worth asking about any sport.

In this area, Rugby League is not much differently served from its winter companions nowadays, though it must be accepted that nothing of consequence happened until after the Second World War. The great library catalogue in the Reading Room of the British Museum seems to suggest that the earliest book was the *Northern Rugby Football Union*

Official Handbook for the Australian and New Zealand Tour, written by
'Forward' and published at Oldham in 1910. Alas, the library's copy
was destroyed in a wartime air-raid and no replacement has been
found. From season 1911–12, however, an official guide appeared
annually in a small format, but nothing else was available until, in
1938, there arrived a slim volume on *How to Play Rugby League*, by
A. J. Risman, who by then had been playing it extremely well for
the best part of a decade. And that was that until hostilities ceased.

The most notable publishing event at home just after the war was
the launching by Stanley Chadwick of *Rugby League Review*, that highly
idiosyncratic but indispensable journal which came out monthly only
in winter at first, but was eventually available weekly throughout the
year. Here was the start of something in which the game has ever
since – sometimes spasmodically – been rich: periodicals. With the
exception of the *Rugby Leaguer*, the newspaper that was first published
in 1950 and is still going strong, most have lasted no more than a year
or two, a few only months, before failing to reappear. The outstanding
Rugby League Magazine ran from 1963 until 1970, when it came to a
stop on the untimely death of its editor A. N. Gaulton, one of the
finest journalists Rugby League has seen; compiler, among other
things, of the testimonial booklets, models of their kind, associated
with Huddersfield players in the '50s and '60s.

In the traditions of Gaulton's magazine are two periodicals with
us today. Harry Edgar's monthly, *Open Rugby*, was a most gallant
venture when a small print-shop in Oxford High Street made 270
copies of four handwritten pages in 1976, and it now prospers as a
glossy with an international circulation. Trevor Delaney's younger
quarterly *Code 13* invaluably complements it, by side-stepping the
present for the most part, and running well-researched articles on
the game's development, more often than not illustrated from old
archives.

The past forty years have seen a number of League biographies –
extolling such players as Gus Risman, Vince Karalius, Billy Boston,
David Watkins, Alex Murphy – which are much the same as their
counterparts in other sports; that is, artlessly repeating mostly well-
known details of the subject's public persona, but conveying almost
nothing about him as a human being. It should surprise no one if we
are ever informed, as we might well be one day, that almost every
British sporting biography for a generation has come out of the same
word-processing plant.

Much more valuable books than these have been written about clubs, including Jack Winstanley's sumptuously illustrated history of Wigan, Ken Dalby's four meticulous volumes on Leeds, and Andrew Hardcastle's model study of Halifax. In Robert Gate, the British game has at last found the general historian it has long needed, someone with an enviable appetite for the hard slog of research, whose inclination is to tackle themes larger than those of the club chronicler; from which we must hope that before long he will give us a full history of the game in this country, comparable to Gary Lester's definitive *The Story of Australian Rugby League*, whose text is marvellously illustrated with archival photographs which in some cases have never been seen before.

Just as important to us as the club and other histories, has been the acquisition of a comprehensive log-book. Although no other sport can ever have cricket's luck in annually keeping track of itself through comforting thicknesses of *Wisden*, this game has at least developed the next best thing with *Rothman's Rugby League Year Book*, which Raymond Fletcher and David Howes have edited admirably since 1981.

The first novelist to pay attention was, almost inevitably, Bradford's most celebrated contribution to English letters, J. B. Priestley. In his collection of essays *Apes and Angels* (published in 1928) was a short piece entitled *T'Match*. This purports to describe a game played in Bruddersford – that invented amalgamation which Priestley uses repeatedly in his works to represent the urban West Riding – between the local team and their rivals from Millsbury. 'If you are in Bruddersford on Saturday afternoon,' it begins, 'you go to t' match.' But you go, in this case, as a self-confessed stranger, Priestley's device to identify himself with his readers, most of whom had maybe never even heard of, let alone seen, this form of rugby.

'As a matter of fact, there were several football matches, of varying codes, to choose from, and when I marched out of the hotel I had no idea at which particular match I should arrive . . . I paid my shilling and then discovered that it was a rugger match, presumably the Northern Union, the professional, 13-a-side all scrimmage game.'

So ignorant is this stranger that he is annoyed when, on reaching the ground, he finds a match has already started and is being played by teams who, 'though sufficiently well-built fellows, were not the giants I expected to find in Northern Union rugger'. He has, of course, arrived in time to see the end of the lads' curtain-raiser. A chap standing next to him on the terrace puts him straight about this and, when the main bout begins, he is suitably impressed: 'The forwards on both sides were colossal fellows, fit to engage in a scrum with a few elephants.'

This remains, from start to finish, an outsider's view of the game. At no stage is there the slightest pretence of understanding technicalities, although Priestley identifies himself thoroughly with the crowd of regular fans. Never does he refer to these people as 'they': it is 'we all waited for Bruddersford and Millsbury to appear . . . we were very angry . . . You should have heard us shout for Nosey . . .' Nosey is probably a winger (we aren't actually told), so inactive for a long time that Priestley decides he isn't worth watching; but then he gets the ball inside his own half and, running 'at a prodigious speed down the touch-line', hands off a couple of Millsbury defenders, and swerves past two or three others before 'curving in exquisitely at last to plant the ball neatly between the posts.'

Nosey's chief function in *T'Match*, in fact, is not to be admired as an athlete conventionally, but to stimulate a different sort of action on the terraces, so that Priestley can describe this in much greater detail than he does the play. The same goes for the visitors' stand-off, who gets sent off, and the home full back, who takes a pounding from the Millsbury prop. The footballers, in short, are no more than a foil for the crowd, and Priestley is much more interested in these people, picturing them vividly with swift, confident strokes. A fellow in front of him has 'an angry, unshaven face . . . one of those men who have no money but yet contrive to follow their football teams wherever they go . . .' Another chap, one of those humourless windbags we all endure, week after week, 'will be the last spectator to leave the ground. He will tell the man who closes the gates what would have happened if Number Six had tried it on with Mulligan'.

Priestley does attempt one judgment of the football, declaring that there are far too many scrums in the Northern Union game; and in 1928 he was right, there were. He trusts himself much more when he weighs up the spectators, and in his description of their natural habitat. His opening paragraph is a memorable miniature of the West Riding landscape, leading to the conclusion that it has bred a special race. 'If you have never seen any of these men, take a look at the Yorkshire cricket team next summer. Or come to t' match.' As an account of the game of Rugby League in the first third of this century, *T'Match* is nothing more than a small cartoon, which ends with an expression of the belief that Priestley was to repeat elsewhere in his writings, that all football is a mixture of art and war. As the

Bruddersford crowd bustles headlong for the waiting trams, 'We are all a little talkative, amiable, relaxed: our combative instincts put to bed for a little space.' The home team, presumably, have won; but again we have not been told. No matter: an atmosphere has been deftly captured, and it is recognisable by anyone accustomed to watching such a match even today, sixty years after J. B. Priestley wrote the piece. That is the hallmark of a classic.

Quite different in its approach is the most recent treatment of the game by a major writer. By the time *A Family Madness* appeared in 1985, its author, Thomas Keneally, had a very considerable reputation which had been crowned by his winning the Booker Prize three years earlier with *Schindler's Ark*. The titular family of his next novel, the Kabbels, are a clan who have come from Eastern Europe to Australia, and their collective madness ends in appalling domestic tragedy. But before that climax, the book is about migration to a strange land and about the relationship between new chums and native Aussies, about collaboration in wartime Russia, and about 'the workers' game, Rugby League'. The Kabbels loom ominously over everything happening here, but Keneally's chief dinkum Aussie, against whom the strangeness of these immigrants can be assessed, is Terry Delaney, a private security guard; also a promising five-eighth, hammering his way through the grades with Penrith in the Sydney competition. Although Delaney's principal role in the novel is his increasing involvement with the Kabbel family, his rugby accomplishments are never allowed to be forgotten for very long. What's more, this is a distinctly knowledgeable enthusiast writing about the game. Thomas Keneally has been a League follower in Sydney all his life.

Terry's footballing background is used to convey a number of stock Australian attitudes. A colleague in the security firm, warning him against getting mixed up with the Kabbels, reckons that involvement with aliens is 'like playing Rugby League in France – you think you know the rules but you don't'. Uncomplicated paranoia about the British is similarly handled. Delaney has a chip on his shoulder about the importation of players in his position 'from Queensland or New Zealand or even from England', seeing these as an impediment to his own progress in the Sydney League. He extends this hostility to a team-mate named Tancred, who functions in the pack.

Tancred's the sort of thickhead who wouldn't work in an iron lung. That's the trouble with Pommy forwards – always knew it was, average bloke watching the game knows it is – they look sort of fast on muddy Yorkshire grounds, but when they get out here on a hard and fast Australian ground they're just as slow as they were back on the quagmire. Yet club officials keep buying them!

Only American football qualifies for greater contempt than that. Delaney's third-grade side reaches the grand final for the first time and, after losing narrowly to Souths, is sent on a trip to Hawaii at discount rates as a cheese-paring alternative to being given match pay. On the island he informs a citizeness of the United States that 'We're bloody supermen down there. Not like those poofters of yours, who play two minutes at a time and all covered with padding.'

The football is also invoked to tell of wider social habits in the suburbs of Sydney. We are not allowed to forget that whatever money the players earn is inseparable from the Leagues clubs and their poker machines, 'smelling acrid with the spilled beer and exhaled tobacco of gamblers, and fed eight hours a day with twenty-cent coins'. One of Delaney's matches occasions a brief glimpse of economic history and its long-term consequences:

> There was always a ferocity in the air at Redfern. They called this team the Rabbitohs, after the Depression days when the unemployed of South Sydney used to hunt rabbits in that low country of sand-dunes and sell them from door to door. Half the crowd seemed to have the toughness of Depression survivors, old men with the shadows of a hard life on their faces, old women who knew their football backwards and wore green and red beanies on their heads. And then, lots of dangerous kids, the kind you saw rioting on English football fields in the evening news. It was exactly the sort of fierce crowd Delaney welcomed that Sunday – an away game and the world against you . . . As he ran on to Redfern Oval, down the wire-caged walk placed to prevent the crones of South Sydney from attacking players or referees, his jaw was retracted, his teeth slightly parted, his mouthguard tight in his fist.

That is virtually the one gesture Keneally makes to Priestley's main interest, the football crowd; and even there, the harsh realities of the sport are close at hand. Far from attempting to disguise the fact that, behind the glamour drummed up by the local *Rugby League Week*, the game in Sydney can be brutal and even sleazy, the author is at pains to reveal how nasty it sometimes is. Earlier in the book we have been told that

> from his years of football, Delaney had learned the game's butt-end range of skills. He liked to depend on penetration and speed, but there were as well eye-gouging and ball-crushing, winding and knees in the back, the clenched arm across the shoulder-blade and the upper cut on the referee's blind side. From this underworld of Rugby League, Delaney produced an elbowing action which left Stanton gagging and devoid of breath.

In the match at Redfern he seriously damages an opponent, which results in his appearance before the judiciary board on Phillip Street. In his defence he tells the authorities that 'It's a matter of inches between a good pass-smothering tackle and a broken jaw. I made a mistake. It wasn't a deliberate one.' They don't believe him, and he is suspended for six months. In the best traditions of Australian mateship, those closest to him on the team take him to a brothel for consolation, footing the bill between them.

Nor is there much of an impression in *A Family Madness* that Rugby League football at this level is played for enjoyment. Delaney is not in it for the sport, but as a calculated attempt to improve his position in life: he sees his football as a career in itself, which will subsequently put him in the way of 'jobs in public relations or writing for the tabloids'. This is a much greater ambition than any of David Storey's characters have entertained, which is another reflection of reality; in this case the bleaker facts of life facing Rugby League players in the North of England both in 1960, when *This Sporting Life* was published, and eleven years later, when *The Changing Room* was first staged at the Royal Court Theatre in London.

The huge crowds that had flocked to the northern grounds for season after season following the war, were no longer in attendance by the time the novel came out; and after a decade of such spectators having discovered other and more fashionable ways of spending their increased affluence at the weekends, the game in England had descended into a trough from which sponsorship had not yet rescued it: John Player & Co's support began within a few months of Storey finishing his drama. There was a certain amount of cash in the game for the players, but not nearly enough to maintain any of them without another source of income. If it provided sufficient to furnish and decorate a rented home and, after that, helped to pay for a car, the average footballer was well content with what his athletic prowess could bring in. Of long-term prospects there was nothing at all except a reputation that a number of enthusiasts would always cherish. This was the Rugby League that David Storey in his novel therefore described as 'a hard game played for money, personal prestige and an enjoyment composed of these two and other elements'.

Storey himself signed professional forms, and used the money he got to pay for an education at the Slade School of Fine Art; one of the more remarkable conjunctions to have been made in the Rugby Football League. While he was playing half-back for the Leeds 'A' team for four years in the 1950s, he was simultaneously picking up prizes for his painting, and exhibiting with Young Contemporaries, the London Group and West Riding Artists. That he then turned to writing was to do the game a much greater service than he could ever have managed if he had been good enough as a player to secure his position in the first team at Headingley, with the prospect – held out to his anti-hero Arthur Machin in the novel – of county and international honours after that.

Although *This Sporting Life* and *The Changing Room* now form but a small proportion of Storey's output as novelist and playwright, and although it seems unlikely that he will ever return to their setting, they stand in a class of their own, whether considered in the cosiness of the library, the flamboyance of the theatre, or the alternative, frequently philistine world of sport. Great footballers are not as rare as all that, but these writings are unique. No other major works inspired by sport – something like Bernard Malamud's *The Natural* rather than the whodunnits of Dick Francis – have come from the pen of someone writing as a complete insider, having played the game whose atmosphere and spirit he is able, with a complementary talent, to give another sort of life.

An interest in Rugby League is by no means necessary to an appreciation of Arthur Machin's story, any more than a fascination with whaling has ever been vital to an enjoyment of *Moby Dick*. This is fundamentally the portrayal of an emotionally stunted and almost insensitive man, struggling to express himself in the way he knows best, through his body. Machin might easily have been characterised as any kind of wage earner who is employed for nothing but his physical strength, self-confident enough in the company of his peers, but regarding all others as potential manipulators, deeply suspicious of their intentions towards him. His clumsy attempts at a relationship with his landlady Mrs Hammond are at the core of *This Sporting Life*, and have little or nothing to do with the game. Yet the novel's richness is very considerably due to the impregnations, one way and another, of the football club for which Machin plays. And all of it ringing with truth. Here is a description of what it is like to be going for the line when you are trying not to admit that you are maybe no longer quite the player you were:

> I ran in close to a play-the-ball and took the pass. I broke into the oblique long-paced run popular with the crowd.
>
> I chose the right wing, a stretch of field more familiar and where the winger was of slighter build. He waited for me cautiously, feet astride, nervously crouched, encouraging me to run between him and the touch. I checked my stride and began to run on the outside of my feet, and moved straight towards him. He moved sideways again, still urging me to pass between him and the touch-line. I hated his mean scheming. I ran at him and shoved out my left fist. I saw his flash of fear, the two arms pushed out protectively, the silly stagger backwards, the two wounds torn in the turf by his sliding heels. I sensed the shape of the full back running diagonally to intercept. I brought my knees up higher and concentrated on the line.
>
> There was Arnie's boyish supporting shout. I'd only to give it to him for a score. I shoved my hand at the full back's head as he came in, and felt the slackening of his arms. I threw myself forward and hit something hard. I fell over sideways into touch.

There's a limit to what an artistically satisfying novel can take of match description, however, and much more is told of Rugby League's character by what happens off, rather than on, the field. Storey is at his best when depicting Johnson, the broken-down hanger-on at the club who is flattered by the title of talent-spotter, or people in management like Weaver and Wade, or the other footballers in the City RLFC. There's a passage where Machin is negotiating a signing-on fee at the outset of his professional career, which conveys an air of dogged resolve on the one hand and seedy closeness on the other. Machin states his price, £500, and is not to be budged, though the directors on the other side of the table try everything from scorn and bullying to false reasonableness and downright dishonesty about the small print in the contract. They even have a last shot at disturbing his composure after they have sent him from the room on the pretext of discussing him privately, in reality to make out the cheque for what he asks. Only after it has been handed over does he learn that several other clubs have been interested in him, as the directors have known all along, which means that he could probably have obtained better terms.

The relationship between directors and players also figures in *The Changing Room*, which is an even more exceptional piece of writing than *This Sporting Life*. For the novelist is not restricted in what he will include in his work by anything other than a need to carry along his readers: he is limited by nothing but the extent of human inventiveness. There are a number of things, however, that no dramatist can convincingly do because they are physically beyond the scope of his chosen medium. One of these is to reproduce in the theatre any sporting contest that normally requires much more space in the open air. (And even in the less confined world of the cinema, attempts to portray field games have usually been embarrassing either because capable sportsmen can't act, or because the actors are no athletes – as was once unforgettably demonstrated by an arthritic Jack Warner in the role of Test cricketer, and again by a young Dirk Bogarde as a medical student playing Hospitals Cup Rugby Union.)

Oddly enough, Rugby League football has twice been featured on a stage: and when John Godber got the Hull Truck Company to produce his farce *Up and Under* at the 1984 Edinburgh Festival, he took the traditional impediment head-on by making his final scene a highly stylised caricature of the way the game is actually played, which one theatre critic described as 'an endearing original triumph'.

In *The Changing Room*, David Storey circumvents the problem by situating the whole of his three-act play within the small confines of the dressing-room on the afternoon of a match. Act One opens with the players arriving to get changed, and closes with them running out on to the pitch. Act Three starts with them in the bath offstage after the game, and the curtain falls on Harry, the cleaner, contemplating the mess left when everybody else has gone home. Act Two posed the greatest technical problem, for although it would obviously take us into the dressing-room for a second encounter with the team at half-time, that ten-minute break wouldn't nearly be long enough for one episode of a three-act play. Storey gets round this by having the chairman and secretary (somewhat improbably) coming in with 15

minutes of the first half still to go; and then (more feasibly) by having
one of the players brought off the field with severe concussion and
a broken nose, just after the second half has started, the business of
sending him to hospital taking up more theatrical time.

The nearest we get to seeing what Rugby League football might
amount to as a spectacle comes just before the players go out for the
first half, when the trainer (the coach was still called that in 1971)
gets his forwards to pack down, to make sure they're comfortable with
the scrummaging drill. Otherwise what we learn about it comes from
listening to the players talk, from hearing snatches of commentary
over the Tannoy, from seeing the state of the injured Kendal and
being told how he got his face kicked ('I don't think Ken wa' even
looking . . . His bloody head came down . . . bloody boot came up . . .').
A great deal about the game's physical hardness is conveyed merely
by a small piece of acting just after the scrummaging. According to
the stage directions 'The players, tense, nervous, start to line up prior
to going out.' Walsh, one of the forwards, tries to hide his own nerves
by being facetious, telling old Harry to 'make sure that bloody bath
is hot. Towel out, tha knows . . . me bloody undies out . . .'

Earlier, the trainer has told them something about their opponents:

CROSBY: (*reading from a list*): Harrison's on the wing this after-
noon, Patsy. Allus goes off his left foot, lad.
PATSY: Aye. Right. (*Rubs arms, legs, etc.*)
(*He and Clegg laugh.*)
CROSBY: Scrum-half: new. Barry: when you catch him knock
him bloody hard . . . Morley?
MORLEY: Aye!
CROSBY: Same with you. Get round. Let him know you're
theer . . . Same goes for you, Bryan.

A hard game, to be sure, but not as hard as it used to be, according
to Harry, whose role in the play is to provide a form of contrast and
relief from the endless vigour and cockiness of the young men. Asked
by the chairman how he thinks they compare with their predecessors
of his own youth, he replies witheringly:

Players? . . . Couldn't hold a bloody candle . . . In them days they'd
do a sixteen-hour shift, *then* come up and lake . . . Nowadays it's all
machines . . . and they're *still* bloody puffed when they come up

o' Sat'days. Run round yon field a couple of times; finished. I've
seen 'em laking afore with broken arms, legs broke . . . shoulders
. . . Get a scratch today and they're in here, flat on their bloody
backs: iodine, liniment, injections . . . If they ever played a real
team today they wouldn't last fifteen bloody seconds. That's my
view. That's what I think of them today. Everywheer. There's not
one of them could hold a candle to the past.

This is a predictable response from an old-timer, maybe, but it is also
one of the moments in the play when Storey is saying more about
Rugby League than that it is a tough and vivid form of football:
setting it in a segment of social and economic history by recalling
when men would come straight from gruelling work at the coal-face
to spend themselves even further on this most sapping of games. From
the beginning he sets out to portray the culture from which the game
sprang, of which it has remained a powerful expression, just as he also
demonstrates the tensions, the comradeship, the rivalry that exist in a
group of interdependent individuals who are collectively facing some
challenge; a theme which many writers have handled by describing
the experiences of a platoon in time of war, a crew on a hazardous
voyage, or some other situation in which a 'team' is involved.

The Changing Room is a remarkable work because of its feeling for
such wider matters, as much as for the veracity of its dialogue, its
insight into the tribal rituals of Rugby League, and its brilliant
solution to the technical problem of dealing with a sporting subject
convincingly in the theatre. Had it not been so, the play might never
have seen a stage except between Doncaster and Carlisle. Not only
did it open in London, but after its West End run it was shipped
across the Atlantic, to be applauded by the most grudging audience
in the Western world, in New York, where it won a critics' award.
That applause and that award were not given to a parochial drama
about a game which most Americans – even when they have heard
of it – hold in amused disregard. They came *The Changing Room*'s way
because it spoke of universal truths.

A very striking thing about these writings of David Storey and
Thomas Keneally, who both know the strengths and weaknesses of
their Rugby League, may be noted by anyone who contrasts them
with the alternative rugby literature produced by Hugh Walpole and
the other novelists mentioned earlier. These, while obviously rejoicing
in the fact that Rugby Union is a tough and character-building sport

(one of its most highly-approved eulogies bears the title *Rugger – The Man's Game*) seem blissfully unaware of dirty play, or of unpleasant behaviour off the field, either in the clubhouse or in those hotels which from time to time have been smashed up by drunken touring sides. Not even Richard Llewellyn, generally faithful to the more dismal facts of life in his valley, could bring himself to admit that Cyfartha Lewis and the rest of the team that Huw idolised were capable of those things which Keneally acknowledges from the 'butt-end range of skills' in rugby football. The game, in such selective hands, must be pictured as a noble endeavour as much as possible, and certainly no worse than a rough and tumble.

World wars, too, have often been dealt with like that by certain authors, of whom John Buchan was assuredly one. And while this contrast in the approach to football may have something to do with a greater degree of realism that has informed all branches of literature in the generation and more since Llewellyn and others like him were at work, it is none-the-less reassuring that similar evasions and concealments do not appear in the writings on Rugby League. Small the game's literature may be, but it is trustworthy at least; and not only in its recognition of sometimes unacceptable violence on the field of play. It allows for the fact that in other ways, too, footballers are not always the heroic figures the rest of us would have them be, that some can be as shabby as anyone alive. By relating the game to other affairs of humankind it reminds us, as well, that some matters are of much greater importance than any sport. It is a function of the serious writer to open the eyes of his contemporaries in such ways. Another is to tell posterity how things really were.

Eight

Incognito in Surrey

The figure coming down the steps is not nearly as solid as it once was and the hair is now white, the face more bone than flesh under the skin; but there's no mistaking the jauntiness in that rolling walk or the clarity of those blue eyes or the firmness of that jaw, even after all these years. Yet this is such an improbable rendezvous. That Joe Egan of Scholes, Wigan, Lancashire and Great Britain should finish up in the Surrey stockbroker belt, where they don't even play a decent game of Rugby Union, is a defiance of natural law as prodigious in its way as water running uphill and the sun rotating round the globe. That he appears content with his transmigration to within a rifle-shot of Sandhurst says much for the character of the man. But, then, he always was composed under fire; which is a reason why he was one of the greatest captains in the history of Rugby League.

Old Wiganers of Joe Egan's era have not been notable migrants, however. Half that team he commanded with such conspicuous success in the '40s are now dead, and the other half are still only a few miles – in some cases a few hundred yards – from where they started out. Joe's old prop and stay, Ken Gee, prospers quietly, a little bit over his fighting weight, in a neat stone cottage at Orrell, on the outskirts of town. Martin Ryan, notable singer as well as dashing full back, lives no more than a cockstride from Central Park. Billy Blan, one of the unluckiest international forwards never to go on a Lions' tour, does a lot of his old club's fund-raising from an office at the ground. Jack Hilton, who used to run down the wing in a three-quarter line of pure class, is now on the Wigan board, giving it that authenticity which businessmen alone, however acute, however enthusiastic, cannot quite match. It is impossible to overstate the loyalty of Joe and his contemporaries to the town of their birth, to the club which brought them fame and which they themselves enriched. It verges on the pathological, and its like may never be known again when they have passed on.

It goes back to those years after the First World War when they were the children of craftsmen or labourers who had large families, feared God, and were obsessed with a need to be thought respectable, one indication being the frequency with which the front doorstep was made spotless with elbow grease and a white or yellow donkeystone obtained for the purpose from the rag-and-bone man. Many of them were the sons of miners, and some even had coal in their other parentage, too. Ken Gee's mother, Polly, and Frank Barton's mother, Mary, had both worked on the pit brow at Pemberton Colliery, and once went to London to demonstrate outside Parliament when their jobs were threatened. There was little money to spare for anything but necessities in such families, so that a Wigan youngster's first rugby ball was invariably a bundle of rags or newspapers tied tightly into shape with bant. Street football was illegal (committing a nuisance, according to the magistrates), but that's where boys usually picked up the rudiments of the game, on cobbles, with clogs on, and keeping an eye peeled for the approaching law. They thus learned to fall properly, because it hurt too much if you couldn't, and to swerve off either foot in the narrow confines of the street, and above all to go like the wind when the bobby came round the corner. Tom Brown's schooldays it wasn't; but it produced some of the finest rugby footballers in the world, in either code.

Joe Egan's father worked at the Maypole pit, but Joe served his apprenticeship as a brass moulder, employed by a local firm which made miners' safety lamps. By then, the word was already getting about that St Patrick's – one of the great seedbeds for Central Park – had an impressive young hooker coming up. Wigan was the only professional club who showed any interest in him, but for someone with his background it would in any case have been unthinkable that he might start to play for some other town's team. He became a Wigan player in 1938, when he was 18, and they gave him £20 for his signature. That represented several weeks' wages, and the football money throughout his career was almost always more than he was earning at his trade. During the triumphant years after the war, when Joe's wage-packet from Naylor's was about £5 a week, he was collecting £12 every time Wigan won and £4 when they lost, which they rarely did. For big cup matches they were more handsomely rewarded. When they beat Bradford Northern at Wembley in 1948 it was worth £30 to everyone in the team. 'It was a wide-open world for us. Big crowds and big money. It was the golden age.' And they were big crowds, even by Central Park's standards, in the post-war years. It was not unusual to have 15,000 turn up for an 'A' team match.

Ken Gee, who'd been working at the Pemberton coal-face since he was 16, was already at Central Park when Joe arrived, three years his junior. This was the beginning of a partnership that was to last a dozen years and dominate not only English forward play, but scrummaging all over the world. But not at once. 'We were only mugs, learners, in those days,' Joe recalls. 'They could never get the ball at Wigan, though they used to fetch forwards from all over the place – Wales, New Zealand, South Africa. Wherever they got them from, they were still handicapped by getting no ball.' His third match in the first team was the 1938 Lancashire Cup Final against Salford at Swinton, which Wigan won, though not in the scrum. 'Bert Day murdered me two to one that afternoon. And I was always up against better hookers until after the war. It wasn't till 1946 that I could look round and say to myself, "There's nobody better than me any more."'

One improvement in his technique came from a bit of fine tuning he made after the match at Station Road. Ken had been his blind-side prop, with George Banks on the more crucial open side. Banks was injured when they were due to play together again, and Joe told Ken to switch positions. That's the relationship they maintained – Gee at 8, Egan at 9 – until their last match in partnership, against New Zealand in Auckland at the end of the 1950 Lions' tour, on which Joe was Ernest Ward's vice-captain. They had already been Down Under before, in the party taken out by Gus Risman in 1946. Fourteen times Joe represented Great Britain in Test matches, and if his England international appearances are added, he finished with thirty-three caps. So did Ken.

Rugby League forty years ago was an appreciably different game in some ways from that played now, and nowhere was this more the case than in scrummaging and in the importance attached to it. There were not twenty scrums in any of the Tests between Great Britain and Australia in 1988, but when the British played New Zealand at Swinton in 1947 there were no fewer than seventy-nine; and Joe Egan, propped by Gee and Elwyn Gwyther of Belle Vue Rangers, took sixty-three of them, in spite of which Great Britain were beaten by a superior side. That's how good at his job he was even when, as in that match, he was playing without the assistance of Tommy Bradshaw at scrum-half, third member of the triumvirate on whom Wigan depended for their scrummaging success.

When it was Wigan's put-in, Joe would discreetly give a thumbs up or down to Bradshaw as the two front rows measured up to each other before going down, telling him to put the ball into the top of the scrum or down at Egan's striking foot. Thumbs up meant that Joe thought they could shove the other pack out of the way without much trouble, thumbs down that some serious hooking, with the assistance of Gee, was required: timing by the hooker himself, above everything.

'It's the biggest split-second job on the field. If you go too soon and pull your legs back too soon, on their put-in, their scrum-half will have fed the ball to their hooker. And if you're a split second too late, you *are* too late. Having a good man alongside you is important, to time the shove and control the degree of wheel, to give you every advantage he can.'

Yet even when Joe was recognised as the best hooker in the world, he was outhooked sometimes. Occasionally this was because a referee would try to even things up for the underdogs by letting them have the ball when a strict interpretation of the laws might have ruled otherwise Joe never minded this much, so long as the beneficiaries were indeed the underdogs. 'The ref was just being a human being. Being too fair, really,' is how he sees it in retrospect. Sometimes, official kindness would have been grossly misplaced. There was no underdog when Wigan faced that formidable Bradford Northern pack of the '40s, with its heavyweight front row of Whitcombe, Darlison and Smith.

It wasn't only in the scrums that Egan excelled. He was a dynamo in the loose as well, in spite of a configuration below the waist that was not obviously athletic. Pit Legs was Bradshaw's name for him and it stuck (only the Warrington full back Les Jones had limbs that were more elliptical). He may have been no great shakes as a runner, but his handling of the ball was such that he had others doing the running about. He had the ability, unique in my experience until the Australian Wally Lewis came along, to see an opportunity long before others did and to set events in motion with an extremely long and precisely spun pass, time after time in the same game.

His understanding with Gee included feeding the big man as he came through on the burst because the prop 'took a bit of stopping' once he had got into his stride (Gee is being modest when he admits this). And Joe relished being tackled by three or four men at once, because invariably he'd slip the ball away and there'd be three or four spaces for Blan and the rest to burst through, where those tacklers should have been. Sometimes, he'd perform the extraordinary trick of walking backwards into the opposition after receiving from the dummy half, concealing his intention, which often amounted to no more than offering the ball on the palm of his hand to any one of several team mates. Such impudence, and such guile. Toughness, too. He wouldn't put up with what Ken Gee calls 'hanky-panky' from anyone and four times in his career he was sent off: 'quite a distinguished record' is how Joe drily remembers this. Twice the referee was just as fed up with the other hooker and dismissed the pair of them. The other two were for 'being too rough'; once in the Second Test at Brisbane in 1946 when, according to an Australian historian of the game, 'Egan . . . was seen by many as a token sacrifice for the fighting and mayhem throughout the match.'

More than anything, though, here was a first-class footballing brain, which showed in everything he tried. If he lost the ball to the other hooker he'd shout 'Gone!' whereupon the Wigan pack would explode like a fragmentation bomb, every man ready to tackle something as soon as the ball emerged from what was left of the scrum. He was a natural for the captaincy as soon as Jim Sullivan's playing days were over and the great Welshman became coach. The lads respected Joe because of his skill, because he was quite a hard man beneath the placid surface, because he was genuine. He never had to do any shouting or ranting on the field. But he was always one for speaking his mind, to the directors as much as anyone, if he thought it necessary. When he told them in 1950 that he was leaving the club, there was nothing they could do to stop him, for he wouldn't have gone to see them if his mind had not been irrevocably made up. He was that sort of person. He didn't play games except on the field.

He left Wigan because Naylor's had told him that if he was picked for the 1950 tour down under, and went, they wouldn't be able to hold his job open for the five months he was away. He didn't begrudge them this ultimatum, for they were a small firm and on his moulding depended the jobs of seven or eight fitters. But he was married with small children by then and needed long-term security. At the same time he badly wanted to make the second tour, now that he was at

101

the height of his powers: another ambition was to keep playing till he was 40, which has rarely been done in a game as punishing as this. In Australia he happened to mention his predicament to the chairman of Leigh, James Hilton, and the upshot was that he was offered the job of player-coach at Kirkhall Lane, which meant a wage on top of match pay; so he went. It was a mutually profitable alliance for six years, though it finished Joe as a player. In a 1953 cup-tie against St Helens, he and Charlie Pawsey tackled Don Gullick from opposite sides, and Gullick fell across Joe's left leg, breaking it so badly that they had to put nuts and bolts into the two main bones. He only played a dozen more matches after the injury healed. The insurance premiums became too steep and at the age of 35 a remarkable career was over.

The descent of a great sportsman from his prime is more poignant than most retirements. Happy to salute in our heroes what we would see in ourselves, we are dismayed when they become less than they were, even though by normal standards they are still virile men. But the waning of their special power reminds us too sharply of all our mortalities. It is as though they have been smitten with some fell disease. It is Samson brought low, a form of tragedy. None need feel sad at the fate awaiting a J. P. R. Williams or an Ian Botham, where the end of a sporting life is merely the start of something else that will present the old hero with alternative powers to maintain or even enhance his prestige. But not many footballers and cricketers have ever been able to anticipate that. The men of Rugby League have been as vulnerable as anyone to the emptiness, the sense of loss and personal devaluation that come with hanging up the boots for the last time. A few, like Jim Sullivan and Alex Murphy, have retained their eminence in association with the game, retirement coming in due season and not before, to be seen as the time for a welcome rest, without any pangs. A traditional haven for others has been the role of publican, where at least something of the old popularity can still be felt. The majority have always had to reconcile themselves to the near anonymity of life at the level of those crowds who idolised them in their ascendancy.

Joe Egan coached for a while longer after breaking his leg with Leigh. In 1956 he returned to Central Park and for five seasons took Wigan to successes comparable to those the club had enjoyed when he was a player, including three trips to Wembley and a Championship. Then he went to Widnes and coached them to a Cup Final victory.

But before the '60s were over, he had left the game and was selling Unit Trusts, of all the unlikely things. That lasted for three years, but he didn't have enough cheek for salesmanship. The last decade of his working life was spent in a chemical factory. At the age of 61, a cycle had completely turned. A couple of years earlier, his wife had died, but Joe soldiered on in Wigan, even though the four children had grown up and lived away. He did some gardening (he'd never known a garden till he was 30) and a bit of fishing on Rivington Reservoir or somewhere along the Ribble. Every Wednesday he would go to see Ken, who wasn't as mobile as he used to be, what with the hip operation, and then needing sticks because a knee was starting to go as well. Old footballing injuries can catch up with you cruelly in later years. The elderly men who had set Wigan alight with their exploits in the '40s and '50s all kept in touch with each other, regularly gathered on some pretext or other.

At intervals, they would meet at the funerals of their contemporaries now. Jack Cunliffe was the first of them to go. Then Tommy Bradshaw, Jackie Fleming, Harry Atkinson, Ernie Ashcroft, Gordon Ratcliffe, Brian McTigue, Harold McIntyre, Ted Toohey, Ted Ward . . . The captain uprooted in the end because he wearied of living by himself; also because, in common with too many pensioners today, he was beginning to worry about vile things that used not to happen when he was growing up, like solitary old folks being mugged by the vicious young. That's why he went South, to live with one of his sons and daughters-in-law. His old mates threw a party for him before he left, naturally; at the Griffin, the pub Billy Boston keeps just across the road from Central Park. It could not possibly have been held anywhere else.

The younger Egans were on holiday when I went to see him, and Joe was looking after his new domicile in the stockbroker belt; which meant doing a bit of decorating, and walking the four dogs, and not forgetting to feed the goldfish and the budgerigar. He'd only been there a few months and was still intrigued by his new environment.

'It's a different world down here,' he said. 'People are flitting in and out of here all the time, making money and selling houses. They move in for a few years and then they're out. At t' bottom of t' road here they paid £114,000 for a place and then they started pulling it down. It was a long bungalow and they wanted a double-decker.'

He shook his head, shocked by the sheer wastefulness of it, which could never have happened in Scholes, where he was raised, or even

in Sedgefield Drive, where he spent his final years in Wigan. But he
was bent on getting the best out of things, determined not to live in the
past. A couple of times he'd been to watch some Rugby Union at the
nearest club and had drunk with them afterwards in the bar; but no,
of course they'd no idea who he was. He'd been to watch Aldershot
play soccer when Wigan Athletic came down, but he'd had to leave
before the end of the match, to catch the bus back home. They only
ran every hour round there, sometimes not even that.

He was determined not to live in the past, yet it is impossible to
be a Wiganer of Joe Egan's generation – and such a consummate
Wiganer as he – then to turn your back on that town at the age
of 67. The place has a long claim to you, and insists on reclaiming
its own. An invitation had come down from the directors at Central
Park, asking him to be their guest at the World Club Championship
Challenge match against Manly, and he had gone, to spend a grand
evening with Ken and Martin and Jack Hilton and others of his
peers. Not that he had been too impressed by what took place on the
pitch, where he reckoned there was a disappointing lack of football:
'T' Manly game was not a lot,' that northern tenor asserts. Wigan
won 8–2 with nothing but penalty kicks on the score-board, and
I had thought it one of the most exciting matches I'd seen in which
not a single try was scored, with play going from end to end all night;
but I wasn't going to dispute the old master's view.

'Well, do you agree or what?' He didn't want polite acquiescence.
He expected people to say their piece, as he had always done.

He has a number of bones to pick with the game today, and one
of them is the tendency to elevate the coach to the level of the soccer
men, giving far too much power to an individual, in Joe Egan's view.

'Sully and I didn't have much power at all. You could do what you
wanted if you could convince the committee. You went into a meeting
and you put forward a team, and they'd sometimes argue against it.
I don't think any one man should have control over a team, a club,
like that.'

He was harking back to the days when Wigan RLFC had a
committee of ten, instead of the quartet who run things now; to
the times when Jim Sullivan used to be in the bath with the lads
after the game instead of closeting himself in a private office in the
fashion of today. All the old-timers are perturbed by the increasing
tendency for Rugby League in this respect to imitate the habits of
what Ken Gee calls, without the slightest asperity, 'that daft game

soccer'. They see coaches as an over-promoted breed, pleasing to no one so much as to themselves. People don't want to know about coaches, say the old men, they want to know about players. And some of the new coaching methods are baffling to the footballers of the post-war years.

Sullivan was a great motivator in a *quiet* way, they say. You'd be injured and he'd tell you there was nothing wrong with you; or 'You're the best, why did you let that man side-step you?' Before a match he'd simply say to them, 'Right, lads, you're the best. Just go out there and show it.' Billy Blan, whose fund-raising desk at Central Park is within earshot of the dressing-room, reckons that whatever it may be that they get up to in there nowadays, it isn't at all as restrained as it was in their time. 'You hear this noise and *screaming*. I can hear 'em chanting. They call it getting psyched up. All for a simple game of rugby.'

What Joe Egan means when he speaks of a 'lack of football' (as in the Wigan v. Manly match) turns out, surprisingly, to mean that the game has become too dominated by the forwards in his view; but not in what he regards as their proper place. This, reduced to its essentials, is an argument about the value of the scrum, about what ideal scrummaging consists of. There is no topic in either code of rugby that has been the source of more irritation, and this should astonish no one. The scrum, after all, like the rule that the ball shall never be passed forward, sets rugby apart from all other sports; but whereas correct passing is easy to define and invigilate, scrummaging has tormented the law-makers and the referees regularly since the game first evolved. The adjustments that both League and Union have periodically made have had one common end in view: simply to make the outcome of a scrum less predictable.

Reviewing the 'almost annual changes in technique because there were almost annual law changes' in the Union version, one of their experts on the subject has written:

And they all failed. No law could eliminate the physical advantage of the loose-head hooker being nearer to the ball as it is put in. Everyone realised this but the law-makers tried. In different years they required the hooker to put his feet together; they bound the hooker with a firm grasp on both props; they prevented him from twisting and lowering; they stipulated that he may not lift his hooking foot until the ball touched the ground; then they allowed him to lift as the ball left the half-back's hands; they demanded that the half-back deliver the ball from below his knees and that the ball go into the scrum quickly; then a year or so later they demanded that it go in slowly; the hooker was prevented from swinging on his props and hooking with both feet; the prop was to assume the hooking position; the tight-head hooker was permitted to hook with his near foot and then the loose-head hooker was allowed to do the same. And so on. Every year the laws committee of the International Board met in London and had a go at the scrum . . .

A little less frequently, and in some details differently, the law-makers of Rugby League have done much the same thing. The scrum has become as much of a vexation in rugby as lbw has in cricket.

Joe Egan, one of the greatest of all scrummagers, believes that a cardinal weakness of Rugby League today derives from a systematic attempt to get rid of the scrum, precisely because its outcome has been so predictable. He sees the origin of this campaign in the 1966 Cup Final, the most deadly dull Wembley occasion of them all, which Wigan lost largely because they were without their hooker, Clarke, and had to press a utility forward, Woosey, into the middle of the front row, with little chance of getting the ball from such an experienced opponent as Bill Sayer of St Helens. Alex Murphy, captaining the Saints with one of the most astute football brains around at the time, quite deliberately played offside throughout the match in the expectation of being penalised repeatedly; which resulted each time in a Wigan kick for touch, followed by a scrum which St Helens invariably won. It was a successful exploitation of the rules as cynical as the touch-kicking to obtain repeated line-outs (111 in all) by the Welsh captain, Clive Rowlands, in his country's 6–0 victory against Scotland at Murrayfield in 1963; another game which brought rugby football into some disrepute.

The purist's argument in favour of scrummaging – that it is a distinctive feature of the rugby game – is to my mind the best one in favour of its retention, so long as it can be insured against such a mockery as that devised by the cunning young Alex Murphy. But Joe Egan's defence of the scrum is pragmatic, not based on principle. In the old days, he argues, when there were perhaps eighty scrums in every game, that meant there were eighty opportunities for the ball to go to the backs, with the forwards interlocked and otherwise engaged for a moment or two. He says:

I think it's a myth that the game is faster today. You think something's happening because the emphasis is on playing the ball out in the open, but all the fellow's doing is playing it to the next one in line, who goes rushing hell for leather till, bang, he hits the wall, then plays the ball in his turn. They don't even pass the ball to speak of. There's too much emphasis on 'driving forward' in the modern game, and not enough on passing. Possession mania's worse now even than it was in the sixties. If you put proper value on the scrum, you'd get proper prop forwards. They shouldn't have to do all that handling and running into a wall. There's nothing rugby about that to me.

As for making the outcome of scrummaging less predictable than it generally is, his prescription is that we would be far better off under the rules operating forty years ago. In all circumstances let one side have the put-in and the other have the head – 'It wouldn't be a 50-50 chance, but it'd be no more than 6–4 in favour of the side with the put-in getting the ball back again.'

He is, of course, speaking from an exceptional experience, for he belonged to a team which won the ball far more often than not from such a daunting number of scrums, and also had the halves and three-quarters (not to mention a full back) to exploit possession more enterprisingly than most back lines in the history of the game. Yet Joe claims that his Wigan side never worked out particular tactics for playing different teams, with a special game plan for Hunslet, say, followed by another one for the week after against Warrington. 'We only played one way, running about at high speed; that's what we relied on. We'd just run the opposition silly and move the ball all round the place. And we lost so few games that we didn't need to change our approach.'

They also had an unusual esprit de corps, which followed from the fact that out of twenty-six footballers playing for the first and 'A' teams on any given weekend, at least twenty would be Wigan lads born and bred. Billy Blan remembers how, when you joined Wigan and came into the dressing-room for the first time, you knew all the faces awaiting you there, and had done since childhood. 'Everyone was so familiar that a newcomer was greeted with "Bloody 'ell, they must be short if we've getten thee!" ' On match days the players would converge by bus or by walking in twos and threes from the parts of town where they lived in adjacent, sometimes the same, streets. The outsiders in the team, Mountford, Nordgren and one or two more, were welcomed warmly enough; but it was made plain to them that their individual flair and talents had to be adapted to the Wigan way of doing things.

On a wall in Surrey are some mementoes of those years. Here is King George VI, presenting Joe with the Rugby League Challenge Cup after Wigan had beaten Bradford Northern at Wembley in 1948; the best side, Joe reckons, he ever played in. The monarch is bareheaded, as he had been when Joe introduced the line of players to him before the kick-off and was asked one of those serviceable questions which royalty are apt to put on such occasions: 'And how long have you been playing together as a team?' Then the king went back to his box to sit alongside Lord Derby, to place a billycock firmly on his head and, thus properly attired for watching a rugby football match in front of his subjects, to give every appearance of enjoying the game before taking off his bowler again for the final ceremony.

Here is another photograph, of Wigan's Lions being greeted by wives and children and sweethearts at Wallgate Station on their return from the 1950 tour Down Under. The club had established a record (which no one has yet equalled) by having no fewer than eight men on that tour; and there they all are in their uniforms of shirt and tie, blazer and grey slacks, with trilbies, badged and ribboned and tilted at a rakish angle on each head. That tour was Joe Egan's finale as a Wigan player, yet what he draws my attention to is a triumph by the club which occurred in his absence. The eight tourists had left England by the time the 1950 Championship Final took place at Maine Road, Manchester, in which Wigan's opponents were to be Huddersfield, who didn't have a single player in Ernest Ward's party. This match was to be the biggest foregone conclusion in the history of the domestic game, and the only relevant question was whether the margin of Wigan's defeat would be embarrassing or not. In fact, Wigan's five first team men and eight reserves ran rings round the Yorkshiremen and won 20–2.

'That,' says Joe Egan, 'was the greatest thing that ever happened to Wigan football; winning that game. It was done by superior football and nothing else.' Then he grins. 'The big joke was that Huddersfield had beaten the full Wigan team at Fartown a month before, even though we'd scored first – and whenever we did that we used to reckon we'd win.'

As I said, a man of powerful loyalties: open-minded, too. The week before we met, the Welsh Union team had just edged Scotland in a great game of rugby at Cardiff Arms Park, which Joe had watched on television. 'It had everything I've been talking about that we are now missing in forward play. The Scottish forwards were all going, and turning round and letting someone else have it. They looked so excellent, didn't they? It's an art that's gone out of our game . . .'

Not, one hopes, for long. Perhaps our new strategists, with their enthusiasm for all that has come from Vince Lombardi via Jack Gibson and Frank Stanton, should pay attention to this voice, too. To dismiss Joe Egan's view simply because it is dated circa 1948, would be as foolish as to contemplate the present with a closed mind from the past.

Nine

Sydneyside

A man goes to Sydney these days as one who is making a pilgrimage. There are many compelling reasons for crossing the world to spend time in Australia's metropolis, and one need have no interest in rugby, or in any sport, in order to appreciate them. Sydney Harbour *is* one of the most beguiling places on earth, whether you are steaming down it on the Manly ferry, strolling beside it through the Botanic Gardens, crossing it along the walkways of the Bridge, or simply dallying with a plate of seafood and a bottle of wine on the terrace beside the marvellous Opera House. The last of these pleasures may be enjoyed in many parts of the city, as well as at the waterside, for in the past generation Sydney has acquired a sophisticated palate to counterbalance its traditional beer belly.

There are visual delights beyond the Harbour, too, like the old terraced homes along Victoria Street and in Paddington, with their balconies of delicately wrought iron, the celebrated 'Sydney lace'. There is also an energy here that one normally associates with the thrusting cities of the United States, which may be detected in all aspects of life, from the arts to commerce. Quite out of place now is Neville Cardus's smart opinion of forty years ago – 'Sydney is exactly like Manchester except that you have the Pacific Ocean at the bottom of Market Street instead of the Irwell.' More recently it has been said that Sydney is part San Francisco, a bit of England, the flavour of New York; and this is more nearly right, except that it omits the specifically Australian essence of the place, which gives it a potency and a flavour that is found here and nowhere else. Sydney may well be the most attractive New World city of them all nowadays, an improved version of anything to be found in the Americas, and certainly unrivalled in the Antipodes.

All this and the most dynamic of Rugby League competitions as well; hence the occasion of pilgrimage by anyone interested in the game who can possibly manage to get there – which may well mean, to many Britons, spending half a lifetime's savings. Yet to come here at any time between March and September is to feel that however difficult it has been to raise the funds, the expenditure has been worthwhile; for it is to be left in no doubt that Rugby League is the leading winter sport in this community, which is not a sensation that many English followers of the game have ever experienced at home. Rugby League is outstandingly better organised than anything else in sight in Sydney, with the possible exception of the horse-racing. It hogs the limelight on television and it gets at least its fair share of space on the sports pages of the daily newspapers as well. In the *Sydney Morning Herald* each Saturday a number of celebrities forecast the result of matches to be played in that weekend's round of the Winfield Cup, and these regularly include the Prime Minister, Bob Hawke, as well as the novelist, Thomas Keneally. Drop the names of Garry Jack, Michael O'Connor or Terry Lamb into a conversation here, and it would be an unusual citizen who didn't know what these men did for a living, even if he or she couldn't connect them with, respectively, the Balmain, Manly-Warringah and Canterbury-Bankstown clubs.

There are considerable numbers of this population whose lives are integrated into the world of Rugby League, even though they may rarely attend a match. Attached to each of the XIIIs in the Sydney competition is a Leagues social club, and it is not necessary to be an active supporter of the first in order to qualify for membership of the second: though anything you may spend there – especially on the battery of poker machines which all Leagues clubs maintain – will assuredly help to keep the local footballers solvent. The clubs are as far removed from a crude spit 'n sawdust image as they could possibly be, in spite of the one-armed bandits that pull so many of the members in.

At the Parramatta Leagues club an atmosphere of soft carpets and urbane decorum prevails seven days a week, from mid-morning onwards; and in this time the customers can enjoy anything from a swim to a session of bingo, a sauna to an elegant meal, an evening in the disco or a programme of movies. This is not by any means exceptional in Sydney, where the Rugby League connection can be encountered at many levels of the city's life. So much is this sport within the experience, in some shape or form, of most citizens that in one of the big department stores along George Street, Grace Bros, there is a shop devoted exclusively to products licensed by the New South Wales Rugby League, where you can buy an inventive range of souvenirs and bric-à-brac – from club key-rings and brollies to videos and jerseys, as well as bedsheets and pillow-slips decorated in the different colours.

The Sydney competition has become much more rambling than once was the case. The Brisbane team, of course, doesn't even inhabit the same state and has to fly by jet for eighty minutes to fulfil most of its away fixtures. Gold Coast are in much the same position, Canberra and Newcastle each a fair step away, while Illawarra's home is just beyond the metropolitan boundary, down at Wollongong, and Penrith are almost as far away to the west, snugged down in the lee of the Blue Mountains, where the bungaloid sprawl of the outer suburbs has finally petered out and the bush has begun. Beyond that gentle range of hills lies rural New South Wales, with its everlasting eucalyptus trees, its sheep-runs, its vineyards and other fertile lands, its corpses of kangaroo hit by passing trucks, its swirling flights of pink galah.

The ten other sides which were also battling for the Winfield Cup in 1988, however, are uncompromisingly Sydneyside, spreadeagled across the city and drawing their support from distinct localities in much the same fashion as a similar number of leading English soccer clubs are deployed around London. Five of the founding members of the New South Wales Rugby League back in 1908 – South and North Sydney, Eastern and Western Suburbs, and Balmain – are still in business, deeply conscious of their traditions, though in some cases the social pattern of a club's home patch has changed perceptibly since the early days.

Balmain's is a case in point. Much of Sydney's industry was located there, on a promontory just above the narrows that, since 1931, have been spanned by the Harbour Bridge. Shipyards and other marine workshops had provided a lot of the wages in that area from the middle of the nineteenth century, as had sawmills, chemical works, soap factories, and a coal-mine. Balmain, in consequence, was a thoroughly working-class football team, both in its playing staff and its support, just like its counterparts 12,000 miles away in the North of England. The club had close links with the Australian Labour Party, which was formed in 1891 out of the NSW General Labourer's Union and held its early meetings in one of Balmain's most popular pubs, the Warwick Castle. Many Labour Party luminaries were on the platform in Balmain Town Hall the night in January 1908 when the football club was formed, and one of them was Harry Hoyle, member of the Legislative Assembly and subsequently Minister of Railways. Another was James J. Giltinan, sporty man-about-town and opportunist, who may properly be regarded as the father of Australian Rugby League, for it was he who first began to interest people in the possibilities of the breakaway code, he who organised the conspiratorial meetings in Victor Trumper's sports shop that led to the NSWRL being set up.

The Balmain district was still what it had always been until comparatively recently. Some see a transformation of the place beginning when the coal-mine was closed nearly forty years ago, and properly under way when the tram service from Darling Street – Balmain's chief thoroughfare – to the city was discontinued in 1958. Soon after that, land prices began to rise in the district and industry started to move out, as did large numbers of people who worked for a weekly wage-packet and not for a monthly cheque. Within twenty years middle-class folk had begun to set the pace in Balmain, and the lingering old-timers sucked their teeth at some of the smart new ways, and remembered days past. As a sign of the times, the transformation of the London Hotel on Darling Street seemed typical to them. For a hundred years or more it had been a classic Sydney pub, in the recognised lineage of mateship, occasional stoush, and the six o' clock swill. In 1988 it was advertising itself as Sydney's newest fun pub, where they now served mystifying fluids known as 'boutique brews' and 'where more than $1.5 million has been spent to create an atmosphere that's refined without being stuffy – perfect for formal dining or a fun night out'.

Something of the sort has been happening in this generation throughout the length and breadth of the Sydney competition; and it is reflected quite clearly wherever in the city Rugby League is played. The backbone of support still comes from men and women who, as in England, would not quibble with anyone who described them as working class. But sitting alongside them in the grandstands today are a proportion of executives and others who are rising through the professions; not so many of these shouting for Souths as for Manly, perhaps, but everywhere a growing number of silvertails from out of the middle class.

One other social revolution occurred at approximately the same time. When the Second World War finished, any Rugby League roll-call here – on a team sheet or among a club's supporters –

would have demonstrated overwhelmingly Anglo-Saxon or Celtic origins. But then Bill Slim advised Australia to populate or perish, which she dutifully did, opening her arms to people from all over Europe and beyond in an epic of immigration second only to the one that transformed the United States a century before. So today there's a mosque in Auburn and a Ukrainian church in Lidcombe and Greek Orthodoxy along Darlinghurst Road, and the spoors of many other nationalities networking the metropolis. And the children of those new chums who sailed in through the Heads a generation ago have become dinkum Aussie heroes in the competition for the Winfield Cup: Fenech and Djura, Gillmeister and Spina, Wurth and Ettingshausen, Schubert and Tronc, Sironen and Elias, Henjak, Geyer, Van der Voort and many more.

You can tell quite a bit of Australian history if you know how to read its football, and not only what has happened in the recent past. The moment Governor Phillip arrived to establish the new settlement in 1788, he had his first encounter with aborigines and remarked on their 'manly behaviour'; which is how, according to Robert Hughes, that well-to-do suburb just inside the North Head acquired its name. Parramatta is where the best agricultural land was discovered in those early days, and where Australia's first farm was created by the time-served convict James Ruse. Leichhardt Oval, where Balmain have played for half a century, commemorates a short-sighted deserter from the Prussian army who, in 1845, made one of the great explorations of the Australian interior, perishing three years later when he attempted another journey on the same scale.

The grounds where the Sydney clubs play are quite unlike anything of the sort in Northern England. Only Belmore, where Canterbury and St George alternate for home matches, is mildly suggestive, with trains rattling past as at Castleford, and with sheds running the full width of the dead-ball lines, as they do at Barrow's Craven Park. But at Belmore they also have two features that recur time and again in Australia and almost nowhere in England: the modern grandstand which is cantilevered so that no one's view of the game is obstructed by columns holding up the roof, and the large grassy bank on which spectators generally sit or lie, commonly known as the Hill. At Parramatta, most sumptuous club stadium of them all, there is a pair of double-decker stands and a couple of hills, together with a large electronic score-board and colossal floodlights at each corner of the pitch.

At North Sydney Oval they have pulled off a remarkable trick almost within a drop-kick of the Harbour Bridge. From the outside this ground manages to hint at something incongruous, like Disneyland (and I suppose it may have taken its cue from Luna Park, which is just down the hill at the waterside). From the road you can see flags flying and other things sticking up; and there's a strange-looking tower suggesting a helter-skelter or some other frivolous thrill. Such speculation could scarcely be further from what actually awaits the visitor on the inside. This is a genuine oval, where cricket is played between October and March, and it feels more like a venue of the summer game than one for Rugby League. The playing area is encircled by an old-fashioned picket fence, the score-board is clearly built with dismissals and bowling averages even more in mind than tries and goals, and the stands are delightfully and inimitably Australian in the traditional style: that is, with pillars and green tin roofs, each with its clock tower, its cupola or simply its pinnacles on top, none overpowering its neighbours and all beautifully kept. One of them is the old Bob Stand, tenderly rescued a few years ago from Sydney Cricket Ground when that shrine of both sports was unforgivably vandalised. To watch Norths battling to reach the play-offs of the Winfield Cup, the players charging to and fro against a background of palms and Moreton Bay figs beyond the Hill, the shadows lengthening as a brilliant mid-winter sun declines, is to know how very far you've travelled from Crown Flatt, The Boulevard or Central Park to enjoy the game that they present, too.

There is something suburban about all the Sydney grounds, whether they're out in the suburbs or not. Each has its own distinctive touch, like those trains passing Belmore, a glimpse of the water from Leichhardt (SHARKS *Swimming Prohibited* says a sign on the edge of Iron Cove just below), the bush-covered hills rolling behind Penrith Park, the sheer modernity at Parramatta, or whatever the distinction may be. But almost without exception they are enclosed by trees, by neat homes standing in their own plot of ground, and there is a conspicuous absence of commerce and industry nearby. This is almost a definition of suburbia. And what could be more suburban than the name Brookvale, where the Manly club is based? It sounds like one of those stations at the extremities of the Central or District line on the London Underground, where the commuters arrive home wearily from their offices and hope to find the lawn already mowed, and other manifestations of domestic bliss.

At each of the grounds there is enough evidence to suggest that it's not as simple as that, though. That long-standing fortification of the sporting masses, beer, is not always available to all and sundry these days: at Penrith a double-decker bus parked behind the pantherine score-board serves as a members' bar, the only place where alcohol can be consumed on the ground. But beer's traditional allies, the hot meat-pie and the carton of chips, are still well-nigh indispensable in Sydney, thank God, though Australia's cultural ambivalence shows in references to the potatoes, which are sometimes chips, sometimes French fries.

The American influence is pervasive. Many clubs now recruit ra-ra girls to posture with pom-poms as the players come on to the field, the grass immediately behind the goalposts is invariably stained with the sponsor's sign, and some clubs – Balmain and Manly come to mind – have characters in grotesque fancy dress to clown around and amuse the fans before the kick-off and during half-time. The enormous banners that many supporters now wave when their teams score may derive from another source. They look much like the pageantry introduced by Italians to the soccer terraces of Europe a generation or more ago, and perhaps this arrived Down Under in the enthusiasm of some Neapolitan immigrant, so eager to blend into his new background that he changed his allegiance to the prevailing football code.

One development can be traced explicitly to the United States. The Sydney competition has always exemplified Rugby League at its best, but not until quite recently has it everywhere been recognised that in this city the game has achieved a dynamic unequalled in other centres: with greater fitness and superior command of basic skills, and with matches played at a higher pitch of intensity than elsewhere. The remarkable feat by two successive Kangaroo touring sides to the northern hemisphere, of winning every game in 1982 and then doing so again in 1986, was the clearest testimony to what had been going on in Sydney for a number of years. In the '60s a national coaching scheme was set up in Australia, making instruction at junior levels much more highly organised than ever before; which was a start towards the objective of galvanising the professional game. And then, in 1970, Jack Gibson discovered Vince Lombardi, and Rugby League in Sydney hasn't been the same since.

Lombardi was an unattractive man, but one of the most successful coaches in the history of American football. Soon after he had taken over an ailing team, the Green Bay Packers, and begun to bully them into an almost unbeatable combination, he was heard to observe that 'winning isn't the most important thing. It's the *only* thing.' The words have since achieved the status of Mosaic law in America, to be applied to sport, to politics, to commerce, to life itself. They have much to answer for.

They registered strongly with Gibson, who was coaching Sydney's St George club at the time, so much that he went to the States to study Lombardi's methods. He appears to have bought the lot, from the use of computers to analyse what went wrong when the opposition beat us, to the application of mascara by prop forwards playing in night games under floodlights.

On his return he introduced everything he'd picked up in Wisconsin to his own programmes, first at St George, later at Newtown and elsewhere, with results on the field so successful that soon every other coach in Sydney was following suit. The elimination of error was the primary objective from then on, ruthlessly pursued: not the encouragement of flair, not brilliant running and handling, not the imaginative thrust by an individual that can leave spectators gasping at its audacity and execution. The most satisfying thing to a Sydney coach under this regime was to see his men stop the other side from scoring. That way he couldn't lose: and increasingly matches were seen as successes or failures by the coaches, almost as much as by the clubs, and most certainly more than by the players. Football was henceforth not so much to be enjoyed for that glorious uncertainty exemplified in the wayward bounce of the oval ball, as to be admired and exalted for its scientific expertise. The age of the puppet-master and his toys had come to Rugby League.

A consequence of this approach was that before long the Winfield Cup competition became renowned for grim defensive battles, with murderous tackling and increasingly serious injuries in spite of more and more protective padding under the shirt (as anyone properly aware of American football might have prophesied). Australian foot-ballers, coming straight from a season in Sydney to guest for English clubs, spoke appreciatively of the greater opportunities for practising their attacking skills during the northern winter, even if in the next breath they tended to scoff at the looser Pommy defence. After a decade of watching football reduced to siege warfare, many of the customers on the Hill at Leichhardt, Belmore, Brookvale and other grounds decided that unless the coaches could serve up the occasional cavalry charge, as in the old days, they would do their watching in future in front of a television set where, when they became too bored with the performance, they could turn the thing off. And, gradually, more open rugby returned.

The obsession with scientific fitness evaluations and with tackle counts has remained and been exported to Europe and New Zealand, and doubtless our game is a far better one for the introduction of both. But in Sydney there is at least one American device that I should like to think will go no further; or, even better, be returned whence it came, as an appliance more suitable for communication with robots than with rugby footballers who can think. It is commonplace now for physiotherapists, conditioners and other acolytes of the coach to run on to the field on various pretexts, equipped with walkie-talkies. On reaching the player whose calf muscle may or may not need massage to relieve cramp, they turn up the volume on the radio, so that instruction on the next tactic to be tried may be heard from Svengali himself, who is mouthing them into his headset from his exalted position on the bench.

The next adaptation from American football – and it has already been advocated by a Sydney doctor who has become dismayed by the sort of injuries, especially to the knee, that now occur in the local Rugby League – might be for each side to consist of an attacking team and a defending team, who will alternate on the pitch in the course of a match, so as to reduce the amount of time any individual player is exposed to the wear and tear of the modern game. And, after that, crash helmets perhaps?

If only Sydney weren't so determined to demonstrate, to itself and all-comers, that here is the *toughest* competition in the rugby world. But Sydney is and does, with degrees of incitement and hyperbole in areas of its journalism that (again) seem to imitate some of the more feverish American models. Issue after issue of *Rugby League Week* goes out of its way to show in colour what a very uncomfortable business football can sometimes be; as if any of its readers had ever been in any doubt. It is not enough to illustrate the bone-crunching (*sic*) tackle and the consequent rictus of pain on some poor fellow's face. Blood must be seen to flow across those lurid pages that form the covers and the centre spread. Here is Gavin Miller with a split nose dribbling gore all over his shirt, but that isn't in as much of a mess yet as Chris O'Sullivan's from that 'shocking head cut'. And how about this one – 'the bloodied face of Peter Wynn typified the mood at Parramatta Stadium last Sunday' – and this beauty that Jonathan Docking copped right on the eye? What bloody man is this?

Alternatively, consider players from the toughest competition in the world dolled up like figures in a dressy pantomime, in order to give the fans some buzz conceivable only by an editor and his art director, or the man trying desperately to promote Toohey's beer. Wally Lewis, looking cuter than ever in a tricorn hat and eighteenth-century naval uniform (Pom navy, too!). Messrs Tunks, Gillespie and Langmack as the Three Musketeers, exquisite in every detail, down to their frilly little jabots. Ben Elias, transformed from hooker to Al Capone for a day. Whose fantasies are these, anyway? Are we *sure* this is the toughest competition in the world?

Well, yes and no; but certainly one that has turned its back on most of its traditions. If there is to be a symbol of Rugby League in Sydney nowadays, nothing is more illuminating than the events that preceded the opening of the new football stadium at the start of the 1988 season. Only a few months before, Manly and Canberra had contested the grand final of the 1987 season at the Sydney Cricket Ground. This was the last game of Rugby League played there, after an association going back three-quarters of a century, with the summer feats of the cricketers – Trumper, Bradman, O'Reilly, Miller, Lindwall and Benaud – being followed by the winter heroics of the footballers: Messenger, Hey, Churchill, Gasnier, Provan and Barnes.

Some of the most memorable games ever played were seen at Sydney Cricket Ground. This was the scene, in 1914, of the Rorke's Drift Test, the most celebrated match in all Rugby League history, when Harold Wagstaff's Englishmen, without half a dozen of their best players, were finally reduced to ten against a full-strength Australian XIII and still managed to win 14–6. This was where, on an awful day in 1950, so sodden that the players were quickly and uniformly a gleaming black, Ron Roberts ran 25 yards through the ankle-deep mud to score the try that won the series and restored the Ashes to Australia for the first time in thirty years.

Sydney Cricket Ground was where every football season came to climax with those tremendous tussles between clubs in the grand finals. It was where State of Origin games between New South Wales and Queensland produced passion and drama such as normally is only encountered in Tests. And because so many fine footballers from the other side of the world had performed on Sydney Cricket Ground, too, it has had as powerful a hold on the imagination of Englishmen and

Welsh as upon Australians: it was where Jim Sullivan and Martin Hodgson and Gus Risman and Billy Boston and Ernest Ward and Alex Murphy had become legends, as well as Wally Prigg and Ray Stehr and Dave Brown and Arthur Summons and Ken Irvine and Graeme Langlands. The first thing any British touring side did when it arrived in Sydney was to be lined up in full playing kit, standing shoulder to shoulder in front of the Members' Stand, where Melba Studios would take their unique team photographs with an old-fashioned panoramic camera, every print destined to become a collector's item.

Melba, mercifully, are still operating in their customary fashion, but Sydney Cricket Ground's unique position at the emotional centre, the historical core of two great sports, had been systematically undermined some time before the last Rugby League match was played there. The destruction began when Mr Kerry Packer's mauling of cricket led to the erection of huge floodlighting pylons in 1978, and was followed shortly afterwards by the demolition of the old Brewongle Stand, which was superseded by a namesake that was up to date but charmlessly without character; which is more or less the condition that Sydney Cricket Ground as a whole has now reached: without its Hill, without its old but perfectly adequate score-board, with scarcely anything that made it an aesthetic as well as an historical delight. Only the Members' Stand and the Ladies' Stand beside it, both of them the work of craftsmen and not prefabricating machines, survive to remind us of an age when both cricket and rugby were played in surroundings of elegance and grace. Seen from a distance across Moore Park now, with those pylons crushing everything else with their mass, Sydney Cricket Ground resembles nothing so much as a municipal waterworks; and on the inside it might without difficulty be supposed that this was some Spanish bullfighting equivalent of Wembley Stadium.

It was, in spite of the rearrangements, said to be inadequate for football, with its oval rather than rectangular expanse of turf, and its dressing-rooms covered in a tin roof; which seemed an odd conclusion to reach after so many decades without complaint. So alongside it there was built the excitingly modern shape of the Sydney Football Stadium (under more or less the same management), a gleaming and silvery roller-coaster outline arising unexpectedly at the foot of those Paddington streets which are dignified, handsome and quintessentially Victorian. It is impossible not to be stimulated by this contrast, between the graciously old and the spankingly new, just as it is difficult not to be disheartened by the mongrel mess to which Sydney Cricket Ground has been reduced.

The Football Stadium has, all the same, had its critics. More than 78,000 people watched the 1965 grand final between St George and Souths at Sydney Cricket Ground, but no more than 40,000 will ever be allowed into the Sydney Football Stadium, because no one is permitted to stand there; everybody has a seat. The radio and television commentators are stuck so high above the turf that they have difficulty in identifying the players with the naked eye. It was promised that something called a 'concept sound system' would make public address well-nigh perfect, but what spectators actually hear is a loud yet largely unintelligible amplification of the announcer's voice. The dressing-rooms are still thought to be inadequate, in view of the long-established Sydney custom whereby on every match day no fewer than three games, one after the other, are played so as to provide entertainment from noon. Worst of all, though most people were supposed not only to be seated comfortably but also to be protected from the weather, a large proportion of the fans nevertheless get wet here when it rains.

Yet in spite of some deficiencies, it is hard not to feel good about the new stadium on the whole. There is nothing else as imaginative, more nearly perfect for watching a field sport on a fine day, either Down Under or Up Top. It is an ornament of Rugby League and it may be that, like Jøern Utzon's Opera House, which also got off to a shaky start, the Football Stadium will before long be seen as something that gives all Sydney much pride.

My fervent hope is that another parallel here will not be followed. There were those who rejoiced when Mr Packer decided that our summer game was ready for his plucking and introduced the spurious glamour of World Series Cricket, because they thought that some notorious ills would be remedied and that this deeply civilised pursuit would thereafter embark upon a future even more glorious than its past. A decade later they could see how irreparably cricket has been damaged, with international matches played so frequently that even lifelong cricket nuts are bored by them, with an alarming deterioration in the behaviour of cricketers on and off the field, and with a depressing sense that money is now the be-all and end-all of the game for everyone involved in it apart from those who merely and humbly watch it and their heroes for pleasure and inspiration;

and ultimately pay most of the bills. All this in exchange for . . . what? Magnificently improved television camera-work. And a new class of exceedingly rich and often unpleasantly overweening young athletes, an élite who prosper mightily, though the mass of cricketers are scarcely any better off than they were before. This doesn't seem much of an exchange to me. I should hate to see anything like that happen to the other great game I have also followed all my life.

But these are almost the only glum thoughts I have had in Sydney, in the sparkling sharpness and warmth of its mid-winter. So many memories, sharp and warm, too, to take back to our own less congenial climate. There is an old man who plays his harmonica to please the lunch-time crowds in Martin Place, with a tonic brilliance that he may have developed as a Digger at Tobruk, or maybe as a roustabout in the Banjo Patterson country to the west of here. There is a young man who entertains the kids beside the ferry terminals on Circular Quay with his gentle conjuring tricks, which he performs with charm and great humour, and with a break dancer's measured nimbleness. There are ghosts in this city from a haunted past. At the Anzac memorial in Hyde Park South you encounter them on sacred ground, and you need no notice to remind you of that, for you can feel it in your bones, especially if you come from Lancashire, where we also are acquainted with Gallipoli. In Market Street, at David Jones's department store, the spirits are without anguish, well pleased with what they did when they met there in what was then Victor Trumper's shop, to launch Australia's Rugby League and invite that diffident and scruffy batting genius to become the League's first honorary treasurer.

For all its toughness and its eagerness to push ahead and be there first, this is an approachable and amiable city, with a native wit that far outdistances the simplicities of Strine. At Leichhardt one Sunday afternoon, Ross Conlon hoists a kick so high that the ball becomes a mere speck in the heavens before it starts tumbling to earth. My neighbour in the stand shades his eye from the sun as he peers upwards, following the ball's flight. '*That*'ll bring rain,' he says reflectively. Next day I read about Arthur Summons and Norm Provan, totting up the injuries each received during his playing days, which are now beginning to give them gyp in middle age. Summons tells how his nose, broken half a dozen or more times in the course of his rugby career, has become something of a trial to him, what with unstoppable snoring and one thing and another. 'My nose is in a bad way,' he says. 'I'm just grateful I don't have to walk on it.'

There's another story that may be apocryphal, but rings with truth for me. It is about Gus Risman's Lions, who sailed to Australia aboard the aircraft-carrier *Indomitable* because no other transport was available so soon after the war. The Navy dropped them off in Perth, and they then had a five-day trip on the train to New South Wales. The last lap of their journey from the North of England was by motor-coach from Sydney's Central Station to the Olympic Hotel, where they were to be based while in the city. On the way there, someone decided that the biggest men should get out of the bus first, so as to impress the Australians who would be waiting outside the hotel to greet them. There was quite a gathering to see the first Pommy footballers in ten long years, and they began clapping as the visitors appeared. First to descend was Frank Whitcombe (17 st 8 lb), then came Ken Gee (15 st 3 lb), then Doug Phillips (14 st 7 lb), then Ike Owens (14 st 2 lb), then Harry Murphy (13 st 12 lb) . . . At which point an aggrieved voice at the back of the crowd was heard above all the welcoming noise: 'Right, then, that's it! No more bloody food parcels to England!'

Incomparable Sydney! Where else, on a Friday night in June, could you choose between Joan Carden singing Leonora at the Opera House, and Wally Lewis leading his Brisbane side at the Football Stadium? And afterwards enjoy rock oysters and a local Chardonnay beside one of the loveliest waters in the world, twinkling with light and movement, and breathing an assurance that all things in the end shall be well?

Ten

Queensland and All That

This is a long, long way from Batley. Castle Hill, which rears above the football ground, is a gnarled pillar of rock, sometimes deep ochre, sometimes khaki, depending on the time of day and the light. Always it tells of Australia's primeval past, when this continent was first scorched by flaring heat. If you stand on Castle Hill you face the bush-covered slopes of Magnetic Island, so called because Captain Cook believed – erroneously, it seems – that its rock formations were affecting his compass. Beyond that, the Coral Sea fills the expanse to the horizon and eventually merges with the Pacific, which is so vast that if you took a tramp steamer out of this little port and sailed East Nor' East, it would be three weeks before you sighted any land, and that would be the isthmus of Panama. If you went on a day trip by fast catamaran, a couple of hours would bring you to the Great Barrier Reef, which runs more or less parallel to this North Queensland coast at Townsville. Topographically, and in many other respects, this part of the world could not be much more of a contrast to the Heavy Woollen District of Yorkshire. What they have in common is the game of Rugby League.

Townsville and its hinterland don't have so very much more in common with Sydney, if it comes to that. The metropolis is separated from North Queensland not only by great distance, but by climate, by politics, and by those differences of regional culture and outlook that the English, too, know very well. The tropic of Capricorn is away to the south of here, which means that although the football season is balmy (the sort of weather Englishmen play cricket in when they're *very* lucky) summers can be desperately hot, with temperatures well over a hundred at times. It can be bad enough in winter in some of the places, farther inland and farther north, where rugby is played. Up at Gove in Arnhem Land – which is as far from Sydney as Widnes is from Bucharest, or Wakefield from Casablanca – it's said that a player can lose anything up to half a stone between the kick-off and full-time.

Townsville is itself something of a metropolis in these surroundings, though it is considerably less than half the size of Rochdale. The norm round here is somewhere like Charters Towers, which at the height of its gold production about the turn of the century might have contained 30,000 souls, but now has probably no more than a quarter that number of their descendants. The gold is virtually done, but instead there are beef cattle to be disposed of in the sale-yards, before being overlanded on great road trains out of the state, or despatched to the slaughterhouse at Townsville and thence by refrigerated cargo vessels to destinations abroad. The Charters Towers rugby footballers are still known as The Miners, though.

Here is the archetypal Outback town. Along Gill Street, men's wear means shorts and Akubra hats, with a good oilskin Drizabone covering a bloke from the chin to the ankles during the Wet, the modest monsoon season that lasts from December to March. At any time of the year, half a dozen aborigines will be found sitting passively round the considerable bar of the Excelsior Hotel through most of the day and, in Stan Pollard's general store, financial transactions are made, from whichever counter you have bought something, by means of an aerial contraption manipulated by a lady who sits commandingly at her cashier's podium in the middle of the floor. It would be no surprise at all to see Crocodile Dundee coming round the corner here; and crocs there are aplenty in the Bohle River, which is not so many miles away across intervening scrub pasture, stippled here and there by termite nests arranged like a series of those concrete cones they built to deter tanks in the Second World War.

At Charters Towers the football ground is an expanse of parched earth on the outskirts of town, with some old gold-tailings behind one touch-line, and fragile-looking goalposts made of thin tubular steel. There is room for maybe fifty people to sit on a roofless little stand, if they hutch up tight, and the dressing-room is so small that the players getting ready for the game have to take care lest they put their arm into someone else's jersey by mistake. Billboards round the pitch advertise some local sponsorship, by a butcher, a car salesman and the like. Half a dozen slender poles have lamps bolted to crosspieces at the top: not exactly floodlighting, but good enough to train by when the sun has gone down. There are English footballers, playing under the supervision of BARLA, who would find themselves perfectly at home on this ground.

Townsville is opulent by comparison, beginning to feed well off tourists who are attracted by its proximity to the Barrier Reef, and who also find here a casino in which, above the click of roulette wheels and the shuffling of cards, may be heard the timeless Australian cry of 'Come in, spinner!' issuing from a two-up school. At the Sports Reserve (sponsored by a couple of breweries and a numerous supporting cast) there are two rugby pitches, the principal one being surrounded by a seven-lane running track as well as a selection of open stands like, but larger than, the one at Charters Towers; and a splendid cantilevered affair with changing-rooms underneath. There are also refreshment stalls, and just outside the ground is a small but modern office block, headquarters of Townsville Rugby League. That's where, among other things, they publish a journal-cum-match programme, containing the team lists for all the matches to be played over the weekend, on the lines of Sydney's *Big League*.

You are most conscious of two things when you watch football in the lee of Castle Hill. One is how far teams and their supporters have sometimes travelled to spend their Saturday or Sunday afternoons here. The motor-coaches and the cars parked round the ground have come down from Cairns, perhaps, or up from Mackay, or from halfway to Mount Isa, which is all but in the Northern Territory. In each case this has meant a journey of 200 miles or more, often along dirt roads; which is why, as well as 'roo bars to prevent the engine being stove in if some heedless marsupial picks the wrong moment to try and get across, the vehicles often have a wire mesh placed strategically in front of the windscreen to fend off flying stones.

The other thing is that never for a moment can you fail to register the sheer tropicality of it all. The homes surrounding the football ground seem to be not much different from those of the Sydney suburbs; that is, standard weatherboard bungalows. But these are generally raised a little off the ground and endowed with more generous verandas, to let as much air as possible circulate round the building and to shelter the rooms inside from the direct rays of the sun. The vegetation is familiar to anyone who knows India, and none of it will be found in Europe north of the Mediterranean coast. There are banyan trees just outside the ground, and some people lounge in the shadow of a mango near a refreshment hut. On the scaffolding and planks of the open stands, men tilt their Akubras so that the wide brims shield their eyes, and women sit with parasols. When play ends on the junior pitch, a flight of ibis settle down to prod the ground for grubs, and a squadron of mynahs rush around noisily, bossing each other about. The players, trooping into the dressing-room under the grandstand, look more drained than any I have ever seen. Men come off in Sydney sopping wet, as if they had just played football in a steam laundry. These lads look as if they have been put through the mangle as well.

Some mighty players have handled the oval ball in these parts, and often enough have gone elsewhere to make an international reputation for themselves. North Queenslanders, in fact, switched from Rugby Union to League six years after the Sydney breakaway, specifically to improve their chances of playing representative football for their state and their country. One of the most famous sons of Charters Towers was Cecil Aynsley, the goal-kicking three-quarter whose exploits for Queensland and Australia in the mid-twenties stirred someone to verse: 'Thoughts of Aynsley's bumping gallop – elbows, hands and hips and knees.' Often playing alongside him in both sides was his townsman Tom Gorman, who went on to captain the fourth Kangaroos on their tour of England in 1929–30. In that party also was the great Toowoomba second-row forward Vic Armbruster who, with Aynsley, finished his career playing for Rochdale Hornets. The state side has not yet been selected without its quota of North Queenslanders, and it will be a rare Australian national side without someone in it from hereabouts. Dale Shearer is a Townsville man, Sam Backo comes from just up the coast at Ingham, Martin Bella from Sarina, on the other side of Mackay. There hasn't been an English touring party since Jonty Parkin's 1928 Lions without a fixture against North Queensland, played in Townsville or Mackay or Cairns. They're thought of as missionary games to help maintain enthusiasm and raise standards in the outback but, whatever the score, they're invariably hard. When Harry Poole's tourists came to Townsville in 1966, North Queensland beat them 17–15 with 6,000 people roaring the locals on.

The vital first step taken by a good and ambitious local player is almost always down to Brisbane, which is an hour and a half away from Townsville by Boeing or twenty-seven hours by train. The Queensland state capital is for the most part a charmingly unsophisticated city, built upon hillocks and separated from the sea by the serpentine Brisbane River; but its city centre is rapidly becoming an architectural disaster as old and handsome buildings are either blasted out of the way or smothered by the domineering and desperately awful new skyscrapers that corporate greed has thrown up with the connivance of cynical politicians. Just on the edge of these ravages stands Lang Park which, for thirty years, has been the headquarters of the Queensland Rugby League and a notable Test match venue. Here is an old-fashioned football ground in the grand manner, but with escalators to convey the infirm and indolent up to the top deck of the Hale Street Stand, which rears high above the terraces in a gigantic Z-shape visible for miles. The Frank Burke Stand opposite is lower and more conventional in outline, and behind it at night matches, just before Lang Park's fine contralto hooter announces the kick-off, sunset produces a great apricot glow in the sky. It's easy to see why many visiting English fans prefer Lang Park to any other ground in Australia. Like the ones they're accustomed to at home it has proper terracing at each end, meant for standing upon rather than sitting in the manner of Sydneysiders on their grassy Hills. Packed with 33,000 Queenslanders, as partisan as they come, Lang Park has, as they say, a tremendous atmosphere.

The trouble with the Brisbane competition, however, is that it has not for many a year been dynamic enough to satisfy the ambitions of talented young footballers from up north or anywhere else in the state; and it simply lacks the money that the Sydney clubs can offer to anyone they fancy. Where the Sydney teams have waxed fat on the income from liquor sales and poker machines in the League clubs ever since the '50s, in Queensland one-armed bandits are still forbidden, along with much else that seems fairly harmless to other Australians (and this may be the only place on earth where it is actually illegal to hitch-hike). So the young man who begins to be noticed as a result of his performances for Wynnum-Manly, Redcliffe, Brothers or one of the other Brisbane clubs, will tend sooner or later to continue his migration south to the rich pickings of the metropolis. Nor does it look as if this tendency is likely to be halted in the foreseeable future. Since a consortium formed the new Brisbane Broncos club in 1987 to take part in the following season's Sydney competition, and bought up the biggest names in Queensland football – Wally Lewis, Gene Miles, Greg Dowling, Alan Langer and Brian Niebling among them – the existing Brisbane clubs, competing only among themselves, have had a very thin time of it, as the crowds have switched their patronage to Lang Park fixtures between the Broncos and the likes of Balmain and Canterbury. It even seemed possible by the end of that first denuded season that one of the local clubs, Brothers, would go to the wall.

The history of inter-state Rugby League matches between Queensland and New South Wales illustrates perfectly the predicament of the Bananalanders until a remedy was applied in 1980. Out of a total of 219 matches since the first fixture in 1908, New South Wales had won 157 and Queensland no more than 55, with seven games drawn. It was fourteen years after the rivalry began before the men in maroon shirts even managed to win at all, and although Queensland held the upper hand with a series of magnificent teams in the '20s, the old dominance of the southerners thereafter reasserted itself. Between 1962 and 1980, out of sixty games played, Queensland could win only three. The fixture was becoming a bore, and the crowds were beginning to give it up in disgust; so much so that, when it was New South Wales's turn to play at home again, instead of turning to Sydney Cricket Ground in accordance with tradition, the organisers took the match to one of the local club grounds, where the handful of spectators would seem less embarrassing.

It was a bore and it was also anything but a fixture representing the footballing skills of Queenslanders versus New South Welshmen. Half of every NSW side consisted of Queenslanders playing for Sydney clubs, which effectively meant a double handicap to the northern state, which was not only bereft of its very best players, but was expected to countenance them as adversaries. The astonishing thing is that it took so long for everyone to wake up to the daftness of such an arrangement. A Queensland politician whose rise to influence had been closely connected with his involvement in Rugby League, Senator Ron McAuliffe, eventually saw light, after noting that elsewhere in the continent Australian Rules had faced up to a similar predicament. Henceforth, he suggested, instead of picking state sides on the basis of which club a man plays for, let us choose our teams according to birthplace – or, at the very least, where a man began to play football as a kid, where he matured. And so the first State of Origin match was played at Lang Park on July 8th, 1980. Twice that season, once at home and once in Sydney, Queensland had already gone down to the Blues. But under the floodlights in front of their own folk that night, the Maroons redressed a little of the imbalance by 20 points to 10.*

State of Origin football has become something of a cult since then, so much so that, in an attempt to beef up English enthusiasm for a weak county championship, someone had the strange inspiration to call such matches County of Origin fixtures; a quite unnecessary aping of the Australian model when, as every English enthusiast knew, our footballers never had been picked to play for Lancashire, Yorkshire or Cumbria except on the basis of where they were born. In Australia, the cult has become so widespread that almost half the nation is known to watch each match live on television. The games, of course, have coincided with Australia's great international supremacy in Rugby League, and are therefore a showplace for many of the finest footballers in the world. But what characterises them most of all is not so much skill, though skill there is in plenty, as full-blooded commitment. They are very hard games indeed with, often literally, no punches pulled. They have begun to occupy a place in the lore of the game Down Under that Anglo-Australian Test matches alone once filled.

This is odd, if you think about it, and not wholly to be explained by the fact that British teams hadn't mounted a serious challenge to the Australian supremacy for almost a decade before the Wigan Test match of 1986. In spite of the traditional rivalry between Yorkshiremen and Lancastrians, I find it hard to believe that they have ever waded into each other in a Roses match with quite the same damaging intent as is evident from start to finish of every State of Origin game. Nor do they show such serious and mutual contempt as would appear to be indicated by the nicknames the two Australian state teams have bestowed on each other: Queensland Toads and NSW Cockroaches. There is real needle in these fixtures, a distinct settling of old scores. The origins of that lie in historical events that have nothing to do with any sport.

It has been said that everyone north of the boundary with New South Wales is a Queenslander first and an Australian second. A number of reasons for this have been advanced and one of them is the simple fact that Queensland is physically demanding. It occupies almost one-quarter of the entire continent. It is a Texas of a state, in

---

* By the end of the 1988 season, the State of Origin tally was Queensland 13 wins, New South Wales 10.

which you have to travel great distances to get from here to there, and regard anyone who doesn't as just a bit effete. It has a summer climate as fierce as that experienced anywhere, and much harsher than anybody knows down south. But more than either of these factors there is the historical experience of Queenslanders, which has been an uphill struggle most of the way. Brisbane began with the Moreton Bay settlement, which was notoriously where convicts were treated more brutally than anywhere else outside Norfolk Island; and this has left a lingering sense of being victimised by those with power, which in the terms of this Commonwealth today means by people who operate down south, in Canberra and Sydney.

I have been told quite seriously by a local partisan that in the Second World War, during the days after Pearl Harbor, a master plan was devised by the politicians down south to draw a defensive line just north of Brisbane, which might be held, but which would concede most of Queensland to the Japanese if they cared to invade; a plan that was only vetoed by the American General MacArthur, who had established his base at Garbutt airfield, Townsville, from which he proposed driving the enemy back across the Pacific. That may or may not be true. Certainly well documented is the deliberate encouragement of industrial growth during the war in all the large Australian cities except Brisbane, which was thought to be a bit too close to the enemy (who had reached New Guinea) to make this prudent.

Nor have Queenslanders been well served by their local politicians. During the great immigrations of the immediate post-war years, which were to transform and vitalise Australia in so many ways, the men running affairs from Brisbane actively discouraged foreigners from settling there because they saw them as a threat to the jobs of their supporters, and therefore to their own popularity. So the vitality, like the industrial growth, went elsewhere, and in time another Queensland grievance was born. State chauvinism, justified by grievances real or imagined, was stoked up most of all during the premiership of Johannes Bjelke-Petersen, a narrow autocrat leading a Cabinet which has been well described as 'a gerontocracy, ruled by men whose . . . horizons are limited to the next paddock or the next mine'. It was parochial Sir Joh who in 1983 exhorted Queenslanders to fly the state flag, not the Commonwealth flag, and told them that 'Queensland has a separate and distinctive civilisation'. It was he above all who massaged their already considerable complexes about

131

other Australians by characterising life in the southern cities as, at one and the same time, less fraught than theirs and yet more despicable. They really didn't need to have it pointed out to them that they generally came off second-best to Sydney: not when one of the biggest constructions in their state capital, the Story Bridge across the Brisbane River, was something they acquired in the '30s, after its design had been rejected in the competition for the Sydney Harbour Bridge.

All this, and the fact that fine Queensland footballers had been obliged, for a couple of generations, to go cap in hand to Sydney. It was more than enough to ensure that when, at last, the inter-state rugby matches became contests between Queenslanders and New South Welshmen, were finally and starkly a matter of Us and Them, not many holds would be barred. At Lang Park the crowds packed the place to its roofs, not wishing to miss one moment of the retribution they knew their blokes would mete out on their behalf, for all the injuries that had been done to them by those smooth bastards in the south; yes, even going all the way back to the Moreton Bay settlement, for in those days that was a New South Welsh abomination, was it not?

It is only fair to say that the animosity is by no means confined to Queensland these days; that when the State of Origin fixture is played in Sydney, the New South Welsh crowd can bay for blood as belligerently as anyone on the terraces at Lang Park. Some of them don't wait for the inter-state matches before hurling abuse in the direction of Wally Lewis, who attracts as much venom in the south as idolatry in the north. One of the more disagreeable evenings I have spent was at a floodlit game in the Football Stadium between South Sydney and the Brisbane team, when I found myself hemmed in by a rabble of South's supporters, who amused themselves by chanting 'Wally's a Wanker' every time the captain of Brisbane, Queensland and Australia did something deft; which was regularly throughout the game.

At Lang Park the compensatory adulation is almost as unbalanced, but at least inoffensive. If Lewis gets a try, the electronic score-board goes into orgasm with 'You Bewdy!'; an act of self-parody which the score-board at Wigan might equal if it flashed 'Eeh Bah Gum!' across the screen. The Brisbane operator follows this first spasm with 'And the Crowd Went Wild!' – as if those ecstatic thousands needed this pointing out to themselves. Lewis plays to the gallery at home for all he's worth. I have seen him heavily, but not unfairly, tackled at Lang Park, and carefully arrange himself flat out on the ground with his arms spread wide, a symbolism that was not lost upon some worshipper near me, whose shocked tones penetrated even the raging chorus of boos. 'Christ!' he shrieked. 'They've crucified him!' These were histrionics in the Latin American mode.

Wally Lewis is for me an enigma. I have no doubt at all that he is one of the most accomplished footballers I have ever been fortunate enough to watch, though sometimes you wonder how this can be, for he is notoriously a lazy trainer and he looks far too heavily built for the activity of a stand-off half. When not going full pelt, when merely trotting from one part of the field to another, he runs like someone on an icy path who is so nervous of slipping that the soles of his feet rarely lose contact with the ground. Yet he has every basic skill to perfection when it is required. His kicking to gain ground may be the best I have ever seen, long, raking punts that find touch time after time behind the enemy: no one can kick as he can from half way and so infallibly *just* squeeze the ball over the line a couple of feet from the corner flag. His other slashing stroke is the long spinning pass which cuts out a couple of men and arrives like a bullet where an unmarked runner near the flanks would wish it to come to hand. He uses his weight to effect, too, tackling powerfully, being himself difficult to stop when in full flight.

But not one of these attributes, invaluable as they are, counts as much as Wally Lewis's ability to read a game, to anticipate what will – or, more often, what shall – happen. During that tedious evening when Brisbane played Souths, I deliberately ignored the other twenty-five players in the stadium and kept my eyes on Lewis alone as much as I could, trying to track his game. The most noticeable thing was how often he was there, in the thick of things. An opening was made, developed, but then began to wane until Lewis strode up and gave it fresh impetus. The Rabbitohs attacked, forced a gap and were about to pour through it, when the flying figure of Lewis came across and stopped them with a huge cover tackle on the man with the ball. These reflexes were to be seen again and again throughout that night.

He also has the crowning asset in the captain of any sporting team: the killer instinct, the ability himself to deliver the coup de grâce. The outstanding example of this that I've seen was at Wigan, in the Third Test of the 1986 Kangaroo tour. Great Britain had started that series with high hopes of at last turning a tide that had run Australia's way without interruption since Bradford in 1978. But they were demolished in the rain at Old Trafford, 38–16 in the First Test, and even more decisively, 34–4, in the Second at Elland Road. They then brought in five new players for the Wigan Test and gave Australia its hardest game in years. Considered opinion on both sides of the world is that the Poms were rather unlucky to lose this match, certainly by 24–15. Crucial to the outcome was M. Rascagneres's award of a penalty try to Shearer as the game entered its last quarter, with the scores level at 12–12: for although Basnett's obstruction of the winger was indisputable, it was doubtful whether the Australian, unhindered, would have got to the ball before it rolled out of play. No matter; O'Connor goaled and Australia led 18–12. Then Lydon kicked a penalty for the home side and Schofield dropped a goal, to make it 18–15 with eleven minutes left, and a British victory well within range. But four minutes later Lewis brilliantly settled it, as any captain might dream of doing, because it looked impossible from where he got the ball, a dozen yards from the corner flag, with several Englishmen strung out between him and the line. He bamboozled the lot, with a side-step, a dummy, a change of pace, another dummy, and a sudden lateral spurt that took him much nearer the posts. The try was converted and that was that.

Yet it is Lewis's captaincy that, for me, raises a question-mark. As you watch him directing the traffic in his half of the field, putting in a word here, waving a man into position there, it is clear that he is in total command of his side out there on the paddock. No one who didn't have the complete confidence of his players could possibly have done what he did in 1986, which was to lead a side in imitation of its predecessors four years earlier by winning every match it played in a tour of England and France. The psychological obstacles in the way of that achievement were tremendous, the odds against it happening incalculable. Wally Lewis must take a great deal of the credit for such a remarkable success, alongside Don Furner, the coach. So where does he fall short?

I think he's too much of a player's captain, perhaps; too anxious to demonstrate to his men at all times that he's their mate through thick and thin, battling for their rights, the first to come to their assistance in a tight spot. There was a perfect illustration of what is missing in Lewis's make-up in the Second Test at Lang Park in 1988. Wayne Pearce had regained his place at loose forward after losing it to Bob Lindner in the Centenary Test at Sydney, and it was clear from the outset that he was not going to relinquish it again if he could help it, laying about him lustily with arms, legs, head and shoulders, whether he had the ball or was simply determined to drop his man.

The first half had been going a while before it was seen that in the wake of some rushing, mauling play, Pearce was on his back, defending himself against Mike Gregory, who was laying into him with both fists. At once Lewis rushed up and began belting the Englishman before anyone else could reach him, and for a moment or two it looked as if we were in for a general brawl. It is irrelevant to say that I don't believe for one moment that Gregory's was a completely unprovoked attack; it shouldn't have happened, whatever his excuse. Nor should Lewis have reacted the way he did. A great captain would have rushed up at the same speed and would have hauled Gregory off, to separate the combatants, not proceeded to demonstrate pubescent mateship to Wayne Pearce and a home crowd howling for English blood.

But it was in character; as was something else that happened when the Australians had comprehensively won that Test and retained the Ashes yet again. It had been a cantankerous match all through, and from where I was sitting in the Hale Street stand I couldn't be sure who'd been responsible for starting all that: possibly Phil Ford for collaring Michael O'Connor too high early on. I was very clear by the end, though, that it was six of one and half a dozen of the other, as near as makes no matter. With the exception of Don Furner, an admirably balanced man as well as a fine coach, the Australians would have none of this. The fault, according to them, was wholly with the Poms for repeatedly tackling high; as though the irreproachable men of Queensland and New South Wales would not sully themselves by ever grabbing an opponent above the shoulder-blades. Apart from those Australian commentators on the game whose livelihoods depend not on careful assessment but on stirring things up, the most vociferous plaintiff was the Australian captain. 'Lewis lashes out at tactics', was a headline the morning after the match, over a story which spoke of his 'disgust over the high tackling'. According to another report, ' "We'll take the victories and they can have the TKOs," Lewis said. "You get pissed off with it and we will be out to make it 3–0 in Sydney. That's the only way you can get back at them." ' He grizzled on in this vein whenever he was interviewed until his team was at last beaten in the Third Test.

There has been some talk of Wally Lewis going into politics when his footballing days are over, the lustre attaching to his name in Queensland making him an attractive proposition there to the Labour,

Liberal and National parties alike. He would be no vote-catcher anywhere else, to be sure, but in his state of origin he would have the cardinal political virtue of being seen by everyone as a man of the people. He is a Queenslander through and through, who disdained the pull of Sydney until an expensive team was built round him to go south at regular intervals and show them there what's what. In Brisbane they feel good when the metropolis is put in its place like that. He is an outstanding athlete who, I imagine, glories in the knowledge that King Wally is not merely a catchphrase for use on newsprint, and the title of his biography, but a sentiment and a tribute heartfelt by every Queenslander with an awareness of football, which means almost all of them. His has been a tremendous success story, with much well-deserved applause. And yet he, too, obviously has a deep psychological need to see himself as victim; even when he's winning. That I don't understand at all.

Eleven

Coasters

When a British touring side goes Down Under, as they have tended
to every four or five years since 1910, there are always some players
who will never have seen anything like it in their lives before. The big
cities of the Antipodes must come as a revelation to any young man
who has been born and bred in the vicinity of their northern English
counterparts, for Sydney and Brisbane, Auckland and Wellington
do not obviously share much with Manchester, Liverpool, Bradford
and Leeds apart from a certain enthusiasm for Rugby League. Yet
I suspect that a bigger shock to the touring system occurs when the
Lions arrive for their quota of fixtures in the remote country districts
where they have a passion for the game. Of nowhere will this be truer
than New Zealand's West Coast. I lived there for a little while some
thirty years ago, and I can remember quite clearly how it affected me.
It had taken me nearly six weeks to sail from England and I felt as if
I had come to an end of the earth; a sensation that had more to do
with the nature of the place than with its latitude.

Here, on the South Island, facing Australia across the Tasman Sea,
is an old mining area whose heyday was in the decades which followed
a gold-rush in 1864, when diggers poured in from the Australian
fields and elsewhere, and set up the shantytowns that eventually
became the permanent communities of Greymouth and Hokitika.
The Coast is a long but relatively narrow strip of land backed by
the high and snowbound ranges of the Southern Alps, and while
this makes for some of the most magnificent scenery in the world, it
also has certain climatic consequences that a Queenslander, for one,
wouldn't much appreciate. Rain-bearing clouds which have formed
over the Tasman tend to drop most of their contents here on colliding

with the mountains. This produces the characteristic forest of matai, kahikatea, pokatea, hutu, totara and other trees, the native bush that smothers the entire region, as well as rivers that can run torrentially half a mile wide at times; or, in dry weather, produce no more than a gentle stream of water wriggling its way through beds of gravel and boulder a full mile across.

When I returned to New Zealand for the first time in 1988, I found that I had remembered those rivers perfectly. But I had forgotten the seething roar of West Coast rain, for hours at a time, on a red tin roof. Wingham Park, lying beyond the bush-covered ridge of Cobden Hill just outside Greymouth, is liable every season to see at least one weekend's fixtures washed out because the ground is up to the ankles in water. Wet winters happen in other provinces, too, though not quite so relentlessly as here. Auckland Test matches have often been decided by which team copes best with the mud at Carlaw Park. When the Kiwis beat Great Britain in the last World Cup decider in Christchurch, conditions underfoot at the Addington Showgrounds were as sloppy as anything known to Odsal or Central Park in the depths of February. Adrian Shelford, in front of his family in his home town, played a blinder, as though he had suction pads rather than studs on the soles of his boots.

Gold is still panned along the West Coast river-beds in small quantities, and it's only in the last year or two that the remaining dredge working the Taramakau has had to close down. The Eldorado period, however, was over long before the twentieth century arrived. By then coal had been found here, and Greymouth's future, in particular, was settled. When I lived there, Friday was notable for the crowds of miners and their wives who came into town for late-night shopping before the Great New Zealand Weekend began and everything shut down till Monday. Every spring they used to line the banks of the Grey River, when the first news spread that the whitebait were beginning to run (not the small fry of herring or sprat we know by that name in England, but a freshwater species of *Galaxiidae* no longer than a matchstick and almost as thin): and with butterfly nets and jam jars they would scoop up these tiny things by the score, to be mixed with batter into the great local delicacy of whitebait patties. Our pleasures were invariably fundamental and uncomplicated.

The mines from which man has extracted coal here were not quite like the pits of my native Lancashire. At home, at the Parsonage, or Mossley Common, or the Maypole, colliers went underground in cages which dropped down deep shafts into the bowels of the earth, and all around them when they returned to the surface was almost unrelieved urban and industrial sprawl. On the Coast the mines have been set in a beautiful, if somewhat damp, landscape, and men have reached the coal by travelling along tunnels driven straight into the hillsides. Otherwise, the life has always had its similarities, including the hazards. There was once an explosion at the Brunner mine, which killed sixty-five; one at Strongman, which lost another nineteen; yet another at Dobson, which took a further nine. These are not the terrible numbers that big pit accidents in Britain have always involved: but every time they happened, they affected tiny communities separated from each other by miles of thick bush. They were major disasters to them.

These hazards, like the crushing nature of the labour itself, help to explain why it is that mining communities, like fishing communities, are a bit tougher, a bit more resilient in adversity, more bloody-minded when crossed, much more cohesive, united, sharing at all times than other societies I have known. They are places apart, whatever their topography; and no outsider can ever have much more than a glimmer of understanding this. I once earned my living as a deep-sea fisherman, and what I remember most of all, apart from the frightening but exhilarating power of the sea, and the stupefying weariness caused by back-breaking hours on deck, was the comradeship, the solidarity against all-comers that we shared. As a young man I went down the Mossley Common pit just once, and I have never forgotten the noise, the coal dust that was still being blown from my nose on to my handkerchief days later, the appalling blackness when all light was extinguished for a moment or two, the ominous creakings and other sounds that were caused by the pressure, terrifying to contemplate, of coal and rock and dirt compressed into a thickness of half a mile or more above my head. This, as I say, was no more than a glimmer of understanding the truth of what was involved in producing for our fireplaces the best Trencherbone.

Like the pitmen in northern England, these New Zealand miners took to rugby, the code they eventually excelled in being the one established as the West Coast Rugby League in 1915. In small settlements the length of Westland a football pitch would be marked out and goalposts cut from the nearest stand of pine as soon as that absolute priority, the hotel with the long bar, had been taken care of. When they started playing they were at first competing among themselves more often than not, because the Coast is separated from the rest of the country by the ice cliffs of the Alps, and even today the road and rail routes over to Canterbury by Arthur's Pass or the Lewis can be severed for days on end by snow or mud-slides or flood; and there is no alternative transport by air.

In spite of, or perhaps helped by, this isolation, the West Coast began to produce some of the finest players the game of Rugby League has ever seen. No fewer than fifty Coasters, at the last count, have worn the silver chevroned black jersey with the kiwi on the left breast, as full representatives of their country in an international match. This might well be the highest striking rate of international honours in the world, given that it is from an area of limited population, probably not more than 25,000 people at any census time. Places that even most New Zealanders might not have heard of have been quite capable of breeding one international player after another in this game.

Such a place is Blackball, just a few miles up the river from Greymouth, on the road to Ikamatua and Reefton. It is a paradigm of the tiny bush township on the Coast, snugged down in a cleft of the Paparoa Range, hills which bristle with vegetation so dense that to walk a hundred yards off the track can sometimes mean being lost without any sense of direction in a sepulchral gloom. This is known as being bushed and is best avoided. Diggings scarred the hillsides here after the discovery of a large nugget in 1864, and the names of the local streams – Moonlight Creek, Roaring Meg Creek, Smoke-Ho Creek and others – are lasting memorials to those frantic days of scrabbling after pay dirt. But Blackball township was no more than an improvisation until coal was found twenty-five years later. It never did grow very large, maybe 500 people at most, with almost every man employed in one of the two mines drifted into the hill above, or else as loggers working in the bush.

As a nursery of footballers, Blackball became phenomenal, especially during the West Coast's period of inter-provincial supremacy, which extended from 1933 to a few years after the war. These were the years when the township's remarkable Mountford brothers – K.H.J., W.F. and C.R. – were learning and playing the game, two of them to become New Zealand internationals, the third missing a Kiwi jersey only because he enrolled as a student at Wigan Mining and Technical College so that he could take a British manager's certificate home, but then became a Rugby League legend at stand-off in the northern hemisphere instead. I never saw Billy Mountford, who was said to be a brilliant centre three-quarter, but I watched Ken twice and Cecil more times than I can count. I saw Ken, playing at loose forward for the 1947 Kiwis in the match at Central Park, harry the Wigan half-backs (one of them his brother) so much that the pair never clicked as usual, and the tourists won a rousing game 10–8. I imagine that, on the whole, the tribe of Mountfords enjoyed that result immensely. Waiting for autographs after the match, I overheard our Tommy Bradshaw, gazing thoughtfully at the passing figure of the man who had just spoiled his afternoon, say to someone 'Wick little bugger, that Montford!', mispronouncing the name in his South Lancs argot, though by then he was familiar enough with the correct version, being deep into his long and usually most fruitful partnership with the peerless Ces.

Those first post-war tourists to England, the Fourth Kiwis, included seven Coasters in a party of twenty-five. The second-row forward Artie Gillman was a policeman from Hokitika, and there were a couple of miners from Runanga – another of Greymouth's satellite townships – in Jack Newton at prop and Nippy Forrest on the right wing. The other four came from Blackball, and no other team in New Zealand, not even the big Auckland clubs like Richmond and Ponsonby, supplied as many tourists as that. All four were in the West Coast side that in Greymouth twelve months earlier had beaten Gus Risman's Lions 17–8, the biggest defeat the visitors sustained in the whole of their Australasian tour. Bob Aynsley, a saw-miller, was hooker; and at full back was another miner, Ray Nuttall, of whom Risman said after the Lions' defeat in the Greymouth mud that he had never seen anyone handle and kick a heavy ball so well. There was Ken Mountford, who was then running a tea-room in Grey; and there was Charlie McBride, one of the greatest New Zealand forwards of all time.

He was only 20, and working on one of the last few gold dredges still operating on the Coast, when he started playing in the second row for Blackball. Within the year he was in the first South Island side to beat the North since 1929, and then in the local triumph over Risman's men. His performance there put him into a Kiwi jersey for the solitary Test of the season. New Zealand won 13–8 and McBride's part in the victory was so unmistakable that he became a fixture for twenty-one Test matches played across the next six years. He had many qualities, including a devastating tackle and the sort of speed now taken for granted in forwards, but not so common then.

But the thing that commentators remarked on time after time was Charlie McBride's hands. 'Beautiful hands and capable anticipation are features of his play . . .' wrote someone before the 1947 Kiwis sailed for England. 'A stocky figure, a determined runner, with beautiful hands . . .' echoed someone else after the Kiwis had arrived, on seeing McBride play against York. After watching him in Bradford, Eddie Waring had no hesitation in declaring that 'The best second-row forward in England today is Charlie McBride, the thirteen-stone Kiwi. He is a wonderful footballer . . .' Yes, a second-row forward who dominated the international scene at only thirteen stone.

When I returned to Greymouth thirty-three years after leaving it, I found some things had changed so much that I felt like Rip Van Winkle; others not at all. Most obviously, the old footballing supremacy had gone. West Coast haven't held the old Northern Union Cup, the inter-provincial trophy, since 1973, and when Mark Graham led the 1985 Kiwis to England, the only Coaster in the touring party was the scrum-half Glen Gibb, understudying Clayton Friend. Gibb comes from Runanga, which always had a useful side, but it has dominated the local club rugby in recent years without being a match for the best Canterbury teams in the annual trans-Alpine tussle for the Thacker Shield. The top Christchurch club, Hornby, came to Wingham Park in 1982 and there wrested the Shield from Runanga after the Coast's champions had held it for three consecutive years; since when the trophy has remained irredeemably on the eastern side of the mountains. This, sadly, is a symptom of other changes that have occurred since my time.

The mines were thriving when I lived here; so much so that the men in one of them went on strike for a few days after objecting to the bad breath of the pit ponies which, they said, was making working conditions intolerable. This was one area of New Zealand that the Labour Party could count on as being rock solid at election time; and it was on a readership and subscription list almost entirely composed of miners that the *Grey River Argus* was able to exist, flaunting its pedigree in huge whitewashed letters on a gable end – 'NZ's Pioneer Labour Daily'. Its fame in the annals of small-town journalism depended on an editorial at the height of the Russo-Japanese war in 1905, which began with the words 'We have repeatedly warned the Czar . . .' In some National Party clean-out after Labour had been voted from office, several mines were closed as an economy, leaving behind a residue of corrugated-iron buildings with broken windows, and little coal wagons tipsily immobile on their rusting rails, which the bush soon began to camouflage and will one day have completely overgrown. In human terms this reduction meant families, after three or more generations in the same small township, leaving the area altogether, for it never provided much else in the way of work. Not one of my old friends lives in the district any more. Those who haven't died have moved away. The ebullient *Argus* in due course folded for lack of readers and advertising, its buildings were bulldozed, and the site is now a parking lot.

I had been looking forward to a weekend's football on my return to Grey, but from the Fox Glacier northwards the rain poured incessantly for days with such force that the programme was abandoned without a ball being kicked. Low clouds streamed over and around the Paparoas, and the Grey River ran swollen and turbulent along its valley, through the town that shares its name, and surged against the Tasman tide over a notorious sand-bar at the mouth. I drove up to Blackball, whose lustrous name rather sadly no longer figures in the rugby news, since the club some years ago amalgamated with Ngahere on the other bank of the river, and they now play as Waro-Rakau. I found no one on the field where Ces Mountford and his brothers learned the game, apart from three sodden children skidding and splashing among pools. Everyone else in the little place appeared to have battened down the hatches until the rains went away. And it all looked drab in that saturated light: wooden homes, working men's club, Blackball Hilton Hotel, down whose veranda rainwater dribbled in thick rivulets.

Runanga was no brighter, but it felt in better shape: at O'Brien Park a load of coal had been dumped beside the clubhouse, so that the foot-ballers could have a hot bath when next they managed to get a game. A home-made scrummaging machine, stoutly fashioned from some nearby tree, stood ready for training outside the fence. Just down the road, back towards Grey, the score-board at deserted Wingham Park told of some recent encounter that must have done something to relieve the gloom: West Coast 14, Canterbury 4. It's an evocative ground, with a neat and well-kept grandstand, a healthy amount of advertising around the pitch, above all an unforgettable setting, lonely beside the highway in the middle of those bush-covered hills. There are football grounds in Sydney that might easily be found in Brisbane, others in Lancashire that one could envisage on the other side of the Pennines. Wingham Park could not possibly be anywhere else but where it is.

Nor could Greymouth which, although it has not quite stood still since I was last there, has managed to retain every bit of its old atmosphere and, as before, feels as if the edge of the world is just out there, where the flooded brown (not grey) river meets the cold and empty sea. Revington's Hotel – where Risman's tourists stayed and must have marvelled at the sight of a train steaming slowly down the middle of the street preceded by a man with a red flag – Revvy's is still a mainstay of local life, being among other things the only place where you can obtain a Sunday lunch. To offset this advantage its rival, King's, can offer the only lift along the whole length of the West Coast, which means that special security locks have been fitted to stop the local urchins from joyriding up and down. The streets are much as I remember them, the buildings low and flat-roofed, with verandas jutting over the pavements outside each store, to prevent the customers from getting wet. At the wharves there are plenty of fishing boats, but not even the occasional trading vessel appears to brave Greymouth's treacherous sand-bar any more. You can still eat whitebait patties, but they told me that the fish comes up from the Haast nowadays.

No, I thought, this couldn't possibly be anywhere but Greymouth; and yet there was a strange familiarity about it that had nothing at all to do with the fact that I once knew it pretty well. I had come across its like somewhere else, somewhere quite different. Just before I left again, when I was standing at the very end of the tip-head, enjoying the threat of a stormy sea from the safety of land, I suddenly remembered where that other place was. With its faint air of depression, of having seen better days, with its workaday and rather bleak dignity, with that loveliness of hills behind it and that blankness of ocean before, with its isolation from the rest of the country, with its taste for Rugby League and with, even, the simple utility of its name, Greymouth is the antipodean version of Workington.

Twelve

The Third Test

The Eighteenth Lions probably carried more good wishes and more fervent hopes from people back home than any of their predecessors who had toured Down Under. The Australians had won every Test match played between the two countries since 1978 – thirteen victories in a row – and never before in the history of their encounters had there been such a one-sided sequence as that. But at Wigan in 1986 the British had come close to pulling one back for the first time. They had then appointed Malcolm Reilly of Castleford as their national coach and under his regime – mettled by his experience of football in Sydney, where he had been a greatly admired Manly player in the early '70s – the signs for the 1988 tour had become distinctly encouraging. It was at last realistic to suppose not only that Australia might be beaten, but that these Lions might conceivably bring home the Ashes. That's why hopes were high from the moment the team was announced. It also explains why so many British Rugby League followers decided that this was the year to be making the trip of a lifetime. From the beginning of June they began to arrive in their organised parties, sometimes kitted out as smartly as the players in blazers and slacks; or as individuals travelling under their own steam, in which case they identified themselves by wearing their club jerseys as often as not. Not many would have the resources to see the tour through from start to finish, though most would manage to watch a couple of the Tests. Someone computed at one stage that there must have been two thousand Poms cheering the Lions on. If true, that would not have been a small migration from one side of the world to the other for a sporting event.

The chosen team, under Ellery Hanley's captaincy, was impressive;

but almost at once it was hit by misfortune, which was to become all too familiar in the next three months. In the penultimate championship match of the season at Central Park, against Salford, Steve Hampson went into a straightforward tackle and was left with a broken arm. This was a cruel blow to the Wigan full back, who not only missed his third Wembley Cup Final through injury but, as it turned out, never recovered fitness in time to take part in even half the tour, as Reilly had hoped on hearing the news. It was bad luck all round, not least on Australian enthusiasts, who had been assured for twelve months or more that Hampson, not their own Garry Jack, was now the best No. 1 in the world. Nor was he the only one who failed even to reach the starting line. For good disciplinary reasons, the Rugby Football League withdrew its touring invitations to Wigan's Lydon and Warrington's Drummond, which meant the loss of two more star backs. Then Goodway, another Wiganer, decided that instead of playing in the pack for Great Britain he'd rather take care of some business venture at home. Many people thought he might have come to that conclusion before his name was announced.

The Lions were only seven minutes into their first match, a Test against Papua New Guinea in Port Moresby, when the jinx struck again. Their first choice at stand-off, Shaun Edwards, the man who was going to mark Wally Lewis, damaged a knee so badly that he had to be sent home on a Sydney specialist's advice. Nevertheless, the team won that Test and another game on the island, as well as its North Queensland game in Cairns, and a fixture with Newcastle, before it ran into trouble at Tamworth, where a New South Wales country side was not expected to tax the visitors overmuch but, in fact, humiliated them 36–12. Worse was to follow a few days later when the Lions met their coach's old team Manly, Sydney's glamour side, especially since winning the grand final against Canberra the season before. This was where I first caught up with the tourists, and it was not a happy rendezvous. They simply were never in the game, whose star was the novice scrum-half Geoff Toovey, a titchy lad who ran rings round, or ducked under the arms of, every Englishman in sight. Platt was the only one of our men to do his reputation any good, and the most awful revelation was Lee Crooks. I'd last seen him in the John Player semifinal just before Christmas, when he damaged a shoulder so much that he missed virtually the rest of the season. Mal Reilly had gambled heavily on this forward regaining not only his fitness but his old storming form, but it looked to me now as if Crooks couldn't possibly make it. He seemed pounds overweight (a report on the previous match said that he had been 'gasping for air after the first 20 minutes . . . well short of match condition') and was mighty aggressive when he came on as substitute in the second half, but not much else. We went down 30–0 and never looked like scoring. We also picked up another casualty. The Leeds forward Paul Medley, who had been expected to raise his reputation from promising young international to regular second-row man in the Great Britain side, sustained a neck injury which worsened so alarmingly a couple of weeks later that he, too, was sent home for treatment.

These setbacks happened under floodlights on Tuesday night, and the hundredth Test match between the two old adversaries was to take place on Saturday afternoon. The Australian press had already decided that there wasn't much point in their team turning up, given the weakness of the opposition. A writer in the *Sydney Morning Herald*, who on Tuesday morning had declared that 'The lights will go out on Great Britain's Australian tour unless they give a luminous performance against Manly at Brookvale Oval tonight', announced twenty-four hours later: 'Reports that the British Rugby League tour is dead are not premature. All visible signs of life were extinguished after last night's 30–0 Manly murder . . .' He was in for a surprise, as were we all, with the possible exception of Mal Reilly.

The adverse publicity and the stiff price of a ticket ($A32) meant that the Football Stadium was not nearly full for the Centenary Test. But the day was sparkling and warm, and a great good humour was in the air as we waited for the teams to appear. A lad in an Oldham shirt was making much noise with a rattle, but the Australian who leaned into him drunkenly from the seat behind seemed to be saying that that was OK by him. Wally Lewis and his men took the field first and there was a pause in which Hanley and his team were nowhere to be seen. A young fellow in St Helens colours beamed on all and sundry, and offered the opinion that 'They're 'avin' to push them on'. Sydneysiders within earshot liked that. Then the British appeared and were greeted by a roar from their supporters. Among these were members of the England Rugby Union team, which was also touring Australia, and John Burgess, stout Lancastrian and current President of the RFU, who had sent a good luck message to the Great Britain manager, Les Bettinson, before the match. If only someone had thought to invite the Union men as our guests. Next time, perhaps?

It was, more or less, a repeat of the last encounter between the Lions and Kangaroos, in Wigan a couple of years before. It quickly became apparent that, far from being outclassed, the Poms were outplaying the Aussies in every department, but especially up front. Kevin Ward, who had had a wretched season with Castleford before the tour began, at last showed us why he had been a Sydney hero during his time with Manly, and Paul Dixon at prop had the sort of game that made one not nearly so depressed about the absence of a top-form Crooks. No one was getting too excited when Loughlin kicked an early goal, but when Hanley ripped in at the corner just before half-time, and the Australians had been nowhere near a score, it felt good to be an Englishman with us leading 6–0. The sight of Sterling clutching his shoulder as he went off at the interval looked like bad news for the home crowd; but that invaluable little man came back and the second half was for the Lions a story of if . . .

If only first Schofield and then Andy Gregory had found touch deep in Australian territory early in the second half, instead of kicking out on the full. If only Sterling hadn't miskicked in front of the British posts, so that defenders went one way in anticipation and the skidding ball another, enabling Backo to dive on it and score. If only, when the Australians had pulled ahead 12–6, Ward's pass to his scrum-half, which put Gregory over between the posts, had not been forward by the thickness of a tram ticket. If only Loughlin had not missed four kicks at goal which, as they say, he would have back-heeled over the bar at Knowsley Road. If only Schofield had held on to a pass with the line wide open before him . . . And if only the Australians hadn't been a different team when they came out for the second half. But they were, and the Lewis-Sterling partnership began to work as usual again, producing two good tries for Jackson on his international debut, and a wily dropped goal by the captain for the one point that might count in emergency: not of any great consequence, as it happened, with the Centenary Test won and lost 17–6. And Australia were well worth their victory, for the way they rallied in the second half. But they were not, I think, eleven points the better side.

I was still warmed by our performance the following day, when I went to see North Sydney play Souths and to watch a curtain raiser of touch football, full of sentimentality and good nature, between old Lions and old Kangaroos (could that *really* be Great Gasnier with the thinning hair and that . . . well, that little pot?); and to cheer with everyone else when the announcer told a nuggety old fellow to rise in the stand behind me; and there he was, the one and only Vic Hey, beaming at us all from behind his specs. I found myself sitting next to a bank manager who said he'd attended some function earlier in the week at which half a dozen of the Lions were present, making the sort of grace and favour appearance that are among the chores of every touring side. 'I hope they behaved themselves,' I said. 'They did,' he replied. 'They behaved impeccably. They were a credit to their country.' It was good to be English at that moment, too. What was it our first tour selectors said, when they chose the side that James Lomas took Down Under in 1910? That they wanted only players who would 'do honour to the Northern Union both on and off the field, so that the Union would have the reputation of not only having shown the best football, but of having sent out the best behaved and most gentlemanly team that has toured Australia'.

Euphoria, alas, was short-lived. The Lions went from Sydney back to Queensland, to play four matches there before the Second Test at Lang Park. They won each of them, though none of their performances was outstanding; and they suffered two more serious casualties. Against a team selected from the Brisbane competition in front of a pathetic crowd at Lang Park, Garry Schofield fractured a cheekbone, and flew home on the same plane as the unfortunate Medley. Four days later in Rockhampton, Crooks lasted nine minutes against Central Queensland before hurting his suspect shoulder again, which meant that he, too, was homeward bound as soon as a flight could be arranged. Reilly's gamble had failed rather miserably.

Although the coach made a number of changes for the Second Test, only one was caused by a need to replace an absent casualty, Phil Ford switching from the right wing to Schofield's position in the centre, with Henderson Gill coming in at No. 2. David Stephenson failed a fitness test, which meant that Hanley came out of the pack to fill his centre berth, with Dixon moving to his usual club position in the second row and Roy Powell taking over at prop.

There was no reason to suppose that this team would do much worse than they had seventeen days before in Sydney. In fact, they were outclassed, and it showed long before half-time. Their kicking was even worse than in Sydney, ball-back being signalled no fewer than five times. Their pack was outmanoeuvred as much in this match as the Australians had been in the first half of the Centenary game, and the defence all round was inadequate, glaringly exposed when Backo, dummy-half five yards from the line, was allowed to burrow his way under three men to score. The Australians afterwards were to make a terrible fuss about high-tackling by the Poms, and there was, in truth, far too much of this – but the Aussies were in no position to complain. There is a photograph, taken by Andrew Varley, of a moment early in the game. Martin Offiah has the ball and is stopped in his tracks by the prop Daley, whose armlock on the winger's throat has snapped back Offiah's head so violently that you can see the sweat spurting from the Widnes man's face.

This was not the sort of thing that won the match so comprehensively, however, and secured the Ashes for the eighth series in succession. Once again, Australia's superb half-back combination had been too inventive, too powerful with the ball for a British XIII to handle. Nor was the scoreline the only reason for acute depression after that balmy night at Lang Park. Bad enough to be drubbed 34–14 in the crucial Test of the series. But to lose yet two more of our best players in the process was almost to resign oneself to really rotten luck. Andy Platt, who had chipped a bone in his wrist in an earlier match, damaged it even more now and had to retire early in the second half. Paul Dixon, tough sheep-farmer from Halifax, broke a thumb in the first ten minutes but went on to make thirty-eight tackles with it strapped up. Within the week, both were back in England, and another emergency call had gone out.

At the start of this run of injuries, Darren Wright of Widnes had been whistled up when Shaun Edwards was invalided home. He had now been joined by no fewer than three other team-mates – the centre Andy Currier (to replace Schofield), and the forwards Paul Hulme (in place of Medley) and Richard Eyres (taking over from Crooks). This meant that Widnes were represented by six men, Offiah and Hulme's brother David having been picked for the original squad. In the wake of the latest setback, just one more man was summoned from home: the Castleford veteran John Joyner, who had first toured Australia in 1979 as a centre but who was now more liable to play loose forward for his club. It ought not to have been necessary to have gone scraping the barrel quite so obviously when there were, after all, in spite of everything, twenty-four more or less fit footballers in the touring party before Joyner arrived. The unhappy truth was, however, that not enough of the men originally picked to back up the Test squad had delivered the goods. That was why some of the results outside the Test matches had been so woeful, because our reserve strength was so inadequate. It was clear that Great Britain could now field a Test match team that, at full strength, would at least give the Australians a very close game. But the Australians could produce at least two fine sides if need be. There, still, was the gap between the two countries.

The most gratifying thing was that not once did Mal Reilly or the British management put forward the injuries as an excuse for the disappointing record of the Eighteenth Lions. They complained about nothing, except that the Centenary Test might have been made more of a festive occasion than it actually was; something on the lines of the cricket celebration at Melbourne in 1977.

The Australians, on the other hand, belly-ached almost non-stop about one thing and another; all except one man, Don Furner, their coach, who carried himself from start to finish of the series with exceptional dignity. But his captain, the senior officials of the Australian Rugby League, and most of all the Australian press, dripped on in the wake of Lang Park about the British tackling; just as they had been moaning without a let-up ever since the First Test match about the supposed inadequacies of the French referee M. Desplas (Great heavens! It was *our* try he'd disallowed in Sydney, not one of theirs). Oddly enough, the Australian Rugby Union coach Bob Dwyer, a few weeks later, was to blame another impartial referee (in this case an Englishman) for the defeat of the Wallabies by the All Blacks, though the penalties had been awarded in favour of his men, 14–6. Once upon a time, I believe we all thought (secretly, in our heart of hearts) that all Aussies were upstandingly laconic blokes like Chips Rafferty. Can it be that they have become a nation of whingers instead?

The next two games were a gift to the numerous critics. In the countryside of New South Wales the Lions barely scraped through against a bush team 28–26, and if the home side's scrum-half hadn't bounced the ball as he crossed the line just before the end, they would probably have lost. They then went to Canberra to play the President's XIII, effectively the reserve Kangaroo side, containing seasoned men like Mal Meninga, Greg Alexander and Gavin Miller, as well as the usual crop of young thrusters who may or may not before long wear their country's green and gold jersey. On a day of continuously pouring rain, the Lions were outdistanced in the first quarter of the match, Alexander demonstrating why he will be a strong contender for Sterlo's place when the Parramatta man retires from the international game. Meninga, too, anxious to prove himself after a long lay-off through injury, broke through our tackles far too often and made himself a try. But, then, in the second half, the British began to come back from 14–8 down, and if Loughlin had managed to convert a Ford try from wide out in the mud, they would have had the game tied at 18–18. He narrowly missed, and minutes later Alexander darted once more through our defence and that was that, 24–16. Not what was wanted with only four days to go before the final Test, but not the shambles that threatened earlier on. Reilly's worst cause for concern was Beardmore, who had outhooked Conescu both in Sydney and Brisbane. He left the field in the first ten minutes, limping badly and holding his hip.

July 9th came in Sydney like a perfect spring day in England, and it would have been nice to report that all roads led to the Football Stadium that afternoon. That this was far from the case – a risible 15,944 people turned up – was due to several things, not least the indifferent playing record of the Lions. But Australian journalism must take its share of the blame, too, for from the moment the touring party arrived, the Rugby League columnists and reporters had displayed a truly remarkable variety of reflexes towards the Poms, running a great gamut that extended all the way from the patronising to the smug. For weeks, a number of typefaces in Sydney had been set in a permanent sneer, and the message generally conveyed to the readers amounted to this: that if these no-hopers can't deliver the goods yet again, and they can't, we may as well stop wasting our time with international rugby and concentrate on the greatest competition in the world, which is right here in Sydney. Even one of the most balanced contributors to the *Sydney Morning Herald*, the former coach Roy Masters, on the day of the Third Test match offered the Lions a 24-point start, and the most restrained shouter of the odds reckoned that Great Britain wouldn't get within ten points of Wally Lewis and his men. The nearest thing to a sympathetic appraisal, on the morning of the match, concluded that 'Captain Ellery Hanley and his patched-up team must now try to salvage pride against an Australian team with no such misfortunes. It is mission impossible. Australia will win today to secure the Ashes 3–0 and the only debate is about the margin.'

Australia made only its second change since the series began, and this was a matter of inter-state politics rather than injury, with Martin Bella from the victorious State of Origin Queenslanders taking over at prop from Phil Daley of New South Wales. The full team therefore was:

Jack; Ettingshausen, O'Connor, Jackson, Currie; Lewis (c), Sterling; Bella, Conescu, Backo; Fullerton-Smith, Vautin; Pearce. Subs: Lindner, Belcher.

A patched-up team was a very reasonable description of what Great Britain fielded, in view of the fact that no fewer than ten men from the originally selected party, most of them proven Test players, were missing for one reason or another. Those picked to wear the white shirts with the red and blue V that afternoon were:

Ford; Gill, Loughlin, Stephenson, Offiah; Hulme D., Gregory A.; Ward, Hulme P., Waddell; Gregory M., Powell; Hanley (c). Subs: Wright, Case.

By playing the Bradford Northern winger Ford out of position, Mal Reilly was at least able to allow Paul Loughlin, who had been full back in the first two Tests, to revert to his normal position with St Helens in the centre. At stand-off yet again, in the absence of Edwards, was David Hulme, normally a scrum-half with Widnes. His brother Paul, the late replacement, was to wear the No. 9 shirt in place of the injured Beardmore, though he had never hooked in his life before. The loss of Dixon meant that the teetotalling, non-smoking Hugh Waddell from Oldham won his first cap against Australia, after having been regarded as one of the reserves for most of the tour. If Richard Eyres, another Widnes replacement, had not been hurt in the Canberra match, where he had played splendidly, he would have been picked ahead of Roy Powell for this Test. But Powell of Leeds, one of the great work-horses of British Rugby League, would not disgrace himself, we knew. At least two of the team were carrying injuries that would have disqualified them, had there been anyone else to turn to. David Stephenson's shoulder, which had kept him out of the Second Test, was still far from right. Kevin Ward, with a sprained ankle, had been asked the day before what his chances were of turning out, and with a gruffness that might have come from the script of *Zulu!* replied, 'I'll have to. There's no one else.'

The Australians were so relaxed that Bella, Belcher and others, changed and in track suits, came outside to sit among friends and watch the pre-match entertainment provided by a large and loud band of students from Stanford University in California, a mixture of music and clowning that belonged to a different culture from the ones known by the two combatants. The Englishmen were said to be so tense behind the closed doors of their dressing-room that not one of them could keep still, each man pacing the floor restlessly unless his coach stopped him to encourage him. But at least when they walked out into the sunlight – slowly and deliberately as always, in contrast to the customary Australian rush on to the field – they could see and hear that they were not without friends. There were English shirts all over the Football Stadium, making an enormous din, with an especially colourful crowd halfway up the East Stand, the hoops and chevrons of Wigan and Halifax, Oldham and Castleford, St Helens and Hull, Leeds, Bradford Northern and York standing shoulder to shoulder with each other and with people wearing the national jersey. A banner, aimed at the television cameras and folks 12,000 miles away, said 'G'day Widnes' and others announced their affiliations with 'Old Globe Wakefield', 'Ship Inn Cas' and plain 'Thatto Heath'. These would have been among the first things our men saw as they walked down the tunnel towards the pitch, and it must have done them a power of good.

They responded to this encouragement straight from the kick-off, with a tearing forward rush downfield which was only halted when O'Connor made a head tackle on Mike Gregory, at which no Australian near me uttered a peep of complaint. Nor was there a sound a few moments later when Lewis grassed Hanley legitimately, but then head-butted the Englishman before allowing him up to play the ball. I was just beginning to wonder, apprehensively, whether this was going to be a continuation of what went on at Lang Park, when Andy Gregory put in a grubber kick to the right-hand corner and Currie fumbled the bouncing ball. There was a flash of white, and there was Ford leaping exultantly after touching down, with only five minutes gone. But M. Desplas was signalling a scrum ten yards from the line, without making his reason clear, and neither the players nor anyone around me seemed to understand why the try was disallowed. This was the sort of thing that could knock the stuffing out of a side coming to this Test, as we had, without apparent hope and in some tribulation; or it might turn the players peevish, which could cost them points. There was a time when Andy Gregory, like a bantam cock, would have chested up to the ref and had such words with him that he would have stood a good chance of being sent off. Today he just stood pinkly with hands on hips, and scanned the rim of the stadium for some sign that the old laggard Justice might yet turn up. Reilly had disciplined his men well for this last battle of the campaign. Very soon it paid off.

Taking encouragement from their escape, the Australians gathered themselves together and surged towards the British line. Too often in this series we had seen the damage we could sustain when they got that close, and when Conescu plunged forward from dummy-half it was odds-on for almost everyone in the stadium that he would put his side ahead. But somehow the defenders held him up right on the chalk. More, they got possession, and began to work their way downfield in short rushes, Waddell, then Ward, then Mike Gregory, then Ward again taking the ball on. Suddenly the Castleford prop was rampaging up the other side of the field and, as Jackson and Conescu tackled him and he began to fall, he slipped the ball round them (exactly the pass that M. Deplas had judged forward in the First Test) to Andy Gregory, who was cut off from Offiah by the tall figure of Ettingshausen, but with no one else between the three of them and the Australian line. With perfect judgment and the trajectory of a trench mortar, the scrum-half lobbed the ball one-handed high over Ettingshausen's outstretched arms, straight into Offiah's reach – and Chariots was away. He had come to Australia with such a reputation, having set up a Widnes try-scoring record in his very first season of Rugby League, but otherwise being acknowledged as a novice in this code. The Aussies had grudgingly conceded that the man was fast, but otherwise, strewth! His defence was pathetic, and he didn't even know such elementary tactics as the absolute rule that you do not let them bundle you over the touch-line on the first tackle. What's more, they said, he was for ever running across the field, not straight, which was useless against such a team as theirs (not many of these critics had ever set eyes on their legendary compatriot Brian Bevan, who used to run defences ragged by long lateral sweeps, before cutting sharply at right angles, in towards the line.) Well, Martin Offiah ran straight in Sydney this afternoon, high-stepping it those last few yards for extra thrust and intimidation before touching down. Loughlin couldn't manage the conversion from wide out, but there we were, 4–0 up. Someone with a sense of humour among the Pom supporters saluted this with a banner, composed under the influence of Lang Park – 'And the Brits Go Wild'.

It was becoming apparent that this British team not only had the measure of the Australians, but was gradually gaining the upper hand, as in the First Test. Again, we were beginning to outdo them in their area of recent strength, with powerful, *running* forward play. Ward was heroic, bandannaed head thrusting like a prow, ball held tight almost under his chin as he charged ahead, and Waddell was a revelation as he stampeded on and on, bursting one tackle after another. Mike Gregory, Powell and Paul Hulme, meanwhile, were harrying and tackling everything in a green shirt that moved, while Hanley had clearly set himself the task of snuffing Lewis's genius above all other things, on the assumption perhaps that if that were done then at least one-third of the battle would be won. From this platform, painstakingly erected by our forwards, our backs – generally Britain's most effective weapon, in good times and bad – began to come into their own. They struck again as the match reached its second quarter.

This time it was blond Mike Gregory who began the move, by breaking a tackle from the rugged Backo. He turned to face reinforcements as he shook himself away, and his namesake from Wigan was there to pounce on the ball when it was jarred from the Warrington man's grasp. Andy Gregory then drew Pearce towards him, away from a position guarding the line, and as Jack also raced in and hit him, he passed the ball to Ford who, for the second time in the match, let his winger's instincts override a full back's. What happened next was very remarkable, given that all Australian football since Great Britain last beat the Kangaroos, has been based, at all times and in all places, on a tenacious defence. When Ford received that ball he was perhaps a dozen yards out, and there were six men between him and the line. Side-stepping and twisting, spinning and swerving, he left Pearce, Vautin, Bella, O'Connor, Currie and Sterling, one after another, sprawling in the grass. Loughlin goaled that one, we were 10–0 ahead, and Englishmen in the crowd were beginning to pinch themselves with disbelief.

In the next few minutes the scales tipped the Lions' way even more heavily. First we came near to scoring once again, but Offiah lost the ball as he dived for the line. Then a real blow befell Australia, when Sterling damaged the shoulder that he had originally injured in the First Test. He left the field, clearly in pain and destined not to return this time. Currie went to scrum-half and Belcher, normally a full back, took his place on the wing. Almost at once the visitors nearly crossed once more, while Australia were mentally adjusting to the rearrangement at half-back. Ford made a darting run up the middle, got the ball to Ward, and the Yorkshireman was over the line, but the defenders desperately flung him back before he could ground.

We were still pressing hard when the hooter went, and us in better heart even than we had been at half-time in the First Test; so elated at the transformation in the Lions, at the sheer one-sidedness of the game so far, that I doubt whether many of us paid much attention to the gyrations of the American students, with their flugelhorns and their other pieces of oompah and toot.

Yet there was the nagging recollection of things falling apart in the second half on this ground in June. The next forty minutes were going to be unbearably long.

Wally Lewis looked grim as he led his men out again, but within minutes his genius had asserted itself for the first time in the match. From the kick-off the Australians swept into the British 25, and began to hammer their way through one tackle after another. Suddenly their captain seized on a pass and took half a dozen swift strides, while Englishmen converged on him in a rush, Waddell, Ford, Ward and Mike Gregory all flinging themselves at the Australian as he reached the line, grappling him below the chest in an effort to tumble him on to his back. Fatally, no one managed to pin his arms to his sides, and he succeeded in keeping his feet. Calmly, swaying under the impact of bodies yet standing firm, Lewis bent double over an obstructing shoulder, reached to his full extent, and dabbed the ball down. This was the powerful and ingenious man's try if ever there was one. Colossus triumphant, right between the posts. O'Connor didn't need to look in order to make it 10–6.

Now was the time for prayer if you were an Englishman; and six minutes later prayer was answered generously. We had taken play back to their 25 and the ball came to Andy Gregory, who did again what he had already done once in this game. He put the perfect, awkwardly bouncing grubber kick into the dirt just to the right of the posts, a little in front of the line. Henderson Gill raced for it, as did Jack and Belcher. These were Australia's two best full backs, remember, though this afternoon one of them was playing another role. Each did what a good full back should do under such circumstances, which is to keep both eyes on the ball until it has been secured. It was exactly the wrong thing this time. The Australians collided heavily and the leaping Gill was past them, dropping on to the ball before turning a somersault. Loughlin kicked the goal and we were ten points ahead again.

It was good to see that cluster of green and gold shirts standing where our men had stood far too often before in the past ten years:

behind the goal line while, this time, an Englishman and not an Australian squatted on his hunkers and carefully lined up the ball before taking the conversion kick. Jack was shaking his head as if he couldn't believe what had happened, and Belcher was just looking sick. Most of the Aussies, with hands on hips, were staring blankly at the figure of Gill, who was strutting back down the field with his team-mates, while the cheers of their supporters again echoed round the half-empty stadium. But Wally Lewis was shouting at his men, and I do not suppose it was polite. Whatever he said, it was effective. Australia surged back, knowing that they had to get something else on the board quickly if this game was not to slip away from them. For an age, it seemed, the teams struggled to take the initiative, absorbing the six tackles then kicking for touch, or punting to make the full back turn and retreat, trying to open gaps and just as fiercely rallying to stop them up. Gradually, though, it was the Australians who were gaining ground, their forwards rushing in a close phalanx, slipping the ball from one to another, allowing the Englishmen no intervening room. Twenty minutes into the half, Backo repeated a move that had come off twice before in this series. Only a stride or two from the line he charged on to a pass from Conescu at dummy-half, put his head down, lowered his centre of gravity almost to the floor, and slammed over the line with Loughlin, Powell and David Hulme stuck to him like limpets. We still hadn't learned that the only way to stop the huge and shaggy Queenslander when he got that close was to be on to him from the front before he gained momentum, and hit him in the gut. For a kicker of O'Connor's ability, it was no problem to convert from only a few yards to the left of the posts. Now, at 16–12, with plenty of time remaining, came the critical passage of the game. I doubt whether many English supporters would have been prepared to stake their lives on the outcome yet; not after the First Test, and Wigan 1986.

Scores of them had by now come down from where they were originally seated and taken up a position together, in an empty space at the bottom of the East Stand, level with the touch-line, as near to the players as they could be. Australian football crowds shout and cheer and hurl abuse, but never do they sing or chant in the manner of the Poms, who now in all their vivid display of club colours began to put their vocal weight behind their team, more than just willing it to victory. 'You'll Never Walk Alone' (inevitably) began to fill the air, and for once I didn't irritably wish they'd either shut up or think of something original for a change. Anything at all was OK today, 12,000 miles from home, with every one of us, man and boy and shrieking girl, in this tremendous thing together. And as the waves of sound rolled around the stadium, with Australian spectators a bit nonplussed at the strangeness of it all, you could sense that Hanley and his men were bending themselves to the struggle even more resolutely, responding to the encouragement.

It was Paul Loughlin who made the break. From a play the ball inside his own 25, Andy Gregory flicked out a pass to the St Helens centre, who side-stepped Currie even as he took the ball, and then left the Aussie standing as he got into his stride. Conescu flung himself in to tackle, but Loughlin changed pace and it missed. He changed pace again, swerving between O'Connor and Vautin, and by now he was into the Australian half, with Gill outside him. As a hand (Lewis's) reached his shoulder, Loughlin passed, and his winger was away. But this was not the Henderson Gill who stirs Central Park to mirth with his crab-like scuttlings across the field, ducking and dodging every arm that reaches for him, to the exasperation of all opponents and in the end, as often as not, a huge white grin illuminating Gill's shiny black face. This, today, was the Gill who sees the corner straight ahead and goes for it like the bandy-legged clappers. He went so well that even Ettingshausen was left sprawling behind, and Jack was still losing way when the Wigan man grounded the ball. Ecstasy for maybe a couple of thousand in the stadium; and Gill showing his own version of it by rotating his backside like a wahine in the tropical throes. It was too far out for Loughlin to convert but at 20–12, dear Lord, surely we couldn't let this match go now.

As the din of acclaim died down, both sides brought on substitutes, Australia replacing Fullerton-Smith with Lindner, the British sending out Brian Case to relieve Hugh Waddell, who had worked himself into the ground from the start, and had surely come to stay as a Test prop. A few minutes later came the reminder, as if one was needed, that no team of Australians can ever be written off until the final hooter sounds. Lewis had sorely missed Sterling ever since the scrum-half went off, and too often he alone had been left to launch attacks, from the scrum or some other set piece. He now came through on the burst yet again, with no one but Ford and Offiah, lightweights both, in the path of his powerful strides, and only ten yards to go. At that point he tripped up and went full length. Then O'Connor, for the first time in the match, received the ball with some space between him and touch. He may not be – though the *Sydney Morning Herald* had tried to promote him as such a few weeks earlier – the greatest footballer who ever lived, but he is certainly one of the most gifted three-quarters to have played in my lifetime, with speed and courage and a rugby brain balanced to a rare degree. When he got that ball, just over his own 25, and began to run, the odds must have been on his reaching the line, for only Offiah stood a realistic chance of getting across and stopping him: but Offiah's defence was not a strong point, derided by every Australian pundit, conceded even by his admirers from home. O'Connor therefore did nothing at all to avoid any threat he may have felt from that quarter; he was going to break through whatever was flung at him. It happened to be an exemplary flying tackle, and it mowed the Australian down, straight into touch.

With only nine minutes to go, victory was clinched in the most perfectly spectacular fashion. And who else should have instigated the clincher but the British scrum-half, Andy Gregory, who had been in the thick of everything in every match he had played, but most especially in this final Test? He had orchestrated every scoring move, had bustled Australians into error when they began to look dangerous, had pulled down men twice his size, had dived into collapsed scrums to tug and tussle for the ball with all the ferocity of a ferret up a rabbit hole, and had run with such unpredictable intent as can make opponents hesitate to tackle because the ball in that moment will almost certainly be gone. The beaky little man was inside his own 25 when he broke through a tackle by Ettingshausen round his chest, and another by Lindner round his neck. As more defenders loomed, he passed to Mike Gregory, with absolutely clear country ahead; but with a good 70 yards to be covered before the Australian line would be reached. The Warrington man simply tucked the ball into his right armpit and went.

He went with Offiah steaming up outside him on the left, in order to take the pass that would probably come his way, for both Lewis and Pearce were in hot pursuit, and it was such a hell of a distance for a forward to run after tackling his heart out all afternoon. Perhaps Mike Gregory could hear English voices all round the stadium urging him on thunderously – 'Go! Go! Go! Go! Go! Go!' Not once did he look anywhere but straight ahead. He was unaware that Lewis had been reduced to pulling Offiah back by the shirt, an act unworthy of a great footballer and Australia's captain. He couldn't have known that Pearce, though he stuck to the chase, was falling farther behind with every stride. All the Englishman could see was the Australian line between their goal posts. He flung himself at it and then lay there, body still hugging the ball, for seconds before he moved, while his team-mates rushed down the field towards him, and every other Englishman in the stadium went dingbats with delight. While Loughlin was teeing-up the ball for the formality of the conversion from straight in front, the English chorus changed. Now they were singing, to the melody of 'Auld Lang Syne', the words 'We're Proud of You, We're Proud of You' over and over again. And the Australians in the crowd for the most part grinned understandingly. It must have been a bit like this for them in 1950, when Ron Roberts, a few hundred yards away on Sydney Cricket Ground, ran in the try that recovered the Ashes for the first time in thirty years. One almost felt sorry for the 24,000 who might also have been in the Football Stadium this day but hadn't thought it worth bothering to turn up.

There was now, at 26–12, with the clock ticking away, no doubt at all who would win. The Australians were in the same plight Englishmen had known too often in the recent past. They were licked, they knew it, and they were doing not much more than go through the motions. The white shirts went raiding yet again, and once more Gill crossed the line – only to be hauled back for a forward pass from his captain. Maybe, maybe not, but it didn't matter any more. When the hooter went, the Lions were coming upfield strongly and Andy Gregory had the ball. They made him man of the match; but, in truth, there were fourteen of those.

The first thing the British players did when it was finished, was to put Mal Reilly on their shoulders, for they knew better than anyone else how much this victory was due to his hard work across a couple of years and, even more, to his ability to stir them for this one last effort after a discouraging time. Then they crossed the field to visit that great and colourful army of their supporters, with whom they exchanged salutes. Many of the players on both sides swapped shirts, and stood around while there was a closing ceremony, with the Ashes trophy presented to Wally Lewis, who then uttered the words expected of someone in his position. It was about the better team on the day having won, and how the losers had been a disgrace; but Lewis, a man unaccustomed to defeat, didn't have his heart in it and it was not very gracefully done. The Australian journalists did better next day, for the most part. They agreed that the Third Test of 1988 ranked with two or three other tremendous matches in the history of Rugby League football, as a classic example of courage and character triumphing over adversity. It was, said someone, pretty close to Rorke's Drift all over again. That was why no Englishman in the Sydney Football Stadium on July 9th could fail to be aware that he was in the grip of powerful emotions by the end of the game. Some quite tough fellows stood, scarcely able to take in the full significance of what had just happened, sniffing and blinking a bit, hoping that they didn't look as soppy as they felt. The light at the end of a gloomy tunnel had been seen at last, and they were no longer to be pitied and held in contempt. That is what those footballers had accomplished on their behalf.

Something else happened that afternoon, at which both Australians and British can be glad. In the West Stand were a couple of rows that, for most of the game, had rustled with animosity. One contained half a dozen young Aussies, the other about the same number of Poms, all of them in beer and each lad eager to put the other lot down. Most of it was posturing, of course, but it was possible that somebody might give the finger to the other camp just once too often, in which case we could easily have a scrap ruining our afternoon. After Mike Gregory's try, the Australians evidently decided that was it; they might as well go home. They rose, turned, and began to shuffle along the row, and I prayed that no Brit would take a last shot, saying or doing something too offensive for them to ignore. It was the Australians, though, who settled things. They stopped, as if struck by an afterthought, and turned towards their visitors. One of them held out a hand, then another, then another, right down the line. The English boys stood up and did the same, and they all bade each other farewell.

'Awright?' asked one of the English, looking his opposite number straight in the eye.

'Yis,' said the Aussie. 'Good on yer, Pom!' Then they were off, into the future, which may be brighter than some of us have feared.

Notes

At the George

2   Barbara Tuchman's thoughts on man and sport, the invention of the wheel and the ball, appear in her essay 'Mankind's Better Moments' from *Practising History* (Macmillan 1982).

3   'Sport provided pleasure . . .' David Smith and Gareth Williams, *Fields of Praise* (University of Wales Press 1980) p. 14.

6   'its progress was impeded . . .' Kenneth Pelmear, *Rugby Football: an anthology* (Allen & Unwin 1958) p. 83.
    'For many years the Rugby Union . . .' Quoted by Smith/Williams p. 118.

9   'that most desiccated of games . . .' Garrie Hutchinson, *From the Outer* (Penguin 1988) p. 186.

10 The scientific methods of evaluation that have been introduced to many sports in the past decade make it possible to make certain comparisons with precision. In an average game of soccer, the ball is in play for about 60 minutes, in Rugby Union for 25 minutes, in Rugby League for 50 minutes. An average Union match will include more than 30 scrummages, 30 line-outs and 40 rucks or mauls. Rugby League, which has neither line-outs nor rucks and mauls, averages 19.4 scrums in a game (when the ball is considered 'out of play'). In American football play rarely lasts more than 10 seconds before coming to a halt. This and more scientific data is contained in the indispensable *Rugby League Coaching Manual* by Phil Larder, the National Director of Coaching (Heinemann, Kingswood 1988).

Class of '46

13 There's an interesting sidelight on football costume in Garrie Hutchinson's *Australian Rules Football: the watcher's guide* (Heinemann, Australia 1988) p. 72. Tracing the development of shorts from the original long

pants of the nineteenth century, he remarks that 'in the 1970s the old cotton button-up numbers were thrown out in favour of tighter yet flexible playing attire. The tightness of a team's shorts is a measure of a team's consciousness of marketing its "sex appeal". In Sydney, aiming to contrast the lithe body of the Australian Rules footballer with the thicker build of the Rugby League player, and hoping to attract young female admirers, the Swans have the tightest shorts in the history of the game, possibly in the football world.'

16   Stanley Houghton's comedy was *Hindle Wakes* (1912). George Orwell noted the clogs and shawls of the young women in *The Road to Wigan Pier* (1937).

Grounds for Reassurance

30   The 'new sports ground near the railway station'. R. Bailey, *The Official History of Featherstone Rovers RLFC* (1956).

35   'a sleeting snow-storm' at Crown Flatt for the England v. Wales match, Rev. F. Marshall (ed.) *Football: the Rugby Union game* (Cassell 1894) p. 192.
After the Dewsbury fire in 1988, the remaining barrel roofs were at Huddersfield and Batley (both condemned), and at Craven Park, Hull (likely to be abandoned when Hull KR moved out to another site).

36   Soccer grounds 'built like medieval fortresses'. Mr Justice Popplewell's *Committee of Inquiry into Crowd Safety and Control at Sports Grounds. Interim Report 1985*, para. 6.5 (Command 9585).

37   'to stop us from getting too proud'. Harold Brighouse, *Hobson's Choice* (1916) Act II Scene 1.

39   'the last fortress of the Forsytes'. Ivor Brown, 'The Best Game to Watch' reprinted in the Pelmear anthology, op. cit.

Cloth Caps and Other Images

43   'Selling the product has priority . . .' Richard Wurman, *American Football: TV Viewer's Guide* (Access Press 1982) p. 16.

45   'I simply followed . . .' From *T'Match*, an essay included in the collection *Apes and Angels* (1928).

49   'There were no perimeter fences . . .' Popplewell, *Final Report 1986*, para. 5.49 (Command 9710).
'The recent Rugby League Challenge Cup Final . . .' Alex Finch, chairman of Wasps Colts, *Rugby World and Post*, September 1988.

50   Tony Harrison's poem is '*v*'.

Tribal Warfare in Post Office Road

65   During the late 1950s and early '60s, a number of British and French teams visited South Africa, in the hope of stimulating interest in Rugby League there; and in 1963 a South African team toured Australasia,

Notes

winning three games and losing twelve. But the powerful South African Rugby Union authorities have effectively stifled further progress by exerting pressure on those who would provide facilities for Rugby League at home.

Small Worlds

72 The report of the Fallowfield/Chadwick libel action appeared in *Rugby League Review* August 7th, 1952.

75 'W. Seddon, a Northern Union full back . . .' W. W. Wakefield and H. P. Marshall, *Rugger* (Longmans Green 1927) p. 16.

76 Captain Crawshay on the touch-line. *Fields of Praise*, pp. 231–2.

77 Relations between Australian Union and League. H. B. T. Wakelam (ed.), *The Game Goes On* (Barker 1936) p. 239.

79 David Kirk in *Sunday Times*, February 14th, 1988.

Not Cricket

81 Anthony Trollope's cricket chapter was in *The Fixed Period* (1882). Charles Dickens referred to cricket in *Barnaby Rudge*, *Bleak House*, *David Copperfield*, *Great Expectations*, *Little Dorrit*, *Martin Chuzzlewit*, *The Mystery of Edwin Drood*, *The Old Curiosity Shop* and *The Pickwick Papers*.

86 The surge of research into the history of the game, this past few years, has been gratifying; and no one can take note of it without remarking on the groundwork that has been and continues to be done by Irvin Saxton, founder and guiding light of the Rugby League Record Keepers' Club. Robert Gate's endeavours so far have resulted in a two-volume study of Welsh players in the game, *Gone North* (1986 and 1988); an account of the Anglo-Australian rivalry, *The Struggle for the Ashes* (1986); and an examination of the Rugby League Championship from 1895 onwards, *Champions* (1987). Apart from the three club histories mentioned, sterling work has also been done by Brian Cartwright on Batley, Len Garbett on Castleford, Alex Service on St Helens, Bill Garvin on Warrington, Michael E. Ullyet and Bill Dalton on Hull. In Australia, apart from Gary Lester's superb general history, there have been some fine club chronicles, notably by Ian Heads on South Sydney, by Neil Cadigan on Parramatta, by Alan Whiticker on Balmain and (with Greg Anderson) on North Sydney. In New Zealand, John Coffey's *Canterbury XIII* (1987) leads one to hope that he may extend his range to the history of Auckland and other provinces. Any mention of football writings Down Under would be deficient without reference to Jack Pollard's encyclopaedic *Australian Rugby Union: The game and the players* (1984). Companion to an earlier work of Pollard's on cricket, it contains a great deal of matter on Rugby League, as well as on the 15-a-side code, and is one of the few books on any sport that can scarcely be overpraised.

92 'I ran in close to a play-the-ball . . .' *This Sporting Life*, p. 249.

At the George

93   When, in 1987, Frank Cvitanovich made *The First Kangaroos*, he tried to get round the difficulty imposed by unathletic actors and unhistrionic sportsmen by filming all the RL action sequences in slow motion. If anything, this made it even more obvious that the actors – as opposed to Wayne Pearce and the other genuine players who had been recruited as extras – were taking *great* care not to hurt themselves.

Incognito in Surrey

105   'almost annual changes in scrummaging techniques'. J. J. Stewart, *Rugby: a tactical appreciation* (Auckland 1987).

106   Some evidence for Joe Egan's belief that there is a concerted attempt to relegate scrummaging to the dustbin of history was perhaps unwittingly provided in the April 1988 issue of *Open Rugby*. In the series 'Tips from the Stars', the Halifax hooker Seamus McCallion mentioned general fitness, attacking, defending and scrummaging. Under the last heading he had this to say: 'Try to be first man to the scrummage mark. Always get your forward pack formed for the scrum before the opposition – it lets them know you're in the driving seat and they have to play catch-up. Make sure that you are comfortable before you pack down. Strike up a good communication line with your scrum-half.' And that was all; not a word about hooking, about techniques of putting the ball into and striking it out of the scrum.

109   Vince Lombardi was an American football coach, Jack Gibson the Rugby League man who introduced Lombardi's ideas to Sydney, and Frank Stanton the coach of the 1982 all conquering Kangaroos, who demonstrated the new approach to a suitably impressed northern hemisphere.

Sydneyside

112   Apart from the five foundation sides still playing in the Sydney competition, the inaugural season of 1908 contained four other clubs. Cumberland did not reappear in 1909 and a Newcastle team lasted little longer. Glebe continued until 1929 and Newtown – the very first club in Australia to break away from the Rugby Union – was disbanded after 1983.

114   Robert Hughes's references to Manly and Parramatta come in his classic account of the Australian convict settlements, *The Fatal Shore* (Pan 1988). Sir William Slim was a wartime commander of the 14th Army in Burma and, from 1953 to 1960, Governor-General of Australia, the most popular Englishman ever to hold that post.
The Bob Stand (now at North Sydney Oval) used to be at Sydney Cricket Ground, situated (together with the old score-board) between the Paddington hill and *The* Hill.

118   One of the more heartening developments at the start of the British 1988 season was the Rugby Football League's announcement that no

166

physiotherapist or other assistant of the coach would be allowed on the field of play with a radio, or be permitted to do anything other than treat injured players, or carry sand for a goal-kicker, if need be.

120 Melba Studios (445 Victoria Road, Gladesville 2111, Sydney, NSW) have been taking their famous panoramic photographs of international rugby teams since 1927 on a Number 10 Cirkut camera which was made in Rochester, New York, early this century. Essentially this is the same appliance that used to pan across entire school groups in this country, so slowly that mischievous children would sometimes dash from one side of the group to the other, thereby appearing in the picture, mysteriously, twice.

Queensland and All That

127 The verse about Cecil Aynsley occurs in a long poem, 'The Reds in Action', about the great Queensland team of 1924–5, by F. J. Freudenberg. I came across it in a booklet, *Sporting Flashbacks* by 'Merlin', published by the Charters Towers Central Sports Ground Committee in 1973.

130 Many English followers of the game lament the fact that the county championship remains a pale shadow of its former self, in spite of recent attempts to hype it up. For myself, I think a great deal of missing enthusiasm might be restored to the potential audience if Lancashire and Yorkshire reverted to their traditional jerseys, in place of the nondescript garments they have been expected to wear in the name of high fashion over the past few years: that is, going back to the plain white Yorkshire shirt and the multiple thin red hoops of Lancashire, such as the Oldham club wore distinctively until they, too, mistakenly tried to glamourise themselves a couple of seasons ago. The Rugby Union men of Lancashire have retained the old jersey design, but I trust that no one is going to see that as a reason why we should not do the same. It would be good, too, to see the Cumbrians back in the county championship, wearing their traditional thin blue hoops.

131 'a gerontocracy . . .' Peter Charlton, *State of Mind* p. 55 (Methuen Haynes 1987). This book is required reading for anyone who wants to understand what separates Queensland from the rest of Australia; and the reasons for it.

Coasters

144 The Grey River and Greymouth are both named after Sir George Grey, the nineteenth-century Governor of New Zealand who subsequently became Premier.

Index

169

Cooper, Lionel, 33
Cornwall, 6
Cow Yed Wakes, Westhoughton, 16
Craven Park, Barrow, 20, 114
Craven Park, Hull, 31–2
Crawshay, Captain Geoffrey, 76
Crawshay, Robert, 76
Crawshays of Cyfarthfa, 76
Crequer, Marty, 19
cricket; and Packer revolution, 54, 55, 120, 121–2; player offensiveness in, 54; Americanisation, 55; writings on, 81, 84; identification with national character, 82, 83; structure of matches, 82; lbw in, 106
Crooks, Lee, 146–7, 148, 149, 150
Crown Flatt, Dewsbury, 27, 29, 35, 48
Cumberland, 18, 63
Cumbria, 6, 28
Cunliffe, Jack, 15, 16, 22, 25, 103
Currie, Tony, 153, 154, 156, 159
Currier, Andy, 150

Daily Herald, 12, 79
Dalby, Ken, 86
Daley, Phil, 152
Darlison, Vic, 100
Day, Bert, 99
Delaney, Trevor, 85
Derby, Lord, 108
Desplas, François, 151, 154, 155
Dewsbury RLFC, 6, 27, 35, 45, 46, 62
Dickens, Charles, 81
Dilley, Graham, 54
Dixon, Paul, 148, 149, 150, 153
Djura, Bronko, 114
Dobson, A. S., 14
Dobson pit, 139
Docking, Jonathan, 119
Douglas, River, 27
Dowling, Greg, 128
Drummond, Des, 146
Dublin University, 82
Dwyer, Bob, 151

Eagles, H., 4
Eastern Suburbs club, Sydney, 64, 112
Ebbw Vale, 61
Eden Valley, 29
Edgar, Harry, 85

Education Act, 1944, 78
Edwards, Shaun, 146, 150, 153
Egan, Joe, 23, 25, 97, 98, 99–109
Elias, Ben, 114, 119
Elland Road, Leeds, 36, 40, 134
Ellenboro, 63
Ellis, William Webb, 3, 6
Engel, Matthew, 83
England, 6, 10, 23, 35, 38, 64, 66
England Rugby Union, 147
Ettingshausen, Andrew, 114, 153, 155, 159, 160
Ewart, Gavin, 81
Eyres, Richard, 150, 153

Fallowfield, William, 71, 72
Family Madness, A (Keneally), 88–90
Fartown, Huddersfield, 9, 16, 18, 33, 71, 108
Fattorini, Tony, 5
Featherstone (town), 29
Featherstone Colliery, 57
Featherstone Rovers, 30, 51, 56–9, 61, 62, 78
Fenech, Mario, 114
Fiddes, Alec, 15
Fields of Praise (Smith and Williams), 84
Firth, Vincent, 70
Fleming, Jackie, 103
Fletcher, Raymond, 86
football strips, design of, 10, 13–14
Ford, Phil, 135, 149, 152, 153, 154, 156, 157, 159
Forest of Dean, 6
Forrest, Nippy, 141
Foster, Trevor, 74
Fox, Deryck, 58
France, 10, 55, 60, 63, 64, 66, 68, 77, 79, 84
Francis, Dick, 91
French, Ray, 44
Friend, Clayton, 142
From the Outer (Hutchinson), 84
Froome, Keith, 50
Fulham RLFC, 61, 78
Fullerton-Smith, Wally, 153, 159
Furner, Don, 134, 135, 151
Furness, 18, 63

Galia, Jean, 64
Gallaher, Dave, 64